# Queenie of Hearts

Julia Bidwell

For Winnie and Vic

Also for my personal collection of Abiders:
Madelyn the QMoHD, Kati Who Did and Does,
and Daddio.

# —Chapter One—
✧

"We brought those beans back from Venice, Reggie. Can't you just taste the *mystique*? No one roasts beans like the Italians."

Rex sat at the breakfast nook in his sister's kitchen cradling his pretentious coffee and trying to pinpoint exactly what the room reminded him of. *Mortuary* edged out *pristine* by a surprising margin and lodged stubbornly in his thoughts. No friendly disorder littered Diana's immaculate white granite countertops; no teddy bear treat jar or Mickey Mouse cookie tin for the Masterson clan. *No cookies at all for that matter.* According to Diana, her family ate strictly '*Paleo*' which she'd described as something of a caveman-like diet.

As far as Rex was concerned, if people were meant to eat like their primitive ancestors then doughnuts wouldn't be so readily available. *Or pie*, he thought. And pie was as close to religion as he'd ever gotten. Diana could keep her trendy food regimen; Rex wasn't quite ready to abandon his faith yet.

He easily visualized the meat in her massive stainless steel refrigerator lined up like tiny corpses ready to be thawed and autopsied in orderly fashion before consumption and experienced a momentary discomfort at being one of two living things in a room so obviously ill-equipped to accommodate his condition. *Definitely mortuary*, he thought.

"We're going, Mom." David, one of Rex's twin sixteen-year-old nephews, stuck his dark blonde head in doorway and gave Rex a brief wave. "Hey, Major."

The boys were fraternal twins, but strikingly similar in appearance nonetheless. Taking after their father in height, their lanky frames stood at just above six feet. Their dark blonde good looks, and blue eyes mirrored his sister's, although not at the moment. Diana's normally honey blonde hair had been lightened and streaked from a color found in nature to something more fashionable.

"It's never '*hey*', David." Diana corrected, shortening the distance between herself and her son, heels tapping across the travertine floor before pausing to straighten the lapels of his navy school uniform jacket and burgundy tie. Despite the early hour, she was dressed for a board meeting in a cream suit with her blond hair pulled up in to some bun-like thing, which was odd, because as far as Rex knew his sister didn't do any work that would require donning a twelve hundred dollar suit at six in the morning.

"It's 'good morning', 'good afternoon', or 'good evening'," she instructed. From the way David was zoning out on his mother Rex guessed his sister had gone into broken record mode.

"Yes, mother." While she fussed, David looked over his mother's shoulder in Rex's direction, expression closed.

"Hey, David," Rex returned the greeting and smiled, purposely disregarding his sister's admonition and wondering how long it was going to take to get the boys to stop calling him 'Major'.

Diana whipped her head around to scowl at him and Rex was rewarded with the first genuine smile from David he'd seen since arriving. *Hey, there's someone in there after all.*

Diana speared Rex with a warning look and turned back to her son. "Where's Drake?"

"Already in the car, I think." David yawned as he glanced at his watch. "I've got to go, or we'll be late." Disentangling himself from his mother's clutches, David made eye contact with his uncle and waved on his way out. *Well, that exchange was about as warm as this kitchen*, Rex thought. No kisses or hugs, no fond ruffling of hair. *Nothing*. Not even a smile beyond the one he'd been working two days for.

"No breakfast?" Rex asked, watching his nephew retreat.

"They'll get something at the school," Diana dusted an imaginary particle from the counter. "Breakfast makes such a mess, don't you think? I'd hate for my family to start the day with chaos and disorder."

"Mm-hmm," Rex offered noncommittally, guessing his nephews were probably on their way to enjoying some non-Paleo McMuffins right about now.

Diana was a very different mother than their own had been, that was for sure.

Not that he recalled Catherine Montgomery all that well, Rex reminded himself. He'd only been seven when she died, and except for a few mental flashes of a woman with a shock of deep auburn hair, clear blue eyes, and a generous smile, very little of his mother lived on in Rex's memories. *But she did feed us breakfast.*

"Did you hear a word I just said?"

"Not one" Rex owned up.

"You're as bad as Bradford." She tsked. "What can you possibly be thinking about?"

"Mom and Dad," Rex answered. "The boys look like him."

"The Montgomery's have strong genes," she agreed, sounding annoyed. "Hopefully, they'll have better judgment than our father."

"Ouch," Rex winced on his father's behalf. "That's a little harsh, don't you think?"

"Not at all," Diana said. "He had a wife and two children that were depending on him. He made the choice to take that plane out. Who does that?"

"He didn't know, Diana," Rex tried reasoning with her, thoughts of his mother leading to his father. Dean Montgomery had been a man cut from the jack-of-all trades cloth. With an amateur skill set that had included a pilot's license that ultimately led to both his death, and that of his wife. "Are you ever going to let that go?"

"You're making excuses for him?" She asked. "His carelessness was the reason you and I ended up in that hellhole."

*By all means, let's bring out that old horse again. We haven't beaten it enough*, Rex thought. "It was hardly a hellhole, Di." *It just wasn't this*, he knew. "And planes crash. It wasn't his fault."

9

At nine years her junior, Rex had adapted to life after his parents' passing, but Diana never did. She'd doubled up on her high school load and finished in record time, making a beeline for the best school that would take her. Efforts that didn't disappoint, if the house was any evidence, but Rex still had yet to see any indication that she was happy.

Of course, he'd only been there a few days. *A few long days.*

"I've got news for you," she continued. "You don't get any excuses when you're a parent, Reggie. Believe me, *I know*." She tapped her chest for emphasis. "I'm always going to be here for my sons. *Always*."

*But sometimes shit just happens, sis*, he thought. "Well, at least there *was* Jasper. If it weren't for him we both would've ended up in the system," he redirected the conversation. "I can't believe he's really gone," Rex said. "Some part of me was sure he'd live forever."

"I can't believe he left you *that* house." Diana replied, her forehead bravely attempted to wrinkle in disgust but lost the battle against the Botox Rex was certain lurked just beneath the surface.

"We were his only family, Di. Who else was he going to leave it to?"

"He should've just had it demolished," she shuddered. "I had my realtor, Cheri, get the wheels rolling. The appraiser will be out there tomorrow. Not that you could hope to get more than a hundred thousand for that shack. It might be better just to bulldoze the site and sell the lot."

"How's the old place holding up?" Rex ignored her last comment, absently fingering the rim of his coffee cup. *Coffee*, now that was something he was glad to have regular access to again. After all the time his taste buds had endured what passed for coffee in the military Rex wasn't sure they'd recognize the real thing, but they seemed to be recovering nicely. He took another sip of mystique.

Someone, probably Leo, had once told him there were over twelve thousand Starbucks in the U.S.. Rex roughly estimated that meant there were at least thirty thousand baristas manning the java mines. The Army could use a few good baristas. Uncle Sam was recruiting in the wrong places.

"I have no idea. I haven't been back since you left." His sister looked around the kitchen, no doubt on guard for any surreptitious countertop clutter.

"Really?" Rex followed her line of sight, admiring the high gloss of countertops that probably cost more than all of the furniture in Jasper's house. "Not even out of curiosity?"

"You mean out of some ill-defined version of nostalgia?" Apparently finding nothing in the area that met with disapproval, Diana raised a finely finished eyebrow at him. "Absolutely not. Jasper's was a dump. The fact that neither of us were ever the victim of a drive-by shooting was a miracle. I'll be relieved to be rid of it." She shook her head emphatically, pausing briefly to study a nail before continuing. "Thank god Jasper had his affairs in order, at least I don't have to deal with that nightmare. I can't tell you how shocked I was to discover that the executor of Jasper's estate was the same Cassandra Woodson you used to run around with in the neighborhood."

"Cece?" He asked, surprised. "You're kidding?" *So, Cece got out. Good for her.* That made them two for three, Rex thought. *Great odds for a neighborhood that digested hopes and dreams for breakfast.* "Doesn't surprise me at all. She always knew where she was going." Rex purposely detoured the conversation away from his childhood companions. "It wasn't all that bad, Di. I've certainly called worse places home." He absently rubbed the shrapnel scar on his shoulder. "And as for the drive-by, speak for yourself."

She waived her manicured hand in his general direction. "Those places were all third world. Not home. They don't count. This is Vegas. In my opinion that whole neighborhood should be slated for redevelopment. I may mention something to Bradford about it."

"Has he been out to the house?" Rex tried to picture Bradford-never-Brad in their old hood but failed. His brother-in-law's over-pressed khakis refused to cooperate with Rex's imagination.

"God, no." She eyed him, and then sighed impatiently. "I left you with Jasper too long, didn't I." Her lower lip jutted out slightly in a pout that might have been pretty on a younger woman. "Reggie, our life with him was a mistake. A hiccup. We were never meant to linger in the lifestyle of the lessers."

*Lifestyle of the lessers,* Rex repeated the phrase in his head wondering if his sister could even hear herself. "I think your money has gone to your head, Di," Rex commented. "It's the house I grew up in. Not a leper colony. Jasper did his best on a limited income. An income he garnered from serving his country and one he used to support your pricey college education until you could access your trust fund, in case you need reminding."

As soon as he said it, Rex regretted it. The subject of Diana's trust fund was an unspoken land mine between them. The fact that she had one and he didn't was an unfortunate by-product of his parents' generally free-spirited approach to life, and more proof to Diana, no doubt, of their father's overall incompetence.

Diana's lips thinned. "Is that what this is about? Me getting something you couldn't have? Please say it is, because *that* I can deal with." She reached across the breakfast bar and kidnapped his coffee cup. She rinsed his cup and set it in the dishwasher with finality. He doubted she even registered how controlling she was.

*So long, mystique. It was fun while it lasted.* He repressed a sigh. He'd been away so long he'd forgotten how challenging it could be to spend time with Diana. His nephews' reserve shifted sharply into perspective. *Just deal with it for a little longer, boy-o. She's all the family you've got.* "As opposed to not being able to deal with other things?" He asked.

"As a matter of fact yes. Our parents never meant for us to have the life Jasper provided. Never meant for you to grow up in the slums, hanging with toughs and going to juvie for drug possession."

*Saddle up, Tex-Rex, here we go,* he thought, immediately wondering where the nickname had sprung from. No one had called him Tex-Rex in nearly twenty years. *Must be this place*, he decided, turning his attention back to his sister. "Will you ever let that go? It wasn't even mine—"

She looked him dead in the eye, hands placed squarely on the counter-top purely for effect, Rex guessed. "And that makes it worse, not better. Don't you see?"

"No. I don't see. I was a sixteen-year-old boy at the time," he shrugged. "I was supposed to get in trouble with my friends. It's in the manual under Teenage Indiscretions." His attempt at humor went unnoticed. *She must've skipped that chapter,* he thought. "We all get the lives we're *supposed* to. No one is out there wearing my skin but me. As hard as it is for you to believe, Jasper was good for me. The toughs were good for me, and even juvie was a life lesson."

"Reggi—" she began, but Rex felt the expensive Italian espresso start to burn a hole in his stomach and knew he was done. "It's enough, Diana. It really is." He rose, carefully pushing his stool back into its designated spot, as much to restore the order of the room as to hide his frustration from his sister. She was who she was. They'd always been different, and Rex had enough combat experience under his belt to know that escalating their differences was a path to nowhere. "I'm glad you're happy. I'm pleased you're at home in your well-to-do zip code, with your Ivy League diploma, and upstanding twin sons to parade around your friends at holiday parties. But not everyone dreams your dreams." He turned, needing to get out before his sister stole his sanity.

"Reggie." His sister's tone gave Rex pause. "Victoria Hart was never going to be anything but trouble, and you know it."

Rex froze. *Victoria Hart.*

Just hearing the name spoken aloud by another person after all this time was enough to shift his thinking into primary colors. Rex's heart thudded against his chest for one long second, as if trying to escape its home and go hunt for Victoria on its own. *Get ahold of yourself, man. You've been in wars that affected you less than that slip of a girl.* He waited for the thrill of the past to settle along with his pulse before replying. "Diana, I think you've always underestimated how much I enjoy a little trouble in my life."

\*\*\*

Victoria 'Queenie' Hart tried not to look too closely at the latest dead thing Cobra Bubbles had just dragged in. Queenie stifled a grimace and gave the monstrous pit mix a pat on her blockhead. "Thanks, girl." The dog eagerly nosed the collection of decomposing small animal in her mistress's direction before turning to pad back through the doggy door, tail wagging excitedly. Queenie's phone vibrated in her hand.

"Ew." She said into the phone by way of greeting, hoping against hope Cobra Bubbles hadn't just deposited the neighbor's recently deceased cat, Señor Pickles, on her tile floor.

"Queenie?" Cece asked hesitantly.

"Queenie of the deadies right now, Cece. Cobra Bubbles is doing her CSI thing again."

"Ew." Cece mirrored Queenie's sentiment, pausing. "She didn't kill it herself did she?"

Queenie repressed a gag at the odor that suddenly assailed her. *Maybe I should post a neighborhood bulletin offering to pay for the cremation services of any future companion losses*, Queenie thought. Anything would beat playing Cobra Bubbles' weekly version of Whose Corpse Is It Anyway. "Not unless she did it a week ago and made it look like kitty kidney failure."

"Señor Pickles?"

"The very same."

"Lord, I thought that cat was gonna live forever."

Señor Pickles, in the tradition of antisocial cats everywhere, had lived much longer than anybody expected, or even desired. Including his owners. The black tabby had been a fixture in the neighborhood since she and Cece were in high school. Señor Pickles had finally succumbed to disease and old age the week before. At his passing the neighborhood breathed a collective sigh of relief.

"His memory will live on." Queenie said, contemplating the nasty scar at the base of her right thumb, courtesy of Señor Pickles and his anti-human campaign. "What's up?"

Cece paused on her end of the line with a gravity that Queenie missed entirely. "He's here."

"Who? Dwayne Johnson? It's about time he replied to those emails I've been sending his agent. You're not getting any younger," Queenie said, looking around the kitchen for something to deal with the dead cat on her floor. *I really should put together some kind of decomposure preparedness kit*, she thought. In the six months Cobra Bubbles had been with them she'd managed to unearth an unnatural number of cherished pets that had moved on to the next world, but left their tiny skeletons behind.

"No, idiot. I've moved on, anyway. Where's Winnie?"

"Moved on from The Rock? Who does that? What would be the point? We agreed he's probably the closest you're ever going to get to meeting the requirements on your Perfect Man list. He's five for seven and you haven't even met him yet, now you're just dropping him? It's like I don't even know you."

"You're right, of course. I don't know what came over me. Let's pretend I called you for a reason other than Dwayne Johnson. It's a stretch, I know, but humor me. Now answer my question, Queenie. Where's Wee?"

"You really should stop calling her that, you know. She's almost six feet tall." Queenie's daughter, Winnie, was nearly seventeen and dwarfed her mother. "She's out. With Talin."

"Talon?"

"Tal-*in*." Queenie corrected. "Less long creepy raptor, more romantically inclined mother."

"Jesus, you white people and your names."

"This from a Casheikah Cassandra?"

"Girl, you just violated our friend clause by bringing that up, but I concede your point," Cece replied.

Feeling like she'd stepped out from a page in Pet Cemetery, Queenie grabbed a kitchen towel and collected Cobra Bubbles offerings. "Who's here, and why do we care if it isn't Dwayne Johnson?" She said a kitty prayer and deposited what was left of a terrifying childhood memory in the trash, following up with a bleach dousing.

"*He* is here. The guy who gave your daughter her height."

It was Queenie's turn to fall silent as her mouth went bone dry and she was overcome with a nausea that had nothing to do with dead cat. She was certain she was about to vomit, but Cece interrupted her plans by continuing to speak.

"Are you listening?"

"Maybe." Queenie said, surprised she managed to choke out the word. "He's there? In your office?"

"No, Queenie. You aren't listening, are you?"

"Let's pretend I am. Rex is somewhere in the city right now."

"Finally."

"Not with you, not with me. But somewhere."

"Same page, same line. He's probably with Diana, come to think of it. She called wanting to know if she could proceed with the sale of Whitey's house."

"Whitey didn't leave her the house. He left it to Rex." *I know. I was there trying to convince him not to.*

"And she had his power of attorney to handle the bequest, until today. He faxed over a letter overriding her POA, and then called to follow up."

"People still fax things?" She asked, giving her mouth something to do while her brain shifted into hyper drive. "You've spoken to him? Why didn't you start with that?"

"I would've, if it had happened," Cece replied with measurable patience. "He spoke to Theodorable. The memo was in my inbox when I got back from my meeting."

The line was silent for a moment.

"So, how do you want to handle this?" Cece broke first.

"Is there something to handle?" Queenie asked. "He can't be here for me. Or her." Queenie's mind raced along, keeping pace with her rapid heartbeat. *Rex was back.* He wasn't supposed to come back. Ever. This wasn't part of the deal she'd made with the universe. *Dammit, world! You can't do this to me, I deserve better.*

It wasn't that she wanted anything bad to happen to him. She just never wanted to see him again. *Ever.* She scowled at the trash bin that now functioned as Señor Pickles' final resting place. *I can smell your fine paw in this, cat.*

"Queenie," Cece dragged her away from the rant she was mentally levying at everything in general. "Rex took over before Aaron could legally acquire full ownership of the gun store from Diana. That means your baby daddy still owns thirty percent until he agrees to sell."

Queenie grabbed the rope of reason Cece tossed her way. At Queenie's insistence, Jasper had a share in the partnership of a gun store known as the Survivor's Hutt. When Jasper died, his share of the business should have reverted back to her, but that salty bastard had changed his will without telling her. She'd heard it from Cece when Jasper passed, but the information failed to register, partly because no one had seen or heard from Rex since he left, and partly because any news that had to do with Rex fell into some kind of weird black hole where Queenie was concerned. But it was registering now. Queenie knew Jasper's niece, Diana, had been in the process of liquidating everything that connected both she and her brother to their past, which was fine by Queenie. But now Rex was here, and faxing things.

"Why wouldn't he want to sell?"

"I don't know. As far as I knew he was overseas, fighting for freedom and the 'Merican way so you and I could sleep soundly in our beds. But as of today, he's here mixing up his business with yours like seventeen years ago didn't even happen."

"Did Theo's message suggest he was here to mix it up?"

"No. Oddly enough the only question my devoted and dutiful assistant noted was about a dog."

"A dog?"

"Yep. Just says 'Wants a meeting, and his dog'."

A few things slid into place for Queenie. Cobra Bubbles was a relatively new addition to her family. About six months prior, Jasper had received a notice to pick up a shipment from the airport. Since he was too sick to manage the pick-up, Queenie and Winnie had made the trek to the airport, where a slightly smaller, but still gargantuan, gargoyle half-breed lay waiting. Queenie doubted the wisdom of even bringing the dog home, but for Winnie it had been love at first sight.

"Rex must've been the one who shipped the Grim Reaper to Whitey." There hadn't been any documentation, except the vaccination clearances. "Damn. Why didn't I think of that before?"

"Why would you have? Rex hadn't sent Whitey so much as a postcard since he left, why would he send a dog?" Cece snorted. "If she really even *is* a dog. Hellhounds are supposed to be the portents of doom, aren't they?"

*Haha.* The portent of doom in question barked outside, a sound that echoed back to Queenie's kitchen. "Maybe. But whose?" Queenie said to no one in particular. She heard a car engine across the street turn off, followed by a door closing, and the hair on the back of her neck rose. She took a peek out of her window and spotted the tail shadow of a man heading into Whitey's house. The nausea thing happened again, but she repressed it with a deep breath.

*Who knew Hellhounds were real*, Queenie thought dismally.

"Queenie, you still there?" Cece sounded far away all of a sudden and Queenie realized she'd let the phone slip.

"I'm here," she answered, "and I think I may know where Rex is right now."

The silence that filled the phone line was deafening.

"I'm not saying that jail may be involved," Cece coughed delicately. "I'm only suggesting that if things get out of control between you two, you don't say anything to the cops until I get there."

Queenie tried to force a laugh, but it came out more like a grunt.

"Queenie...?" Cece pressed.

"Understood."

Queenie hung up and went to face her doom.

*** 

Rex stood in Jasper's living room, Cher's *If I Could Turn Back Time* sounding in his head. Sure, there were little changes here and there: the old carpeting had been torn out and replaced with tile, the light fixtures had been updated, the hallways repainted, and kitchen appliances replaced with stainless steel. But the essence of everything was exactly as he remembered it. Even the smell hadn't changed. Jasper had passed on, but the scent of Old Spice and baked potatoes remained.

The ancient T.V. still occupied the corner of the front room like a toaster on a heavy dose of steroids, but someone had managed to hook up a gaming system and a DVD player to it. *When did that happen, Jasper? Weren't you the one that said technology was the devil?* Rex checked some of the games resting on the console, trying to imagine his uncle playing any of them. A well-used Call of Duty case sat near the others, a controller still resting on the arm of Jasper's favored recliner daring Rex to disbelieve at his peril. *Okay, so maybe some things had changed.*

Despite the new paint, the doorjamb leading to the kitchen still bore the telltale pencil marks of his ascension into adult hood. But at some point another set joined his. *What the...?* The more recent set started before Rex's and looked to have stopped just a few inches short of him. *Almost there*, Rex thought, gleaning a tiny bit of satisfaction from the fact that whoever had replaced him hadn't outgrown him.

As he walked through the hallway, Rex noted more little touches that someone had made. He paused at the doorway to his old room. The mystery decorator had struck here too, but only marginally. His childhood posters had all been framed and re-hung on freshly painted walls. The bed looked new, but the rest of the furniture had been left untouched. As if Jasper knew some day Rex would return and wanted him to know he'd still be welcome. *You old softie.*

Rex crossed the hall to Diana's old room, curious to see how his sister's living space had been reworked. He pushed open the door to find any sign of her completely gone. Replaced by someone with distinctly girlish taste.

Lavender and white stripes lined the walls. A white bookshelf stacked with haphazard piles of children's volumes filled one wall, while a white, canopied bed filled the opposite corner. The closet still held random bits of young girl's clothing and stuffed toys.

Rex took his curiosity into his uncle's room hoping to find something that would offer answers. Instead, he was suddenly drowning in more questions. The smell greeted him first. There wasn't enough Febreeze in the world to disguise the odor of hospital grade disinfectant. Not that anyone would have tried in this house. Rex stepped through the doorway, realizing it was the first time he'd even been inside his uncle's bedroom.

Oh, he'd seen inside it, just never had any reason to *be* inside it. Jasper had made it clear that the house had enough room for everyone, and it was important to respect other people's space. Not much had changed from what Rex recalled, except for the random presence of hospital paraphernalia. The bed had been stripped down to the mattress, revealing the mechanical bones of the adjustable frame beneath. Rex sat on the side of the bed, picking up one of the many random prescription bottles on the bedside table.

*Take for as needed for pain.*

Rex replaced the bottle, reading the same set of instructions on most of the others. He grouped all the scripts together making a mental note to dispose of them, and found a picture of an ancient, grizzly, smiling Jasper standing with an arm around a small grinning redheaded girl. She was gamely pinching one of Jasper's cheeks while he looked on in obvious pleasure. The photo had the immediate effect of easing the guilty conscience Rex didn't even realize he'd been carrying around. *I've no idea who you are, but props to you kid for putting that smile on that face. I know I never managed it.*

Jasper hadn't been much of a parent, but Rex knew that the old marine had never planned on having his own family. Rex and Diana had been dumped on him in his golden years, and he hadn't complained about the responsibility one time that Rex could recall. He'd done his best by them, so how was it that the man who'd been a second father to Rex had died like this? How had he let this happen?

"It shouldn't have been like this, Uncle Jasper." Rex said more to himself than the room. "I failed you."

"Don't be an idiot, Rex." A voice said behind him. "You know Whitey always said there's no such thing as shoulds, only dids and didn'ts."


Two hundred pounds of alarmed Rex spun to face her, hand reaching for what Queenie guessed was the weapon that no longer hung off his belt.

*Smooth, Queenie,* she forced herself stand her ground, though the urge to run was tempting. "Whoa, there Tex-Rex," she raised her hands in mock surrender, while Cobra Bubbles growled menacingly at her side. She'd thought she knew what she was doing when she'd abandoned the relative safety of her home with her personal Hellhound as company to face her fears and confront Rex. She hadn't even been certain it was him until he'd spoken. He wore jeans and an army green tee shirt, and was taller than she remembered, although that should have been impossible since he'd been six foot three at least to her five foot four. He'd filled out all over. The wiry gaggle of limbs he'd been had matured into broad-shouldered frame well defined by firm muscle. Even his face had changed. His jaw line was wider, his mouth fuller, and the light dusting of tawny facial hair was new.

He had more hair than she was accustomed to seeing him with. Whitey had always made certain it was cut short. A habit Rex continued in high school. Now, the dark blonde locks had been allowed to grow, and like her own had a tendency to curl. He'd tamed it with some kind of product and the result was fit for an episode of True Blood.

"Victoria?" As their gazes collided, disbelief melted into pleasure and Queenie felt her insides flip completely over when he smiled at her. *Get ahold of yourself, girl. Don't forget he's an ass of the highest order.*

In two strides, the ass had her in his clutches. The floor dropped out from under her from the force of his bear hug, and despite herself Queenie's own arms slid around Rex's back feeling the hard warmth of his body. When his warmth spread into parts of her that she'd forgotten existed, Queenie forced herself to let go, withdrawing from the intimacy of the moment.

*It's official; I'm still an Idiot*, she berated herself. *Have some self-respect. He doesn't want you.*

"What are you doing here?" Rex released her and stood, same ridiculously crooked grin in place on his handsomely scruffy face.

"I live across the street, remember?" She replied, taking a step back. *Distance is what you need, Queenie. He put it there for a reason. Respect some boundaries, won't you, Hussy?* "What are *you* doing here? Last we heard you were off in Afghanistan, or Germany. I forget."

"You heard?"

"Whitey had his connections," Queenie supplied. *Which he wouldn't have needed if you'd called.* She bit her tongue, the flicker of rage on Whitey's behalf replacing the gooey warmth his hug had left her with.

"I came when Diana wrote to me about Jasper." He was still smiling down at her. *Damn him.* "Victoria, I can't believe it's really you."

"Believe it," she said, laying a hand on Cobra Bubble's head. "Now you. What brings you back to the hood?" *Did she sound normal?* She hoped to god she did.

"Jasper left me the house. Diana has a realtor coming by tomorrow, so I thought I'd come by and see the place one last time."

*Thank the treelike biceps of the mighty Thor.* Queenie heaved a huge and silent sigh of relief. "And then you're off on your next adventure?"

He shrugged impossibly broad shoulders and Queenie had to force her gaze elsewhere. "I guess. I don't have any plans yet."

*Well then, we're going to have to get you some, because I sure don't want you here.*

Cobra Bubbles, tired of holding up the backdrop of the conversation, nosed her head into Rex's hand. He patted her head and ruffled her bat ears. "Hey girl."

"Cece gave me a heads up that you might want her." As soon as she'd said it, Queenie wanted to kick herself for being so vague. *Don't bring Winnie into this, fool!*

"Her who?"

"Cobra Bubbles—the dog." She snatched at the lead he offered. "I'm assuming she was yours. Not too many other people in the world would ship Whitey a dog."

Rex's eyebrow drew together in confusion and he looked down at the dog. "Fiona?"

Cobra Bubbles instantly began wagging her whip-like tail rhythmically against the tile floor. She sat with renewed energy and began emitting the high-pitched whine she generally saved for begging.

"Hey, girl." Rex knelt down and it was all the sign Cobra Bubbles needed. She bowled towards him, knocking him flat, and began vigorously dosing him with wet dog kisses. "Nice to see you too."

*I know how you feel, girl.* Queenie felt her heart break a little and left the two to their reunion. "I think there's still some soda in the fridge."


Rex sat on the couch across the coffee table from Victoria, cradling a bottle of soda in one hand, and drinking in the view. She'd changed, but in all the right ways. She'd cut off the mane of curling black hair that had always hidden the deep blue of her eyes. Now soft curls framed fair skin, giving him a clear view of the cheekbones he dreamt of all these years. She'd called herself Thairish because of her mixed heritage. It was a combination that leant an interesting angle to her eyes when they were kids, but was striking in the adult version.

Rex realized he was staring and forced himself to say something. "So, she's been with you all this time?"

"Pretty much," Victoria played with the corner of her soda label. "Jasper was too sick to take care of her. We didn't know where she came from, and after a while she kind of grew on us, you know?" As if she knew they were talking about her, Cobra Bubbles lay her massive head in Victoria's lap and was rewarded with a stroke. Rex watched as the dog's eyes closed under her mistress's touch. *Lucky dog.*

"I do know." He watched her pull a swallow from her soda, admiring the long line of her neck as her head arched. The Victoria he remembered hated her lack of height, but Rex had always enjoyed her elfin proportions. An admiration that lingered apparently, if the sudden tightness in his loins was any indication. *Slow down there, boy.* He caught himself. *That bridge self-destructed a while ago.*

"How'd you pick her up?" Victoria wanted to know.

"Someone called in a bomb threat. When we arrived to investigate, all we found was an abandoned litter of puppies." Rex put his bottle aside. "Fiona was the last of the brood after every one had their pick. So, I took her. A buddy of mine handled the transport. I sent word to Diana to pass the info along, but I guess it slipped her mind." *It would have*, Rex realized. There was no place in the Masterson McMansion for a dog.

"You taking her?" Victoria interrupted his thought.

"You want me to?" He asked, realizing for the first time that Victoria was different. The old Victoria would have told him to eat glass before she would have offered to give her dog away. Not that she'd ever had a dog as a kid, that would have meant her father would have had to get off his drunk ass and give a damn about something.

"No. Not really." She shrugged lightly, "But I don't want to separate a soldier from his canine companion either."

"I think she's more yours than mine at this point. Please keep her. It's the least I can do after everything you did for Jasper." He gestured around the house. "I'm guessing this was you, wasn't it?"

"I figured I owed him something after all those hours of Scooby-Doo he let me watch on your T.V."

As a kid, Rex had always wondered why she didn't watch them at her own house, but as he grew older he realized that it was the need to escape the effects of her father's Friday night drinking binges that drove her out of her house at a time when other kids slept in. "I can't believe that T.V. is still around. It has a tube in it, and used to take fifteen minutes to display the picture."

"Now it's more like forty-five minutes, and it doesn't have a remote." She grimaced. "I think the Smithsonian may want it for one of their American History displays." Victoria shook her head. "If they contact you, offer to throw in the telephone, will you?"

Rex's gaze went to the wall where the same mustard yellow rotary phone of his youth still hung. "Does it work?"

"Sure. Just not in this century." She blew a lock of hair out of her eye. "These days it's all: press one to hear your message in Bangladesh, or zero to speak to an operator."

Rex felt himself grin. *Damn, it was good to see her.* "Couldn't get him to switch that either?"

"Nope," she grinned back. "In fact I think he liked it more because it meant he could just hang up."

"That work?"

"Well enough. He was fond of saying that if people wanted to get in touch with him, they knew where to find him," she gave up on trying to blow the hair away and tucked the errant curl behind one ear. "Turns out to be true."

Rex wondered if her last comment was directed at him or if he was imagining things. "Seems like he was lucky to have you nearby keeping him connected."

"Did you think that because you and I had our differences that I would stop being there for Jasper?" Victoria asked.

*Shots fired,* Rex thought. "What do you mean, 'we had our differences'? What differences?" Rex asked. "We practically lived in each other's pockets for ten straight years. We had all the same classes from elementary until the day you stopped going to high school."

"That was a while ago," she said.

"I punched Brent Lewis for saying you let him kiss you in the quad."

"What? For god's sake why? I *did* let him kiss me in the quad," she covered her face with her hands.

"I know that, but he didn't need to go around telling people."

"You're ridiculous," she let her hands fall away from her face and shook her head. "Besides, I paid you back for that when I filled Lynn Dooley's backpack with condoms for saying you took her virginity the night of junior prom."

"That was you? You didn't even finish your junior year. How'd you know?"

"Cece told me." Steely blue eyes narrowed on him. "Do *not* tell me that you did what she said."

"Absolutely not," Rex replied, forcing an earnest expression on his face and trying not to laugh.

"Rex."

"Seriously," he raised his hands in the spirit of open and honest communication. "She was lying to make some other poor schmuck jealous."

Victoria crossed her arms over her chest, steely blue eyes evaluating him.

"You're doubting me now? Me, of all people? I went to jail with you. Twice."

"And then you left. For good." She said flatly.

"You always knew I was going to." He replied automatically. "You always knew I was going into the service. *Always.*"

He watched as she opened her mouth, then shut it and chewed on the corner of her mouth. The gesture was alien to him and he didn't like it. This was a Victoria he didn't know, one who could keep her thoughts to herself. *Come on, let it out.*

"I never expected you to just back out of my life like you did," she said finally.

"You're one to talk. You left all of us long before I finally walked away. Besides, I never really thought you would live this long." He wanted the words back even as he said them. *Geez, Rex. A dick much?* He tried to cushion the blow, tried to make her understand. "Victoria, you—"

She held up a delicate finger and he stopped talking, reflecting that such a petite digit shouldn't hold that kind of power over a

25

man who'd been through three tours of duty and then some. Even the dog opened a cautioning eye.

"I know what I am, Rex. You're not Willy Wonka, don't bother trying to sugar coat it." She laid a hand on the dog's head and the eye slid closed, signaling the crisis moment had passed. "I made poor choices and you got caught up in them on more than one occasion." Rex started to object but Victoria waved him off. "I don't blame you for thinking what you thought. And of course I knew you would grow up and go soldiering one day. That was a no-brainer from the first time I saw you with your crew-cut hair and camouflage cargo pants. What eight year-old dresses like that unless he's hell bent on becoming the next real-life G.I . Joe? Which you managed apparently, so congrats." She went on. "What I'll never understand is why you felt like you had to cut yourself free of everyone in order to do it. Leave me? Sure, I get that. I would have left myself if I could've, but Cece, J.J. and the rest? And Jasper?" Blue eyes pinned him. "You were all he had left."

The truth warred with his pride and lost. There was no way he was about to tell her that he wasn't strong enough to break ties with her without cutting himself off from everything that reminded him of her. Rex knew better than anyone that he was a grown-ass man now, but sitting in awash in youthful memories he finally understood that a man never sheds his childhood dreams. And his had matured into a doozy.

*And you've been trying to kid yourself all this time, boy-o,* he reminded himself. *What's the longest you've ever gone without wondering what happened to her?* Hell, he'd been mentally preparing himself to hear that she'd died of an overdose. And here she was, now. Against all odds, sitting in his uncle's house with his dog, telling him she felt what..? Betrayed.

Could he blame her? He'd left her before she could leave him. What had his therapist called them, abandonment issues? Common side effect of losing his parents so young, he'd said. He'd been abandoned, not intentionally, but left all the same. And now he was the abandoner.

"So, you're saying what exactly? That I may be back, but you've already erected a wall against me?"

"You built the wall, Tex-Rex. I'm just reminding you of where you left it." Rex struggled to put his thoughts into words, but Victoria stood before he managed it, her dog rising with her.

*She's right and you know it, Old Son.* You ran away and now the world you left isn't here anymore.

"It was great seeing you again, Rex. I'm glad you made it home safely." She waved goodbye and walked out the door.

He watched her go, wondering what the hell just happened.

\*\*\*

Queenie could feel her phone vibrating almost out of her pocket before she reached her door. "I'm not in jail yet and there are still no bodies to bury."

After a split second of silence her daughter spoke. "Mom?"

Mentally cursing herself for not even bothering to check the caller ID before she answered, Queenie scrambled. "Oh, hey honey."

"What's wrong? You sound angry."

"Do I?" She exhaled, shoving Rex onto the backburner and willing her heartbeat to slow. "I'm not. Bubbles keeps bringing me dead things. Thank god we don't live near a graveyard."

"No kidding. But why would you be in jail?"

"I thought you were Cece." Queenie explained. "We had some business to discuss. Never mind that. Where are you?"

"On my way home. Talin wanted to stop for food. We're at DeMarco's and Dante wants to feed you."

"If it were up to Dante I'd be three hundred pounds."

"You're the coolest of the kids, Mom, but I don't think even you could rock that look."

"Rollie-pollie-mommie." She entertained the visual for a nano-second, and shuddered.

"What should I tell him?"

"Tell him to send whatever, but no pasta tonight." Cobra Bubbles's ears perked up at the words. "For you either, dog."

"Dinner for the reaper?"

"Nope. I stopped at the pet store earlier and picked up some horse feed." Queenie was joking, but only a little. The dog ate more food than Winnie and Queenie combined. "And honey, try to pay Dante."

"We're a negative on that, Mom. You know how Dante is when it comes to you, but never fear. The infallible Talin dropped forty dollars in the tip jar when we came in."

"Infallible is he now?" Queenie had to admit she liked him a little more for not trying to take advantage of free food.

"So far. Let's give him another twenty-four hours and see what develops," Winnie said. Queenie heard Talin's voice in the background, and her daughter laughed at something he said. The sound was more powerful than Valium and some of tension drained out of her. "See you in twenty. Love you."

"Love you back." She hung up and went inside.

After feeding Cobra Bubbles, Queenie looked out the window, relieved to find that Rex had gone. Since the coast was clear Queenie went out to sit on her patio and enjoy the mild October weather. After inhaling her kibble, Cobra Bubbles joined her, sniffing around the yard for any tiny corpses she'd overlooked before coming to settle nearby.

*Damn you Rex for thinking you could come back here.* "He named you Fiona?" Queenie scored a small emotional victory when the dog's ears failed to perk up at the name. "What was he thinking? You are obviously a Cobra Bubbles." The dog's tail wagged against the concrete.

Queenie felt uneasy, uncertain if she was more angry or relieved.

He hadn't even asked about Winnie. But then again why would he? He'd made it clear to her from the very beginning that he was out. So, why did she feel so betrayed by him all of a sudden? Sure, they'd been inseparable as kids. But like other kids, they'd grown apart.

*No*, she reminded herself. *You fell apart and despite that, some part of you still thinks that Rex should have hung on to you just because you managed to get yourself knocked-up with his daughter.*

"I'm an idiot." Cobra Bubbles smacked her tail on the ground in what Queenie assumed was empathetic agreement, glossy black eyes trained on her mistress. "What are you looking at, Fiona?"

At that moment, an old mustang pulled up to the curb. The driver killed the engine and exited. Queenie watched as the tall, dark-haired figure of Talin came around to the passenger side of the car and let Winnie out. Alerted to the familiar scent of DeMarco's, Cobra Bubbles sat up suddenly and began her half-whining/half-begging food song. "Leave it," Queenie commanded as the pair approached.

Talin saw the dog and slowed his step. "She okay?" He asked Winnie.

"Me, or the dog?" Queenie put on her best maniacal grin. "She's had all of her shots, so you can't give her anything. If that's what you mean."

"Mom, stop it." Winnie dead-panned without missing a beat. "They're both fine, Talin." She took the food bags from him. "Thanks for the ride."

"Anytime, Winnie," he said, his youthful smile beaming, then looked at Queenie, uncertainly. "You have a lovely daughter, Ms. Hart."

"I also have a shotgun, access to a backhoe, and an alibi on speed dial. All of these things should come to mind whenever you think of how lovely my daughter is."

"Mo-om," Winnie shook her head.

Talin, more uncertain than ever, laughed awkwardly and settled for a wave before making himself scarce.

Winnie joined her on the patio. Now that she'd just seen Rex again, Queenie couldn't help but pick up on what suddenly seemed like the endless similarities between her daughter and Rex. *Goddamn those Montgomery genes.* Cece was right, Winnie certainly got her height from him, along with a smile that never quite straightened out. Queenie took credit for her kidlet's stormy blue eyes and fair skin, but the red hair was all Rex's mother. Whitey had once shown Queenie a picture of his sister-in-law from her wedding day. In the photo Rex and Winnie's smile was mirrored on the face of a stunning auburn haired bride, her brand new husband fresh out of the package at her side.

"So, what did you think of Talin?" Winnie interrupted Queenie's thoughts.

"He seems nice, if you like tall, dark and handsome." Queenie answered, trying not to recall Rex at that age and failing.

"Do I ever," Winnie grinned, dimples puckering.

"He in the running for your affections, Miss Hart?"

"Perhaps," Winnie gave the dog a scratch behind the ears.

"He sure has some pretty manners."

"The car door?" Winnie asked. At Queenie's nod, her daughter laughed. "It's a project car. The handle on the inside sticks. Hence the manners."

"Stop disillusioning me," Queenie said. "I need my dreams."

"Sorry," Winnie laughed. "How was your day? You play today?"

"It's Tuesday. Of course I played. Except I called it work."

"Riiight. Sitting at a poker table all morning is work." Winnie winked conspiratorially, and Queenie laughed. "Actually, I didn't go downtown. I worked from home."

"I thought you hated on-line poker." Winnie squished Cobra Bubbles face into a grin. "She said so, didn't she, beautiful?" She let go and the dog's features melted back to normal, a normal that included licking Winnie's face.

"I wouldn't let her do that just yet," Queenie warned. "She had a mouthful of Señor Pickles about an hour ago."

"Who's my creepy baby?" Winnie cooed over the dog and Cobra Bubbles lapped up the attention, tail wagging madly.

Queenie took the food from her daughter and rose. "As for the online thing, the dynamic isn't usually there. You need to see people in person to take their money in any meaningful way."

"Any good?" Winnie joined her, brushing the dog hair off her skirt, then opening the door for them.

"Enough to keep you in the style to which you've grown accustomed." Cobra Bubbles beat them inside.

"That good?" She applauded lightly. "Me likey."

"I went all-in on an aces high three of a kind." Queenie bee-lined for the kitchen.

"Nice one. How was the pot?" She asked, grabbing a plate for her mother and bringing it to the table.

"Extra crunchy." Queenie pulled out a foil-covered baguette, "Much like the crust of this tasty bread."

"That *is* crunchy." Winnie whistled. "We car shopping this weekend?"

"I'm not sure I can afford you." Queenie's mouth began to water as she put together a plate of the DeMarco's chicken marsala.

Winnie laughed, stealing a bite from her mom's plate. "If you can't, no one can."

## ∽—Chapter Two—∾
⚜

"Cassandra Woodson, Esquire." Rex said as she stood from behind her desk to greet him. "Look at you!" He admired the way the expensive, cream silk suit she wore accentuated the pale mocha of her skin. The awkward collection of knees and elbows she'd been had grown into a confident and lithe, cinnamon beauty.

"Forget about me. Ranger Rex is all grown up and home from the wars!" Cece squealed, grinned and came around her desk to embrace him. When she pulled away Cece gave him a long, measuring look, tugging on his facial hair. "Nice," she approved. "I've always liked a man with a little scruff." She gestured for him to take a seat in one of the leather chairs opposite an enormous polished desk. "Isn't this just like old times? You hungry? Thirsty, maybe? My assistant makes a mean espresso."

"Your assistant?" Rex grinned. "Would that be the elegantly attired, multi-tasking

Theodore attempting to see to my every need in the lobby?"

"The very same. Did he flirt with you? He has excellent taste in men."

Rex chuckled. "I'm sure he has excellent taste in everything to be your only Guy Friday. I can't believe you make do with just one. You always wanted a crew of

minions to do your bidding. Wasn't six the magic number?"

"It's seven now. My needs have multiplied as I've aged." She grinned. "As for the paltry number of minions: I'm only a junior partner, and I'm still waiting to see how the cloning thing pans out. I could certainly do with more Theodorables in my life." She winked, and continued. "And you're right, of course, I did have a villainous streak back then. Still do, actually, but no one notices because it's expected in my line of work. So, for now I make do with one minion, and while he does sometimes complain about the workload, deep down I know he doesn't want to share me with anyone else. He'd have to split the perks."

"And they appear to be many." Rex made a sweeping gesture around the room and the view.

"And multiplying all the time now that you're here," she said.

"I shared a tent with a squad of fourteen men that was smaller that your office."

"You and fourteen men all in one room?" She gave him a playful onceover, green eyes gleaming with mischief. "You're making me think twice about the military, honey. Tell me more."

He couldn't help but chuckle. "Damn, it's good to be back."

"You're reading my mind. Lord, it's good to have you. I can't wait to tell Angel Baby I've seen you in the glorious flesh."

*Angel Baby.* It was Rex's turn to grin. "How is your mother? Life's treating her well, I hope?"

"Spoiling her rotten and no one deserves it more. Seems like we're all living proof that the old neighborhood was just an address, not a destiny, Rex." She took a seat across from him. "I'm so sorry about Whitey, sugar."

"Honestly, it was the last thing I expected to hear." A whisper of guilt twisted through him at the memory of the prescription bottles at Jasper's bedside table. "He was tough as nails. When Diana let me know he'd passed from pneumonia I was shocked. I was sure he wouldn't give up the ghost for anything less than a nuclear blast."

Cece's dark curls bobbed in agreement. "Well, I think the pneumonia was the last straw. He'd hung on as long as he could." Her phone beeped discreetly and she pressed a button to silence it, turning her attention back to him.

"Last straw?" Rex asked, confused.

Cece's finely sculpted eyebrows lifted delicately. "Whitey had lung cancer, Rex. Didn't Diana tell you?"

Rex sat back, dazed. "No. No, she didn't mention it."

"She probably didn't want to worry you." Cece's body language broadcast a fraction of doubt that Rex picked up on. "He was diagnosed nearly two years ago."

"That long?" *Two years.*

Cece nodded. "I remember it because he came in to have me draw up his will the same day he was diagnosed. I tried to talk him out of it, but you know how Whitey was."

"Stubborn as an armed bear when he wanted to be," Rex acknowledged, still floored that he'd had a two-year window to come visit and he'd missed it. The sharp edge of Victoria's anger shifted into perspective. Jasper had still thought enough of his nephew to leave him what little legacy he'd manage to build despite his abandonment. Rex felt humbled.

"Too true," she agreed. "So, what brings you in? I got your message yesterday about retracting Diana's POA. You keeping Whitey's crib?"

"Probably not. Diana's hot to sell it. I think dumping it would bring her some kind of closure." Rex suddenly found himself wondering if his sister had an ulterior motive for wanting him to sell so quickly. His only living relative had been terminally ill for two years and she never said a word.

"She never was a good fit for the neighborhood." Cece's mouth thinned sympathetically.

Rex snorted. "And that's a very diplomatic way of putting it."

Cece grinned, dropping her business facade. "An Ivy League shine changes a girl."

He looked around the office, admiring the oak desk and the polished chrome. "Are we talking about you, or her?"

"Both maybe." Cece shrugged. "Although I don't think she's changed much, just sort of found her proper context. Queen's Heights was never going to be a good fit for Diana. Not enough Tiffany & Co. stores."

"Queen's Heights? I've heard it called a lot of things, Cece…"

Cece smiled and shook her head. "A nickname the neighborhood picked up a few years ago. I almost forgot you've been away. It was like picking up where we left off."

"Ditto, and with Victoria last night too."

Cece nodded lightly. "You talked to her, then? She mentioned something about you being in the old neighborhood."

"The two of you are still thick?" *Of course they are*, he realized. Loyalty was the trump card in their neighborhood. It's why the gangs lasted so long, and why his defection stung so badly.

"As thieves," Cece affirmed. "I can't un-friend Victoria Hart. I may run for mayor one day, and she's alphabetized all of the skeletons in my closets." Cece winked and sat back, hands resting demurely on her lap. "How'd your reunion with her go? I'm dying of curiosity."

Rex searched for the right phrase to describe the schooling she'd given him the night before.

"That bad?" Cece blanched.

"I would've expected worse, to be honest. Especially considering everything." Now that he knew what *everything* was.

"Everything is a lot," Cece agreed neutrally. "Were the two of you able to come to some sort of agreement at all?"

"She made it clear that I wasn't welcome," he admitted. Not that Cece looked surprised. "Not much room for me to agree or disagree really."

"Do you blame her?" Cece asked. "She's been the responsible party all this time."

"I really never meant for that to happen. Of course, I had no idea Jasper was sick." Rex felt the need to explain. "And I sent word to Diana and expected her to fill Jasper in. I really didn't think it would be much trouble for Jasper to care for her until I made other arrangements."

Cece's brow wrinkled. "So, you intended for Jasper to take responsibility? That was a big assumption, don't you think?"

Rex couldn't put his finger on it, but he knew Cece was suddenly annoyed with him. Outwardly she was the picture of friendly professionalism, her smile was present, but not too bright, her body language leaning in with interest, but something about her eyes broadcast irritation swirling just beneath the surface of her cool demeanor. He tested the waters. "In retrospect, of course. Victoria has done a great job with her, though. I'm sure they'll be fine together."

Cece opened her mouth, then closed it again, reinforcing Rex's instinct that their conversation had navigated him down a map-less road. "Mmm, so you're just going to leave her to it?"

"Well, Fiona seems to be doing fine." He sat back, waiting for Cece to broach the subject of her irritation, his line of sight falling on what had to be the most hideous porcelain clown figurine he'd ever seen resting on the nearby side table.

"Fiona?"

"Cobra Bubbles, I think her name is now." Rex looked around the room, noting the clown had friends, all equally horrific.

Cece coughed delicately, bringing Rex back. "Of course. So, the *dog* is...uh, fine?" And just like that she was Cece again.

"Happy and healthy. Victoria offered to give her back, but that didn't seem right. She's found a home. That's all I really wanted for her anyway."

"And you and Victoria?"

*You and Victoria.* He liked the sound of that more than he wanted to admit. "I don't get it."

"What part specifically? Maybe I can help you unravel the mystery that is our third musketeer."

"That right there. How can she still be hanging on to anger from seventeen years ago?"

"She's Irish," Cece shrugged. "It's her God-given right to be bat-shit crazy at any moment. Fortunately for all of us those moments are few and far between these days. Let's just be glad she survived self-medicating her emotions, shall we? I swear I thought she'd die before sobriety settled in."

"And that. She's completely clean, isn't she? I could tell by looking at her."

"Has been for a long time," Cece acknowledged.

"So, what's she still doing in that house? Why the hell didn't she get out?" Restless, Rex stood, and shoved his hands in the pockets of his jeans. He moved to study the bookcase lined with law books only to be confronted with another grotesquely grinning miniature clown. This one holding out a red balloon as if ready to offer it to a passing child. When he took a closer look, Rex realized the balloon was actually a man's head floating on the end of a string.

"Where was she going to go?" Cece asked simply.

"Anywhere. You and I got out." He forcibly turned away from the clown spectacle, and back to her.

"And how much of our self-motivation to leave the Heights was inspired by watching one of our besties get sucked down into the muck of the neighborhood."

Cece hit a nerve. Rex recalled his last memory of Victoria and the scars of guilt from walking away from her. "You think that was it?"

"Rex, we always knew you were going to join up. But I don't think either of us thought you were going to go off after boot camp graduation and never look back."

"Victoria said as much last night. I think she feels like I betrayed her."

"Didn't you?"

"Did I? I didn't want to watch her destroy herself any more than she already had."

"So you bailed. People do. You weren't the first; don't beat yourself up about it. She was always stronger than either of us ever gave her credit for. Praise the Lord, as my mama would say, and has said, many times when it came to Victoria. When her mother left and Colin got sick, it was the beginning of a bad run for her. The good news is: it didn't last. If I were you I might try to be happy for her success even though I wasn't there to be a part of it."

"Happy? I'm ecstatic. I honestly thought she was going to burn out at nineteen."

"I know, Rex. We all did. Fortunately for us, she's hard to put down." Cece glanced at her watch, frowning. "Well, damn. As much as I would love to hash over old times, I'm squeezed with clients all day."

She stood and went around her desk to her computer, retrieved a file from her outbox and passed it to him. "That's all the legal pertaining to Whitey's bequest. All the highlighted portions pertain to you. Besides the house, there's the small matter of the Survivor's Hutt."

"Survivor's Hutt?"

"It's a combination gun, ammo, survival gear store that Whitey held thirty percent of. He left his share to you, and Diana was ready to sell it back to the owner, Aaron Matson, but now you're here, so you'll have to decide what you want to do with it. I rep Aaron also, and he's offering market value within reason if you decide to proceed with sale." She tapped something into her blackberry and an instant later Rex's phone dinged in his pocket. "That's Aaron's info. Stop by and see the place before you decide." Cece smiled up at him. "Any other pressing legal matters? Custody issues? Palimony cases you want me to take over?"

Rex laughed. "Thanks for the offer, but I'm still free and clear on both counts. How about dinner tomorrow night? I'll go by Victoria's and see if I can play nice and get her to come along."

Cece's eyes narrowed slightly and for a fleeting instant Rex couldn't read her expression at all. Then the moment passed. "You're on for dinner. Don't worry about our girl. I'll pick her up. Let's do the Commonwealth at seven. It's downtown. You'll love it."

"Cece, I have to ask," he gestured to the nearest figurine dripping with malice. "What's up with these? I didn't think I suffered from PTSD until I saw these."

"They're atrocious aren't they?" She agreed, patting one on the head as she came around her desk. "They're horribly expensive. My mother won't stop giving them to me no matter how much I beg."

"She need to be on medication?"

"I may tell her you suggested it," she laughed. "She claims being able to waste perfectly good stacks of money on something that ugly sends people a message."

"At least one." Rex agreed. "Couldn't she just give you a Maserati or a Tesla instead? I'm not sure these convey the kind of message you want to broadcast."

"Think so? I don't even notice them anymore, but the Governor's sister never fails to praise them."

"Well, if the Governor's sister likes them, who am I to judge?" He tried to shake clown collection as he headed to the door and Cece called after him. "Hey, Rex? Can I ask you something?"

"Sure."

"Why do you care so much what Victoria thinks of you?"

"Damned if I know." He shrugged. "Never really learned how not to, I guess."

Cece watched Rex leave. When she was sure he'd gone, she pinged her assistant.

"Yes, oh venerable one?" Theo answered without hesitation.

"Theodorable, how open is my schedule this afternoon?" Cece tapped the file on her desk lightly, her thoughts whirling.

"About as open as a nuns legs in a whorehouse."

"That tight?"

"I can give you twenty minutes at noon."

"I'll take it."

\*\*\*

Queenie had just called the pot with two pair when the Lin, the dealer caught her attention. "You have company, Queenie." She looked over her shoulder to see Cece standing just beyond the velvet ropes of the high limit table looking expensive and authoritative.

"Can't escape our fans," Bandit said, folding his hand.

"She's got nice legs, whoever she is." Cowboy admired next to her.

"I'll tell her you said so. You in?" Queenie tapped the felt of the table in front of her.

"Sure, Queenie. I came to play, after all." Cowboy tossed in a hundred dollar chip and matched. "I'll pay to see." He winked at her.

"If you weren't old enough to be my grandpa, I might take you up on that, old man."

Her playmates showed their hands.

"Oh, pick me." Queenie swept in the pile, loving the happy sound the chips made clicking against each other as they comingled with her growing stacks. "Gentlemen, it's been a pleasure." She grabbed a chip from the pile and slid it to the dealer. "Lin can I get a cash out?"

"Sure thing, Queenie." The dealer gestured to a runner while Queenie grabbed her bag and went to meet Cece. "You never come in here. What's up?" A moment of panic washed over her. "Is

Winnie okay?" She pulled out her phone and checked for messages.

"I'm assuming she's fine. Isn't her over-priced private school supposed to be baby-sitting her during the daylight hours?"

"And the learning thing. Don't forget about that."

"Remiss of me," Cece shrugged. "I'm here about Rex."

"I'd almost forgotten about your meeting with Benedict Arnold," Queenie lied. "What does he want?"

"As nearly as I can tell, nothing. At all."

"You came all this way to tell me that?" Queenie said doubtfully.

"I'm assuming you're up."

"Aren't I usually?"

"Go get your money and meet me at the café."

Queenie tried to keep herself from imagining the worst as she did as she was told. When she finally slid into the booth across from her friend she her palms were sweating. "You're freaking me out. You said he didn't want anything. He seemed fine yesterday. So what's the deal?"

"What *is* the deal? He came to see me and imagine my surprise to find him in one very handsome piece. No bruises, no burns, no open wounds."

"I've matured." *Is that what you're calling it? Don't pretend you weren't entertaining thoughts of a physical nature around that boy.* But then, she couldn't blame herself really, he had grown into quite a tast—

"I'd hate to think so." Cece examined her silverware for cleanliness.

"Stop that. It's insulting to the servers. As for Rex, your mama's endless preaching about living a moral life must have finally taken hold on some level." Queenie said. "Also, I try not to leave marks anymore. Now, get to the point if you don't mind too terribly."

"In your conversation with him yesterday, did he say anything at all about Winnie?"

"No." She paused while the server laid out two Caesar salads with dressing on the side. "Thanks, but I'm not hungry."

"You don't find that odd?" Cece arched a brow, but didn't look her way.

"That I'm not hungry? No. You just came out here to talk to me about Rex. He and I have kind of a screwed up history, if you'll be so kind as to recall. Rex and my appetite are mutually exclusive these days. If he moves back to Vegas I may never eat again."

"Queenie. Pay attention." Cece gave her a look that could stop a felon in their tracks. Being no better than the average criminal, Queenie fell prey to the expression and settled. "Don't you find it odd that Rex had nothing to say about Winnie?"

"Odd, no. Insulting, yes. But considering our past it wasn't anything new. He wanted to be free of my poor choice, and he is. Why?"

Cece went back to her salad, meticulously distributing the Caesar dressing to suit her dietary desires. "When he was in today, we were going over some particulars of poor Whitey's estate. I assumed that at some point he would ask about you and Winnie."

"Did he?" Queenie held her breath.

"Not a single word."

She exhaled, and Cece continued. "He mentioned your chat last night, but never said anything at all about our dulcet darling. He was very complimentary, however, about the level of care you've lavished on the reaper."

"*Fiona,*" Queenie said with scorn. "Who names a Hellhound Fiona? Face it, he just doesn't care, Cece."

"Oh, he cared all right. Just not in the way we expected him too. He actually seemed disturbed that you felt betrayed by his decision to leave. Like your response was out of proportion to his action."

"The dick." Queenie stabbed her salad with more force than necessary, and took a bite of what ended up being just lettuce.

"Also, FYI, Diana never told him that Whitey was sick."

She swallowed her plain raw roughage and lay the fork back down, energizing her right to go hungry rather than eat plain lettuce ever again. "That bitch. They deserve each other then."

"Of course." Cece agreed, her attention on her own salad, a relationship that seemed to be humming along a lot more smoothly than Queenie's culinary efforts.

"Why do I feel a 'But' in here somewhere, Cece?" She asked. "It's virtually hanging over me, however, I can't see why it would be applicable at all under these circumstances."

Cece did the head bob gesture she used whenever she was about to float something crazy by.

"Stop doing the bouncy head thing and just spit it out."

"Okay, so, I got tired of dancing around the subject. When we were wrapping up I threw out an open-ended offer to help him with any of his legal needs. I specifically mentioned custody and palimony thinking he would bite. Why not? We're old friends. He must know that I kn——"

Queenie's head exploded."Wh——Why would you do that?!"

"You *know* why. If he had any designs on the Wonder Winnie I was ready to set him straight. But he just laughed and said he'd managed to steer clear on both counts."

Queenie was speechless, but she didn't know why precisely. Was she more shocked by Rex's ability to act like they were still best buds after sixteen years of him pretending she didn't exist, or by Cece's rash behavior? *My friends are all crazy.*

"Queenie," Cece reached across the table for the pepper. "Is it possible that he really doesn't know?"

"No. Not at all. Not remotely," she replied blindly, then paused. *Was it possible?*

Queenie had spent the better part of Winnie's life trying to get over the fact that the boy she had loved had grown into the man who'd left her behind to raise his child without a by-your-leave. The idea that he somehow might not have known...

"How could that even happen?" Queenie wondered aloud. "He *has* to know. We sent him a picture of me with a belly the size of Venus and a letter. He sent me that awful reply." To her bitter shame, she still had it somewhere but a single line had burned itself on her brain: *The choices you're making aren't what I would have wished for either of us. You'll always have a part of me, but I have to make my own way in the world now.*

"I know, I know. But something is seriously off track here." Cece said, picking through her salad deciding which leaf lived up to her standards. "Maybe he had a brain injury or something."

"Even if he did, it happened later. That still makes him a jerk."

Cece studied her longtime friend. "I'm not saying it doesn't. You loved him. He obviously loved you back. The pair of you tried to make a go of it and he left you on your own to raise our darling girl with no means of support. He's a jerk of the highest order."

"At least we agree on that."

"That's always been settled. Don't be so defensive, Mama Bear. I've been on this ride since the beginning, remember?" Cece placated her. "All I'm saying is that something isn't right. I can feel it. I don't know what it is, but we're going to find out."

"*We* are?" Dread gripped her.

"Yes. We're meeting him tomorrow night."

Dread took a stranglehold. "For god's sake Cece, why?"

"Really, Victoria?" Cece's no-nonsense tone spoke volumes. Dread won.

"Fine," Queenie said, with absolutely no intention of complying. "Where and when."

"Nice try." Cece pinned her with a look. "I'll pick you up."

\*\*\*

With time to kill and no one to kill it with, Rex cruised his old stomping grounds with the intention of hunting down the Survivor's Hutt Cece said he now owned part of. He fed the address she'd given him into his phone and let the GPS direct him. A few wrong turns later he managed to navigate into a Queen's Heights strip mall and locate what he was looking for.

Rex parked, noticing for the first time how relatively clean everything looked. The neighborhood in general seemed like it had undergone a refresh in the time he'd been away. Empty lots had been developed, new merchants replaced what he remembered as mostly seedy, rundown business fronts, and there were even a few banks. He pushed through the door, not quite knowing what to expect. A buzzer gave him away, and a dark haired man sporting a goatee and tattooed arms acknowledged him from behind a glass counter. "Hey."

"Hey," Rex returned the greeting. "Aaron Matson around?"

"You're lookin' at him." Aaron stood about a half a foot was shorter than Rex, but his shoulders were broad and all muscle.

"Hmm, not too many people around here know me without me knowing them first." Aaron gave Rex a studied glance. "You've got the look of a cop, but the walk of a soldier." He eyed the folder in Rex's hand. "You serving me? You're not the regular guy." His toothy grin invited a kind of rough trouble Rex was familiar with.

"You expecting to be served?" Rex asked easily.

Aaron shrugged as if not caring. "Fortune cookie say: Every day is filled with unexpected gifts."

"Cookie no lie, but I'm not serving you." Rex shuffled his paperwork around and held out his hand. "I'm Rex. Jasper was my uncle."

"Jasper?" Aaron's dark eyebrows drew together in cautious confusion. "Oh, you mean Whitey." He took Rex's hand, shaking it firmly before letting go. "Cece said you might stop by but I wasn't expecting you so soon." He gestured to a tall stool nearby, and Rex sat. "I know Whitey was a retired marine, but you don't have the look of a jarhead."

"Army Rangers," Rex answered. It wasn't something he usually talked about, but Aaron looked like he knew his way around a combat zone.

Aaron gave a low whistle. "Seriously? You just leveled up in my book. That's some hardcore shit."

"It was a living," Rex shrugged it off, not really wanting to get into it. "You, on the other hand, reek of leatherneck." He knew the look. Something about the stiff set of Aaron's shoulders broadcast Marine.

"Guilty as charged," Aaron gave a short bark of laughter.

"So, how'd you end up here?"

"I followed in Whitey's tracks for a while. Now, I just dabble."

An ex-marine that 'dabbled' was generally code for a range of unsavory activities Rex never understood. If he planned on staying he'd have to get his buddy Leonardo to take a hard look at Aaron Matson. "Cece said I'm your new partner."

"If you're interested." Aaron gestured around. "All this could be yours. Along with myself and Queenie, of course."

"Queenie is an actual person?"

"Hell on wheels when she wants to be, but yeah." Aaron grinned again. "A babe after my own heart. If only she'd stop giving it back to me." He winked. "I've got forty percent of the store, she and Whitey split the rest. I'll tell you what I told Cece: If you're looking to unload your shares I'll be happy to buy them off you."

"Shouldn't I offer them to both you and Queenie?"

Aaron shrugged. "I'm sure Cece already did. Queenie could pay you two or three times what I could offer if she wanted to, but it's not likely, man. She's pretty hands off. Kinda has to be."

"Why is that?"

"She's into most of the businesses around here."

"Into them how?" Rex suddenly pictured a matronly Italian woman with a fat gold ring he was going to have to kiss for approval.

"Sponsored them." Aaron said. "I don't know if you spent much time with Whitey, but it used to be pretty ghetto around here."

"Spent my formative years on Adams and J Street." Rex said.

Aaron gave a low whistled. "Presidential suites? That used to be a wasteland. Good on you for getting out. I'm a D-streeter myself." Aaron replied. "You know what it was like. Gangs everywhere, taggin' shit like they owned it. It wasn't great to begin with, then the recession hit, and everyone was dirt poor. Not even the gangs could afford spray paint. No one to rob."

"But not Queenie?"

"Not her. She lives in her own bubble. Never sailed the same waters as the rest of us, if you know what I mean. Does her own thing."

"Her thing sounds profitable."

"Ups are finally balancing out the downs in her case." Aaron said. "She came into some money right about then. Bought up most of these spaces and started leasing them out to anyone with a business plan and a dream."

"Sounds like a fairy godmother."

"Did a Cinderella number around here, that's for sure. A few years back people started calling the area Queenie's Hood. She didn't like that too much, so we changed it."

"And Queen's Heights was born."

"You got it, brother. She's a good partner. I can't speak for anyone else, but she's been great to me and for me. She comes by on Friday to do the books and manage payroll. I'm the guy you want in a tight spot, but I never had a head for numbers."

"I know what you mean." Rex said. "How'd my uncle get involved in this?"

"That was Queenie. When we opened the store ten years ago we split ownership sixty-forty in her favor. I'm not always around, and she had Cece and Walton in her pocket, so it made sense."

"Cece I know. Who's Walton?"

"Her accountant. You probably won't see too much of him. He's a West-sider. Doesn't come down here too often." Aaron smiled. "Probably with good reason. He smells like money. I mean, the area is relatively safe these days, but good old Walton has the look of a man asking to be rolled, if you know what I'm sayin'. *Expensive*."

"Sure," Rex nodded. *Probably enjoys dinner at the club with Bradford and Diana.*

"About two, maybe three years ago, Queenie and Walton brought in an insurance broker to put together a health plan for all of the business owners and their employees. She incorporated under one name and we all signed on as employees so we could qualify for bennies. You probably have military benefits, but out here in the civies health insurance was a bitch before the reform kicked in."

"I've heard."

"Yeah, I guess everyone has," Aaron said. "So, after that she tells me one day Whitey owns a third of the store and I'm the new bossman." He shook his head. "I found out later that Whitey had the big C and needed the insurance."

"He had military benefits."

"I suppose, but the VA hospital is quite a ways from here, and Whitey couldn't drive anymore. Even if he could, he was on a fixed income and the gas to trek out there three times a week would have put him in the poor house."

*You couldn't get much poorer than Whitey's house as it was*, Rex knew. "I never knew it was that bad. Looks like I have some gratitude to express."

"Whitey wasn't a man to advertise his troubles. And stubborn as hell most of the time." Aaron shrugged. "She did it for him, not you, man. She's like that. See's a problem, finds a solution. He was like family to her."

*Because god knew, Jasper Montgomery's own family wasn't around.* Rex's curiosity about the mysterious Queenie multiplied. "Still. I don't quite know what I'm doing around here yet. Think I can come by on Friday and meet her?"

"Don't see why not. She usually comes in around six thirty before the Z.E.R.T guys get here."

"Zert?"

"Zombie Eradication Response Team. It's a local group mostly, cops and ex-military, that get together for tactical training. We run drills all over the valley. It's a friendly competition. If you're interested, we're always looking for new blood."

"Sounds like fun."

"Starts at seven. We meet here, usually run some target practice on the range, then head out. My cousin Bobby is in charge of the details, but he doesn't suck. We have fun, dust the rust off our recon skills, and drink until we can't stand up afterwards."

"Sounds like old times."

"Thought it might. If you have your own gear go ahead and wear it, we'll supply you with anything you're short on."

Rex shook on it. "Can't wait."

## ๑—Chapter Three—๑
♔

Queenie sat at the bar of the Commonwealth awkwardly stroking her Cosmopolitan like a virgin trying to get to second base. She'd never been a cocktail drinker. Never saw the point, really. Drinking was for numbing the senses, not for using as a flirtation device, at least not for her.

The twenty-somethings of the Commonwealth were nothing like her, though. They glowed with an urbane confidence Queenie never felt in her life. *Leave it in the past where it lived and died, Victoria. You're not that girl anymore*, she reminded herself, wishing she'd never ordered the drink to begin with. *One cocktail isn't going to kill you.*

Cece was chatting up a client she'd seen on their way in, consequently abandoning Queenie and leaving her to wait for Rex on her own. She tried to calm the chainsaw-wielding butterflies in her stomach with some deep breathing, but the butterflies just ignored her and continued their deadly ballet. So, she'd given in and ordered the cocktail, and now was staring down the damn thing trying to decide if she was brave, or foolish, enough to drink it.

"Drink okay?" The bartender, a fit and friendly young man with an engaging smile and an eye for a set of broad shoulders, brought her back to the present.

Queenie nodded and took a small sip, faking a smile as she swallowed, betraying seventeen years of sobriety in a hummingbird's heartbeat. "It's great."

The bartender looked behind her, his eyes widening appreciatively at something, or someone, before falling to her and winking. "As much as I wish that were for me..." Queenie felt her stomach drop into her lap, disappointment in herself marrying the anxiety of impending doom and turned to see Rex's lopsided grin aimed her way. Suddenly she was twelve again.

"Victoria," he embraced her.

"You again." She returned the gesture, inhaling the freshly washed scent of him. He withdrew just as Cece approached, eyeing the Cosmopolitan with ill-concealed curiosity, but saying nothing. She hugged Rex, and before she could broach the subject of the drink the hostess arrived to seat them. The nouveau vintage backdrop of the Commonwealth suited Cece. It was artsy enough to feel comfortable, but elegant enough to dress up for.

The server came and took their drink orders and Cece kept the conversation flowing easily while they were served. When she paused to take a drink, Rex broke in. "I can't believe we're all here enjoying a drink together. This feels surreal somehow."

"No kidding," Queenie muttered to herself. She felt the pressure of Cece's stiletto against her foot beneath the table and acknowledged the warning with a vague nod. "So, Tex-Rex, give us the high points of the past eighteen years."

"You pretty much nailed it the last night, Victoria. Just soldiering."

"Toting a rifle across the planet to keep America safe?" She took a long sip of her drink, trying to do something with her hands besides fidget.

"Something like that." He gave her a penetrating look and Queenie realized her tone was sharper than she meant it to be. On the off chance that Cece was right and he really had no idea that he'd left her in the lurch, she should give him the benefit of the doubt. Of course, since the odds of that being true were so far from the mark, Queenie bottled up her angst for later.

"I'm more interested in hearing what you've been up to."

"Same old, same old. You know."

"I doubt that very much," he eased into the wing back chair and the fabric spanning the shoulders of his shirt groaned at the seams.

*Get a grip,* Queenie berated herself.

"It's true," Cece filled in. "She pretty much just sits on her ass all day abusing people."

"Hey," Queenie objected. "When you put it like that, you and I have the same life."

"You know what? You're right. We're more alike than I thought possible."

"I'm intrigued now." Rex glanced from Cece to Queenie.

"Don't be. I'm not that interesting," she tried to put him off. Rex's interest was the last thing she needed. "Cece's definitely the more dynamic of this duo. She was named Most Influential Woman of the Year by people who know that sort of thing. Tell him Cece."

"Don't let her snow you, Rex. It's on par with being voted best chewing gum by four out of five people who chew gum." Cece waived aside the accolade.

"Only if the mayor were chewing the gum, and chewing gum could be elected the next district attorney." Queenie added.

"Wow, the Mayor wants you to run for DA? That's big."

"It's in the early stages. I'm still trying the title on in my mind. In fact, I think my first act would be to change the job title to something with a little more cache."

"Lady Justice?" Queenie suggested.

"That has promise." Cece approved.

"Harbinger of Righteousness?" Rex offered up.

"That's awful," Cece laughed, pulling out her Blackberry and started working the keys. "I'm making a note to have Theo add that to my next order of business cards." She finished, then tucked the device away. "I can't believe no one thought of it sooner."

"Are you seriously thinking of running?"

"I'll tell you, the me of five years ago would've laughed it off. But now..." she shrugged, non-committedly.

"What's changed?"

Cece looked at Queenie then back to Rex. "I've seen the impact a single person can have on their community if they refuse to let anything get in their way."

*Stop it right now, Cassandra Woodson Esq. The last thing I need right now is for you to spill my life allover this fine oak table in front of Rex.*

"Your mother is a truly remarkable woman," Rex said, and Queenie raised her drink to prevent Cece from making any clarifications. "To Angel Baby and her dogged determination to keep us on the narrow straights of decency. May she live long and prosper."

Cece gave Queenie a questioning look and Queenie replied with a nearly imperceptible shake of her head, willing Cece to say no more. Cece appeared to heed the request.

"That's enough about us. It's the Rex Montgomery show we came to see. The boy soldier has gone off to the wars and come home in one piece. Have you abandoned the thug life permanently, or are you and the other Joes just on a break?" Cece asked.

"The other Joes and I have agreed to see other people permanently. I'm out." He folded his hands on the table. "When I heard about Jasper, it forced me to drop everything and take a look at my life. It felt like the right time for a change."

"Think that's likely to stick?" Queenie asked. Cece leaned in, nodding. "That's a good question. I have several clients that took some time off and realized that the structured lifestyle of the military had left them ill-equipped to deal with life out here in the asylum."

Rex rubbed his shoulder in a gesture Queenie didn't recognize. "I'm certainly going to try it on for size. I can always go back if I can't cut it out here."

"You staying with Diana?" Queenie asked. *Please, God do not let him tell me he's moving in to Jasper's house.*

"For now, but the Masterson McMansion isn't a good fit for me." Queenie choked out a laugh and Rex winked at her. "She still thinks she can take care of me."

"Like the mother you never wanted," Queenie observed.

Cece beamed at Rex. "Maybe she just thinks you need a woman's touch after spending so much time in the company of the rough and readies."

Rex chuckled. "If I let her, I'm sure she'd pick me out a suitable bride."

"Not interested?"

His gaze momentarily flickered in Queenie's direction. "Let's just say Diana and I vastly disagree on my type."

"Not in the market for a Stepford wife, then?" Queenie asked, Cece ignored the comment. "I know Diana had plans to sell off your uncle's place. You thinking of going ahead with that?" Cece smiled into the question, her glance sliding to Queenie, then pointedly to the drink in her hand.

*Easy girl*, the look said.

Having never achieved mastery over the art of interrogation, Queenie relaxed and let Cece guide the conversation. She finished off her Cosmopolitan and felt the vodka do its work. They talked about Diana and her family for a bit. One of the great ironies in Queenie's life was that she had never managed to get clear of Rex's sister.

Rex left. Jasper died, but Diana was the tired penny that kept casting her shadow over Queenie and Winnie's life. Winnie attended one of the few private high schools in the valley. She hadn't wanted to send her, but her daughter had her sights set high when it came to academics and Queenie wasn't going to ruin her chances by indulging the reverse snobbery she felt when it came to private education. Lady Luck may have been her seat-mate at the tables, but by some unfathomable stroke of ill fortune Winnie attended school with Diana's twins, Drake and David.

While she tried to avoid them, she had still managed to formulate some opinions regarding the boys. She was well into her second cosmopolitan when Rex started talking about them and the vodka chimed in. "Someone needs to keep an eye on Drake."

She knew she'd made a mistake when Cece's green gaze drilled into her.

Rex turned curious eyes on her. "He seems like a good kid to me."

Her mouth took over and she made a noise that was just short of a snort. "You've spent all of what, two days with him? He and I have been crossing paths for the past two years, and he's got trouble coming out of his pores. You can practically smell it on him, if you get past the weed."

"How can you have been anywhere near Drake or David?"

"Victoria's daughter goes to school with the boys. Didn't Diana mention it?"

Rex looked from Cece to Queenie, his expression confused. "No. I think I would have remembered."

*Here it comes,* Queenie thought readying her angst.

"You have a daughter?" Rex looked as shocked as Queenie felt. "I'm speechless."

He took the words out of her mouth.

The look Cece gave her was a mixture of victory and caution. She gave an airy wave like it was old news. "Winnie's circles sometimes mesh with your nephews'."

Rex sat forward, his full attention on Queenie. "And you think Drake is what, a bad seed?"

Queenie's angst, unwilling to remain cocked and unfired took flight. "I'd know if anyone would. Wasn't that the point you were making the last night?" *Easy girl.* She hadn't meant to say anything aloud, but two cocktails and her internal inertial dampeners were off-line. *Great, two drinks and I'm nearly three sheets to the wind.* "Drake is trying to get anyone who'll bother, to notice. I just happen to be the only one paying attention."

"Explain."

"Girl," Cece warned, but sat back to watch the show unfold in all it's glory. Her body language broadcasting that Queenie was off the reservation and Cece was going to give her all the rope she wanted to hang herself.

Queenie grasped for a place to start. *He's Diana's son,* that was enough for her, but Rex would probably need a more compelling argument.

"Have you had a chance to ask him why he doesn't drive?"

"I didn't even notice it until you mentioned it."

"David does the driving for both of them because Drake's license was revoked after he almost plowed another student down and ended up crashing into the principal's car at the beginning of last year."

"I remember that," Cece nodded. "It made the news didn't it?"

"People have accidents," Rex offered.

"Mmm-mmm, honey," Cece gave a miniscule head-shake. "Trust me when I tell you that sweet boy was as high as a kite."

"And then there was Boobgate," Queenie continued. "Drake lost a bet to one his friends and the payback was to go grab some poor girl's chest."

"Please tell me it wasn't your daughter," he grimaced.

"Her best friend Rachel." Cece offered. "We got the account first hand because her parents consulted me about prosecuting Drake."

"Whose side are you on?" Rex asked.

"The side of justice," Cece raised her glass to him. "Also, the one who calls first. Which as you probably know wouldn't be Diana."

"Shouldn't he be expelled by now, then?"

"You'd think," Queenie tipped her head in agreement. "But the school is privately funded and not in a position to refuse the tuition of a future felon."

"Ouch. Is that really necessary?" Rex gave Queenie a direct look, which she answered.

"Not to mention the fact that he's a drug dealer. A fact which you may be tempted to dispute, but as we all know, who better than me to recognize my own kind?"

"Victori—"

She barreled through his objection. "There are always one, or two, like him, you know? Friendly, good-looking kids out there to help you enhance your joy, or help with that semester-exam stress. Guys that make a major moral misstep seem more like stubbing your toe than pitching your future down the toilet. That's Drake." Queenie held Rex's stare, alcohol bolstering her fury with all things Montgomery. "He's decided to crash his personal life and while he's at it, he'll be more than happy to pilot your plane into the Bermuda Triangle so he'll have company at the campfire."

Rex broke their shared gaze, sending a look to Cece, who only shrugged.

Queenie felt her rage balloon burst and she dropped back into the moment, realizing what she'd done. *Booze - 1, common sense – negative infinity*, Queenie slid the half-consumed cocktail purposely away from her and stood, shaking her head disgusted with herself. "Once an addict, always an addict. You'll have to excuse my mouth. It's running as usual. You two enjoy your evening."

"Don't be stupid, Victoria. I drove you." Cece argued, but Queenie waved her off ignoring the concern in her friend's expression and hating herself for putting it there.

"I can cab home, Cece. I'm a big girl now. I know how."

They watched her go and Rex turned to Cece. "She hasn't changed much, then."

"You'd be surprised." Cece picked up Queenie's half empty glass, pondering it. "I haven't seen that side of her in years. Trust a Montgomery man to bring it out of her."

"Something I said?"

"Someone you are, may be more likely." She shrugged easily and eased into the wingback chair, legs crossed elegantly.

"You think I made her regress somehow?"

"I don't know the person that can make her do anything, so don't give yourself that much credit, buddy boy. What I would say is that some behaviors are ingrained in people and it can take time to work them out. You and I had the benefit of strong role models to keep us on the straight and narrow. The first time I met you, you were dressed in fatigues and hiding in Angel Baby's pomegranate tree."

"And you were yelling at me that if I fell out of that tree and broke myself, good luck suing your mama because '*ain't nobody got nothing worth havin' in this hood*'."

Cece laughed out loud. "I can't believe you remember that."

"It was a formative moment in our relationship, as it turns out." A smaller stick-like version of Cece popped into Rex's memory and he tried to reconcile the image with the striking woman across from him now.

"I was wrong, you know." She took a demure sip of Victoria's abandoned cocktail.

"About the tree?" He grinned.

"Mmm-hmm. Turns out it's covered by homeowner's insurance."

"Thank god, it didn't matter." Rex chuckled.

"Yeah, J.J. broke you instead."

Rex rubbed his wrist. "Your cousin had a strong grip."

"Still does. He's a UFC trainer these days. Equal parts tattoos and muscle. Scary to behold. Once a force of nature, always a force of nature. Do you remember why he handled you that day?"

"I had finally pinned down the shadow that had been trailing me since moving in with Jasper." Rex was suddenly eight years old again and sitting on top of a black haired spitfire half his size. "You know, J.J. didn't need to be so rough. She'd already punched me in the face and knocked my front tooth out."

Cece chuckled. "Welcome to the hood. Lord, no wonder your sister hates it."

Rex took a long pull of his lime and soda and shrugged. "Diana's list of dislikes runs the length of my leg."

"Oh my. You sound like you're on it these days."

"Maybe. Hell, probably. Her husband and sons are on the list, why not me? We're all disappointing her in one way or another." He raked a hand through his hair. "I think she's afraid I'm going to move back here."

"That likely?"

"It wasn't." *And now?*

"But now it is?" Cece's eyebrow raised slightly. "You miss combat that much, sign up for another tour."

Rex laughed. "I cruised the neighborhood today. Went to visit the Survivor's Hutt, as a matter of fact."

"And?"

"And I didn't get shot, so it beats most of the places I've been in the past few years."

"What did you think of Aaron?"

"I think he's probably scary as fuc—, er, hell when he's on his own time, since you asked." Rex shrugged. "If you'll pardon the expression."

Cece laughed. "He said nearly the same about you."

"Well, that's something then." Rex nodded, deciding full disclosure was the best route with Cece. "I'm pretty sure he's up to no good in as many ways as it can be manufactured."

"Seriously?" Cece's eyes widened.

"Most likely. But probably not in this country. When I asked him about his service he said he dabbled. That almost always means a guy is mercing abroad. I'm guessing one of the reasons he wanted a business partner was to leave a credible paper trail and give himself a verifiable income."

Cece gave a low whistle. "I'm fairly certain his business partners never suspected him of anything below board."

"Jasper would've known the minute he met Aaron." Rex shrugged. "He was old, but a merc is merc. If Jasper didn't care, there's probably not much to worry about, but all the same I'm going to drop a buddy of mine a line and see what comes down the wire."

"Talk about buyer beware." Cece finished off Queenie's drink. "Sounds like you're planning on planting some roots in Queen's Heights."

"Maybe. Depends on what I'm likely to harvest." Rex said. "What can you tell me about this Queenie? Aaron said she owns the rest of the shop. Hell, from what Aaron said she owns most of the area."

Cece paused, contemplating the empty glass in her hand before speaking. "She's lived in the area all her life."

Rex suddenly felt like his friend was hedging, but chalked it up to client confidentiality. "She comes across like the love child of Don Corleone and Mother Teresa."

"That's her in a nutshell," Cece smiled broadly and laughed. "But she's all legal."

"You make sure of that?"

"Of course."

"She have any shady past I need to be aware of?"

Cece pressed her lips together in silent humor. "I vetted her myself and I can tell you that despite her best intentions, she's a law abiding upstanding member of the community."

"How did she come by her capital if she's a hood rat?"

"The old fashioned way."

"She was a prostitute?"

Cece burst out laughing. "No, idiot! She swindled it out of from under the noses of rich men with too much ego and not enough sense."

"And she didn't put out for it?"

"I sometimes wish she would," Cece sighed. "But no."

"Now I'm curious."

"I thought you might be." Cece smiled.

\*\*\*

"Jesus, Queenie, you're killing us here," Cowboy watched the dealer slide the pile of chips towards his opponent. "Your tells are off by a mile."

"I don't have any tells," she tossed her cards towards the dealer and began loosely sorting her chips into piles to get them out of the way.

"You have two," Bandit replied automatically, then cast a shame-faced look around the table. "Sorry."

"Do I?" Queenie looked around at the nodding heads, then at Lin, the dealer who only shrugged. "What are they?"

"Bandit, if you plan on giving that information away, you might as well just give her your credit card too." Elliot Bryant said from the far end of the table.

Bandit, otherwise known as Lucas Randolph, lifted his hands. "Not me."

"Cowboy?"

"Nah, sugar. You're sweet, but I've got three girls in college and a wife with a rather unhealthy affection for Louis Vuitton." He tipped his head apologetically. "I'll go to my grave with your tells."

"Amazing Rando?"

As expected, Amazing Rando said nothing, just smiled and adjusted his mirrored sunglasses.

Lin dealt and Queenie checked her cards and anteed. There was a collective groan from the table and they folded. "What is wrong with you all? Never played poker before? If you buy-in I'll show you how."

"You're no fun without a little read, Queenie." Elliot said. "I don't know what's going on in your head today, but it's like you're not even here."

"She's here. She's got our money to prove it." Bandit said with humor.

"Maybe it's time to take a break," Cowboy looked around the table.

"Seriously?" Queenie addressed him. "I'm only up ten thousand. You've lost more and never cried about it."

"I had a chance then, Queenie. You've only been here an hour and had nothing but aces up your sleeve. Lady Luck is sitting in your lap tonight, sugar. I know when the tide isn't flowing my way."

Queenie looked around the table and saw the sentiment mirrored in the other player's eyes. Even Amazing Rando seemed somehow in solidarity behind his ever-present shades.

"Besides, you don't usually play tonight. What gives?"

What gave was that she had nothing else to do. It was Friday night and Winnie was staying over at a friend's house, and Queenie had no desire to call Cece and listen to her rant about her performance the night before. She didn't know what to say. She'd acted like a child.

Her phone buzzed in her pocket for the hundredth time that day and she ignored it.

"There she goes again."

Cowboy's comment jerked her into the present.

"Fine." Queenie took three chips from her winnings and passed them to Lin. "Cash me out please, Lin."

"Of course, Queenie." He gestured to the pit boss.

"It's nothing personal, Queenie." Elliot said. "Just come back when you're a little less lucky."

Queenie accepted her receipt from the pit boss and looked at Elliot. "I'll come back when you've found your balls."

"Damn, if you're not cute when you're angry." Cowboy laughed before turning back to the table.

Queenie walked away as Lin dealt. Her phone lit up her pocket again and she pulled it out, seeing that it was Aaron. *Oops.* Queenie checked the time and answered it before it could go to voicemail.

"Hey, Aaron. I'm sorry. I totally forgot what day it is."

"It's all good. I thought you might have. You're usually pretty prompt. I've got Z.E.R.T. in tonight. You coming now? If not, I can leave the flash drive in the safe and J.J. can get it out."

"J.J. has the combo to the safe?"

"Not exactly, but I'm pretty sure he could get into it if he felt the need."

"Be there in ten."

"I'll be here, babe."

By the time Queenie reached the shop the carnival of zombie apocalists was already in full swing. Men and women in varying degrees of tactical gear loitered in and out of the store, haphazardly organizing themselves for the evening's mission. Queenie made her way in and recognized a familiar face near the entrance.

Jerome was Cece's cousin, and as menacing in an octagon as Cece was in a courtroom. He filled in as security for the store when Aaron planned on being out. "J.J., you see Aaron around anywhere?"

"Hey, sweet thing." He bent down and gave her a quick squeeze. "Aaron's in the back with his latest recruit. Probably signing waivers as we speak."

She nodded her thanks and headed back to the inventory room that doubled as an office, waving at the regulars she recognized along the way, relieved to be free of the crowd when she finally pushed through the door.

"Hey, Queenie my love, you made it." Aaron smiled at her, but her answering smile died on her lips as she lay eyes on Aaron's newbie. "This is Rex, latest new recruit and our new business partner until he decides otherwise."

"*You're* Queenie?" Rex's floored expression almost made up for being jacked from the poker table. "And you're a wild card this week, Rex." Queenie ignored the chainsaw wielding butterflies that had once again chosen this moment to manifest, and stepped over to Aaron to give him a hug. Aaron hugged her back, but his eyes never left Rex.

"Is there a problem here?" He asked her, looking from Rex back to her, body language broadcasting battle readiness.

"Dial it down, Zombie Killer." Queenie commanded with more confidence than she felt. "Rex and I have known each other since we were kids." She smiled at Aaron hoping none of the anxiety she felt bled through. The last thing she wanted was to have Aaron digging into her past.

*Stop it, Queenie. You belong here. Rex is the outsider now.*

"Did you say hi to J.J. yet?" She gave Rex a half-hearted grin.

Rex grinned back and the tension eased in the room. "Oh, god. He's here too?"

"He's on the door tonight," she looked at Aaron. "I take it that means you're leading the charge this evening."

"Yeah, Bobby has a thing. So J.J. and Jimmy have it covered." He opened the desk drawer, pulled a flash drive out and tossed it to her. "The week's numbers."

"Can I get a look at those when you're done?" Rex surprised her by asking.

"Sure. How far back do you want the accounting?" Queenie tossed her bag on the desk and grabbed a pen and paper.

"How much do you have?"

"Little over ten years worth." She told him.

"Ten years will do."

"You really thinking about joining us, then?" Aaron asked, closing up his desk and filing away whatever Rex had just signed.

"Still too early to tell." His gaze met hers briefly, before busying himself with adjusting the obnoxious collection of man toys cluttering his utility belt.

"I, for one, would love it. I've got other commitments coming in, and it would really help if we had a third around." He tightened the strap on his Kevlar vest. "You're still good to cover me next week, right Queenie?"

*Damn, he'd asked her a month ago and she's completely forgotten about it.*

"Yes, of course." She mentally reworked her schedule.

"Maybe Rex could do some time in the store. Get himself acquainted with the biz." He patted Rex on the back. "How about it, Queenie? That work for you Rex?"

"Sure."

"Great." Queenie offered her brightest smile to the duo, hoping her internal cringe wasn't showing. *A week with her baby daddy. What could be better?*

"It's all settled then. You'll watch out for my girl, and learn the ropes." He grinned. "Let's go kill some zombies!"

\*\*\*

Aaron tossed back a shot and called for another round from Richie the bartender as he tried to figure out just what it was about Rex Montgomery that set his teeth on edge. Army Rangers were never his preferred arm of the brotherhood, too much Boy Scout, not enough hell raiser if you asked him. Even Navy SEALS could be a little tight for his taste. But a brother was a brother and plenty of the Z.E.R.T. crew were from other branches of the military.

Watching Rex kick back with the others, Aaron had to admit he'd fit in with the gang right from the start. Clear-headed, a clean shooter, friendly and even-tempered. What wasn't to like?

He hadn't made it out before Whitey kicked it, but Aaron recalled from his own days in the service that the military wasn't always the most accommodating employer at times. It was one of the many reasons the two of them were no longer in a relationship. Rex was a Ranger, there was no telling what kind of missions he might have been on when Whitey got sick. And knowing Whitey, Aaron doubted the old man had been in a hurry to cry to his nephew about his illness. So, that wasn't it either. Clearly no one expected Rex to show up.

*And why would that be?*

He worked the thread of reasoning. Hadn't Rex said he'd grown up in the neighborhood? That had to have been with Whitey. Yet Whitey had never spoken of his nephew. There were no Army proud stories of his Ranger nephew, no commiserating tales, or photographs. Rex had been almost non-existent, but Jasper had still thought highly enough of Rex to leave him his share of the business when he could have just given it back to Queenie.

*Queenie.*

Aaron survived on instincts, and right now those instincts were waving a bright red flag over his best girl and Rex Montgomery. Then there was the thing that passed between Rex and Queenie. It was a no brainer that they'd have known one another if Rex lived across the street from Queenie, but she'd never mentioned Rex either. In fact no one had. It was like he'd materialized out of thin air. J.J. acted like Rex was a long lost brother, but Aaron couldn't recall ever hearing about him. It was like he'd fallen off the scene and then just walked back on the set one day.

Aaron was tempted to go to Queenie for answers, but they'd agreed a long time ago to leave the past alone. *Your brilliant idea,* he reminded himself. It seemed like it at the time. She was a single mom living in a bad neighborhood, and he had more than a few indiscretions he'd rather not mention. So, he'd suggested a fresh start for the pair of them and she hadn't argued. Over the years he'd been tempted to amend the suggestion, but never did and now it was too late. He had a whole new rash of troubles he didn't want coming to light. But sometime in the near future he'd be looking at all his issues in his rearview mirror, with Queenie at his side.

If he brought the subject of Rex up now with Queenie, he'd be coming across like some jealous ex-lover. *Isn't that what you are, bud?* He ignored the thought. It was only a matter of time before she came to her senses and took him back. He knew she'd been close to giving in a couple of times. And she'd never even tried dating anyone else after they'd broken up. For Aaron that was the whole story.

He was getting ready to cash out and settle up his side life and he wanted Queenie with him when he put down new roots. It wasn't going to be in Vegas, he had too many loose ends in town. Maybe San Francisco, or Florida. Some place close to an airport so the kid could visit. He hadn't ironed out all of the details yet, but he would.

Rex laughed at something someone at his table said and an idea began to form in Aaron's mind. He tossed back his drink and gestured to Richie.

"Another round, boss?"

"Set up some Jaeger shots for my friends at the table, would you, Richie?" Aaron stood up. "And keep them coming."

"Sure thing."

Aaron joined the table accompanied by the first round of shots. "Richie says these poor drinks are lonely. You guys know the drill. Everybody buddy up."

"I'm good," Rex gestured to his beer as hands converged on the liquor.

"A little bit of Jaeger can turn good into great, my friend." Marshall, a cop on Rex's left took a shot and placed it into Rex's hand. "Besides, it's tradition."

"And it's on Aaron," Randy, a Z.E.R.T. regular, grabbed his own shot and lifted it up, the others following suit. "To the disease ridden fallen, and surviving another week among the healthy."

"The fallen," the group murmured and tossed back their drinks in one motion. Aaron pulled another shot and slid it Rex's way. "You need to catch up, friend. My girl would tear me a new one if I didn't take care of you."

"I'm good, really." Rex objected.

"You have a girl now, Aaron?" Marshall asked, taking another shot for himself.

"Same girl I always have." Aaron picked up his whiskey and knocked it against Rex's waiting shot glass. "You wouldn't leave a brother hanging, would you Rex?"

\*\*\*

Queenie finished crunching the Survivor Hutt's numbers for the week, closed her laptop and looked at Cobra Bubbles. "Not much of a Friday night, eh?"

Cobra Bubbles whipped her tail against the couch, and scooted her dense black body along the sofa until she could lay her massive head in her mistress's lap. Queenie absently began to stroke the dog's ears while she reached for the remote. She turned on the television, surfing the channels until she ran across a broadcast of You've Got Mail.

She fell asleep waiting for Meg Ryan to realize Tom Hanks was her true love, only to be awakened a short time later by Cobra Bubbles' thunderous bark and a pounding at the door.

"Stella!"

The dog, eager to prove her security chops, leapt off the couch and sped to the door with Queenie following at a slightly less anxious pace.

She barely had the knob turned when the weight on the other side pushed the door forward. "Hey!" Queenie thrust her body against the door to stop it from coming completely open and allowing some random inebriate to enter, but Cobra Bubbles was on the side of the intruder and the task suddenly became tantamount to getting a ring of power to Mordor. "Bubbles, leave it!" She commanded, but the dog only wagged her tail and nosed the door open further.

"Ah, Fiona. You do remember me."

"Rex?" Queenie yanked the door open and Rex spilled through it, barely catching himself. *And tonight's anxiety attack is brought to you by the US armed forces.*

"In the flesh." His breath broadcast his condition.

"Geez, you're drunk." She turned her face away.

"It's my turn, Queenie, don't you think?" He smiled crookedly.

He was standing, but Queenie didn't know how long gravity would spare him. She kicked the door shut behind her and with the help of Cobra Bubble's herding instincts, maneuvered him to the sofa.

The thought of him driving in this condition was horrific. Queenie wondered if she could expect to find his rental on her lawn, but she hadn't heard a car at all, come to think of it. "How'd you get here?" She left him melting on the sofa and went to the door to bolt it closed.

He displayed the long fingers of one hand and began ticking off on his digits. "Helicopter, air craft carrier, military transport aircraft, rental car, and feet."

Queenie followed along as he related his transportation trail, and paused trying to sort out the end. "You mean you walked here?"

"Yes ma'am." His head rocked sloppily.

"From the Survivor's Hutt?" It was a good five miles from the store to her house.

"Affirmative."

"You're an idiot." She checked the clock. "It's after midnight." But then again, even in his obviously impaired state Rex looked dangerous. And he was still wearing his Kevlar vest from the Z.E.R.T. event.

Cobra Bubbles jumped up onto the couch to keep Rex company and he ruffled her ears, bringing his face down to hers. "We've been in worse places. Haven't we Fiona?" The dog licked the side of his face and Rex turned up to Queenie. "See?"

"I'm sure you have," Queenie sighed, undone by the ridiculously adorable sight of an intoxicated soldier reunited with his former Hellhound. "What are you doing here, Rex?"

"Dunno." He shrugged. "Your boy dropped me off at the store. Can't drive like this." He slurred slightly, the end of his sentence turning slushy.

"Cab out of the question?" Queenie was going to kill Aaron.

"To Diana's? Not an option, ma'am. She'd lose her sh— er, mind if I came home like this." His hand made a loopy gesture that his eyes followed. "And I don't think she's got a good grip on it as it is, if you really want the truth."

"I'd figured out as much already," Queenie said. "You're ridiculous. I thought you military types could hold your liquor."

"I'm not a drinker. That was always you, but your boy Aaron was laying it on pretty heavy with the welcome shots."

"He's not my boy," Queenie said automatically.

"But he was once," Rex looked to Fiona for confirmation, taking the dog's tail wag for a yes. "See. Even she knows."

"Once, yes. For a little while. But not anymore." The words were out of her mouth before she could stop them.

"Thought so." Rex laid his head back, and his body, deciding that gravity wasn't all that bad after all, slid over until he was half lying on her sofa. "I saw how he looked at you."

Queenie went to the kitchen, returning with two aspirin and a glass of water. "Aaron and I were over years ago."

"Not to him." Rex waggled a finger in the air, and Queenie choked down a laugh.

"Sit up, Tex-Rex." He pushed himself upright. "Open up soldier." When he did, she popped the aspirin in his mouth and pressed the glass into his hand. "Drink. I know you can do that."

"Ha! I see what you did there," he slurred over the aspirin in his mouth, then drank deeply and handed the glass back, missing her outstretched hand completely. Queenie grabbed for it as is passed, fingers reaching it just as an arm snaked around her waist pulling her down.

"Rex."

He ignored her, pulling her down onto his lap until his face was inches from hers. "He calls you *his girl*."

He was so close she could detect the sweet scent of Jaegermeister on his breath. It was enough to make her feel like she was sixteen again.

"Rex, you're *so* drunk."

"He calls you his girl," he repeated, ignoring her, "but you were mine first." He pulled her closer, his mouth capturing hers. Queenie had a split second urge to push him away, the inclination melting into desire. As the kiss continued, he withdrew enough to trace his tongue over her lips, pausing to suck gently at her lower lip.

Queenie heard the moan, recognizing it as her own and Rex deepened the kiss, turning his body and laying back, pulling Queenie down on top of him. The position should have put her in control, but Rex's hand slid up into her hair, gripping it slightly, controlling the pace of the kiss. His tongue darted in and out of her mouth, then plunged deeply, only to withdraw so he could suckle her lips again.

The sensation melted her in ways she'd forgotten she could feel, leaving her lightheaded and breathless. When she was sure her heart would burst out of chest Queenie broke off the kiss, pushing herself off slightly. "Rex, you're drunk. We have to stop."

"Do we, Queenie?" Hazel eyes clouded with desire met hers and she felt the power of his arousal against the inside of her thigh. Unable to look him in the eye anymore, she lay her head on his chest. "Yes."

He sighed, his large frame sinking into the couch. "If you say so." His arm settled around her, fingers drawing circles over the fabric covering the small of her back. When his hand rested and his breathing settled, she knew he'd fallen asleep. Queenie extracted herself, careful not to disturb him, at the same time not sure if she could.

She took off his shoes and retrieved a blanket. Before covering him, Queenie unfastened his batman belt and denuded him of his Kevlar vest, maneuvering it around him to make him more comfortable. As she drew it off the arm wedged closest to the sofa back his shirt started to come with it and she ended up pulling both his t-shirt and vest off in one motion. She dropped the gear on the floor near his shoes where he would see it in the morning and grabbed the blanket. As she spread it over him, she caught sight of the scars.

Queenie caught her breath in the semi-darkness, forcing herself to absorb the damage that he'd taken. When he'd left her he'd stopped being a real person somehow. In her living memory of him he was untouched by age, and definitely lead. Before that moment if he'd never come home she was certain she would have taken the image of a nineteen year-old Rex to her grave. But the sight of him now, so obviously changed from the younger version she knew forced her ego aside, softening the hard edge of the resentment she'd carried for him. Resentment that it turned out he somehow hadn't earned on his own.

Things between them had somehow gone wrong, and stayed that way. But no matter how angry she'd been at Rex Montgomery, Queenie would never have wished upon him what the legacy of the scars on his body were telling her. Some new, some old, some that she could readily identify as bullet wounds, others that just confused her, and one particularly nasty scar along his shoulder. "Goddammit, Rex, you weren't supposed to get yourself shot."

He ignored her, one cheek dimpling against the couch pillow. Despite whatever he'd been through, and the scruff he was sporting he'd still managed to hang on to the boyish innocence she remembered.

"Hello, what's this?" She identified the telltale edge of a tattoo with a design she couldn't quite make out in the dim light. *Just when you thought he couldn't get sexier, Queenie.* "You showed me, Rex." Queenie pulled the blanket over Rex and Cobra Bubbles stepped lightly onto the encumbered sofa, insinuating herself into the little space that was leftover.

"Goodnight, girl." Queenie gave the dog's head a stroke and slipped away to her own bed.

## ᑎ—Chapter Four—ᑎ

ₒₗₒ

Rex stirred uneasily Saturday morning to the bizarre sensation of having two heartbeats. His first thought was that he'd passed out in the bar and someone had seized upon the opportunity to use his body to host an illegally harvested human heart to get it out of the country and into the body of a billionaire, Vietnamese War Lord. Then he remembered that was the plot of the CSI he'd been watching with David the other night and he came to his senses.

An immense weight shifted on his lower extremities and Rex made an emergency assessment of exactly how drunk he'd been the night before. He had no real way to measure. He wasn't a drinker, except for a few memorable teambuilding experiences with his fellow Rangers. Years of watching Victoria's father, Colin, and then Victoria drink themselves into numb stupor had turned him off the stuff. But Aaron had exerted a kind of man-card peer pressure the night before that tagged Rex's button like a bull's eye.

He couldn't recall how many Jaeger shots he'd downed the night before; he'd lost count after the first dozen. His head didn't hurt exactly, but it was seriously considering it. Rex cracked an eyelid, but the sunlight had him jamming it shut again. When he tried to lift his hand to shield the light so he could try again and it failed to respond, Rex experienced a moment of real alarm.

Heedless of the sunlight his eyes sprung open to discover he was blanketed in well over a hundred pounds of dog and being watched by a young woman sporting chin length red hair framing a heart-shaped face armed with a blue-gray gaze that could pierce titanium. She sat in the chair opposite the sofa studying him.

She, or someone, had been thoughtful enough to provide a Coke and a bag of what Rex's olfactory senses defined as drive-thru french fries. Both were tantalizingly out of reach considering his situation.

"Hi." She said, a trace of a smirk in her crooked smile.

"Hi," Rex replied with a mouth that felt and tasted like lint covered cough drops.

"Nice pecs. You work out?" She asked.

Rex looked down, discovering he was indeed bare-chested. Finding his hands, he jerked them out from under Fiona and pulled up the blanket he had no memory of. "Sort of."

The girl's smirk disappeared, crooked smile widening into an even grin, eyebrows drawn together. "You're awfully shy for a half-naked man."

"You have a lot of experience with half-naked men?" Rex asked, pulling his blanket up to determine if he was really only half-naked. *Pants, check.*

"It's Vegas, buddy," the girl shrugged. "Since the Hangover movies came out this city has been lousy with dudes in various states of undress. I think there's even a website. Where have you been?"

"Everywhere but here, the Middle East mostly," Rex looked around finally getting his bearings. The house, like the girl, looked familiar in a vague way. The girl was an older version of the one in the picture by Jasper's bed frame, and the house had the same floor plan as Queenie's old one, but the inside of that one had never been this nice. His only real clue was the dog.

"That explain the holes in you?"

"As much as anything," he tried to keep up, but the latent hangover was making it a challenge. He reached for the name Cece had mentioned at the Commonwealth. "You're Winnie."

She gave him a thumbs-up, still grinning. "Good job getting your diagnostics back on-line so fast. I am indeed Winnie, though I prefer Wonder Winnie, but I'll let it pass this time." She nodded to the dog. "Okay, Bubbles." The dog gave Rex's hand a lick and let herself onto the floor. "She seems to like you. You're lucky she didn't bring you a tiny corpse as a testament to her adoration."

"Thanks." Blood rushed back into his legs, and he suffered the momentary unpleasantness of a million pins and needles in his feet before he was able to sit upright completely. "I think."

"You're welcome." Her head tilted prettily. "Who the heck are you anyway when you aren't the drunk guy on my couch."

"Rex. An old friend of your mom's." He pointed to the food, suddenly equal parts hungry and thirsty. "That for me?"

She got up and opened the bag and fished around for something before taking out a handful of tater-tots and handing it to Rex. "You see anyone else around here in need of the Hangover Special?" She made a kissing noise to the dog and wandered into the kitchen where Bubbles sat while Winnie filled the dog's bowl with kibble, dropping the tater-tots on top before setting it on the floor. The dog dug in and Rex did the same. "I didn't know what you preferred, so my friend Rachel and I picked a little bit of everything from the menu. Mom said it was always fries and a Coke for her, so I took the liberty." Winnie grabbed a bowl from the cupboard and poured herself a bowl of cereal, before adding milk and rejoining Rex "I hate to eat alone, don't you?"

Rex inhaled the contents of the bag and half of the coke by the time she joined him. The greasy salty mishmash of his makeshift breakfast had reached his stomach and was working its magic. "Your mom around?" He asked, trying to remember the path that had brought him here and failing.

Winnie shook her head, her mouth full. She chewed and swallowed. "It's past noon. She had to go to work for a little while and sent me a text recommending I bring food."

"Your dad?" Rex looked around realizing he had no idea what Queenie's living situation was at all.

"No takers. My real dad bailed while I was in utero, and Mom has yet to fill the position."

"I'm sorry." Rex said, suddenly overcome with the urge to punch Winnie's father in the face.

"Don't be. His loss." Winnie took another spoonful of cereal and Cobra Bubbles, having finished her kibble, came to sit by

Winnie, soulful black eyes gleaming with hope that the cereal fairy might bequeath her an errant marshmallow charm.

"I lost my dad when I was a kid. It was tough."

"You've gone from the drunk-guy-on-the-couch, to someone I'm sharing absent father stories with in fifteen minutes flat. You're smooth, I'll give you that much." Winnie tucked a piece of hair behind one ear and frowned. "Your dad story. That was probably worse. My mom may be the only biological unit in the line-up, but I have plenty of other wanna-be-rents watching me like hawks."

"Rents?"

"As in pa-rents. You know. The people who tear holes in the fabric of your life on a daily basis."

"I see. So, who's on your rental agreement these days?"

Winnie smiled at his joke and for some reason Rex felt better about himself. He wasn't just the hung-over guy in her mom's house. Now, he was the slightly less than hopeless hung-over guy with nice pecs in her mom's house who could make her laugh.

"You know my mom's friends?" She asked, bringing him back.

"Some."

"Aunt Cece and Cousin J.J.?"

"Oh, yeah," Rex said. "J.J. broke my arm when we were kids."

Winnie's eyebrows reached for the roof as she nodded. "You're big, but J.J. is a house. You're lucky he didn't break all of you." Having finished the cereal, Winnie drained the milk and set the bowl on the table. Cobra Bubbles looked on with longing. "Then you probably know Angel Baby. She's on the list. And Uncle Jasper until recently because he died. And JP."

"JP?" Rex knew everyone except the last.

"Short for Jiffy Pop. His real name is Aaron, but he's like the crazy step-father I never had. He filled the dad role on demand when I was a kidlet, which explains the nickname, but not much else unless you know him."

"We've met." *Aaron. Again.* Rex had a flashback from the night before. *He calls you his girl.* There's only one person he would have said that to. An uncomfortable feeling niggled through him. *Oh, hell.*

"You know JP?"

Rex scrubbed his hands over his face. "He's the reason I'm on your couch, actually."

"Now, come on Rex. You don't really believe that do you?"

Her tone sounded so much like his sister's that Rex startled and Winnie laughed. "I'm B-S-ing you of course. JP is nuts. He drinks like it's his last day on the planet. It's one of the reasons he and my mom never worked out."

"Oh?"

"Yeah, she says she has addiction issues. She never touches the stuff." Winnie shrugged. "Hard to picture her that way actually. How long have you known her?"

"Strictly speaking, we were introduced on her seventh birthday. I gave her a My Little Pony Tea Set, and she drew a skull-and-crossbones on my cast in red sharpie. We would've probably gotten around to meeting a little earlier than that, but J.J. intervened before I could get her name."

"Oh." The story seemed to give Winnie pause. "That's really sweet. Did you know her when she was an addict?"

Rex looked around the house. It bore little resemblance to the pigsty that Colin Hart lived in with his only daughter, but Rex could still picture Victoria the last time he saw her, strung out on the couch after her father's funereal, a new fifth of scotch and a bottle of valium on the floor near her head. He let the memory fade into the Victoria he knew now.

"Yes. Yes I did."

Winnie shrugged again and rose. "There's a shower down the hall if you want to wait for my mom to get home. Towels are in there. I have manual labor to attend to, so if you'll excuse me."

"You work too?"

"Nah. Mom won't let me. She says school is my job." Winnie went to the fridge and grabbed a bottle of water from it. "I have to box up my things from Uncle Jasper's house. It's just across the street. He died a little while ago and Mom says she thinks the house is going to be sold."

"You stayed with Jasper?" That explained the room.

"You know him?" She looked surprised.

"He was my uncle."

"Ah, it all comes together now," she slid her palms together. "You had an amazing collection of boy toys."

"Guilty."

Winnie grinned. "You almost got me kicked out of school."

"Pardon?" Rex sat back, hands raised.

"Turns out not all of your goods were rated G." Winnie sat again, tucking a leg under her.

"I plead the fifth," Rex said, trying to sift through the mental fog to figure out what she was talking about. "Care to elaborate?"

Winnie gave Cobra Bubble a knowing glance then took pity on him. "When I was in grade school my mom took on the arduous task of revamping Jasper's house."

"That doesn't sound like Jasper's thing."

"I'm pretty sure Mom never asked him. He was going out of town for a military reunion."

"Sneak attack, then?"

"Go with what works, Mom always says," Winnie supplied. "Anyway, Mom set all the stuff that was going to Goodwill out in boxes and told me to take anything I wanted. I was going through a pineapple phase and there happened to be a pen in the box that had pineapples all over it."

"That sounds fortuitous," Rex tried, and failed, to recall ever owning the item she was describing.

"You'd think, right?" Winnie agreed.

"You should thank me."

"Maybe. Let's hear the rest of the story before we decide. Deal?"

"I don't know you well enough to make deals with you. I'm beginning to feel like this might be a good place to end the story."

"Don't be impatient," she shook a finger at him. "Now, where was I?"

"You had a fancy pineapple pen," Rex prompted.

"Yes. So, after the weekend passed I put said fancy pineapple pen in my fancy pineapple backpack and went to school."

"Was it like pick your favorite fruit day?" Rex asked, trying to keep up.

"Stop trying to change the subject. As a matter of fact it was let's learn to write an essay day."

"And there you were with your fancy pineapple pen, thanks to me."

"Thanks to you," she nodded. "So, I whipped it out and prepared to lay down some fierce and fruit-licious sentences, but it no worky."

"That's a shame," the grim awareness of enlightenment began to dawn on him. "That wasn't my pen."

She hitched an eyebrow at him. "Are you sure? A minute ago you were all about taking credit for the awesomeness the pen brought to my life."

"I just had a vivid memory of the writing implement you're speaking of. It was most definitely not my pen. "

"So, what I'm hearing is that you don't want to take credit for the awesomeness that occurred when Mr. Erving unscrewed the pen to see what was wrong with it and a doobie fell out?" She giggled. "It was quite a show. The police and Child Protective Services even got involved."

"I am so sorry." Rex scrubbed his face with his hands, trying not laugh at the awful scene she'd described. "Your mom must've been thrilled." *Who wouldn't be?*

Her eyes twinkled with merriment. "Oh, it was thrilling for everyone. I'd never been in a real police car until then."

The image of the pixy-ish girl Winnie had been from Jasper's photos being escorted into the backseat of a black-and-white police vehicle and taken down to the station was too much. "It really wasn't mine." *Lame, Rex.*

"I said the same thing at the time," she told the dog, who licked her knee reassuringly. "I bet it's probably one of the first things a cop expects to hear."

"I mean—," he stopped himself, really not knowing what else to say.

She leaned forward and gave him a pat on the knee. "Relax. J.J. has since copped to the illegal substance. And it was a long time ago, I doubt Mom even remembers it."

"I'm not a parent, but your grade-schooler going to jail doesn't seem like the kind of thing that slips the mind in a hurry." Rex said. "I'm so sorry."

"Geez, don't be. Up until that point I was invisible. The pineapple incident bought me enough street cred to see me through middle school." She gave him a thumbs-up. "No regrets, brah." She glanced at the clock on the wall then gently dislodged the mammoth canine at her feet as she rose. "But I digress, and there are things to be done." Winnie headed to the door, Cobra following at her heels. "It was nice meeting you, Rex."

"Same here, Winnie." Rex waved as she left.

After she'd gone, he sat on the sofa trying to put the pieces of the previous evening together without much success. Deciding a shower might help, Rex helped himself. He'd finished and was toweling off when he heard the front door open and a voice call out.

"Winnie?" Queenie called from the living room.

Rex cracked the door of the bathroom. "She's across the street with Fio—, er Cobra Bubbles." He brushed the funk from his mouth with his finger and some toothpaste, pulled his jeans on and went out to meet his savior of the previous evening.

Queenie was seated at her kitchen table, her laptop open in front of her and a small pile of color-coded flash drives nearby. "How you feeling this morning, Tex-Rex?"

He sat in the chair across from her. "Probably better than I deserve, thanks to you."

"Well, you may recall that I achieved mastery over hangover management at a young age."

"Please don't," He reached across the table and took her hand. "I'm sorry, okay? Let's not start this again. I feel like enough of an ass as it is."

"You don't have anything to be sorry about." She tried to tug her hand away, but he refused to let go. "Look at me please, Victoria."

"I can't. You're half-naked. The sight of your abs might ruin me for other men. You wouldn't want that for me, would you? What would Angel Baby say?"

He laughed despite himself. "She would tell you to give me a chance to say what I have to say. And as for the abs she'd probably tell you to enjoy the show while it lasted."

"God, she's predictable," Victoria sighed. "Fine." She did as he asked and whatever fear Rex thought he might see there was blessedly absent. "Well, at least I didn't try to force myself on you."

Her face flushed and she snatched her hand away, turning determinedly back to her screen.

"Oh, hell," Rex pulled back, self-loathing washing through him. "I did, didn't I?"

"No. No, you didn't. Really." She verbally assured him, her eyes never leaving the computer screen.

"What then?" Rex asked, purposefully closing the lid of the laptop with a fingertip, before turning her face to his. Her mouth thinned and he could tell she was trying to frame her reply. "Dammit, just spit it out, Victoria."

"Ease up, Major," she said. "Relax. Nothing happened."

"Don't lie to me, please."

"Okay, something very much like nothing happened."

"That's almost the same as telling the truth. You're getting closer. Care to try again?"

"Not really," she patted the table, "Sit down, please. Looking up at you is giving me a crick in my neck."

He obliged and settled into the chair she offered. "Fine. I'm sitting. Start talking, Pinocchio."

"Rex, you remember all the times you poured me into my house?"

He shrugged non-committedly hoping she wasn't going to drag them down memory lane. He'd lived it with her and once was enough.

"The times I was so loaded with valium and oxycontin that you and Cece had to put a mirror over my mouth to make sure I was still breathing? The time I came to visit you at Fort Bennington and got so hammered I almost threw up on you while you were relieving me of my virgini—"

"—that's enough of that." Rex held up a hand, unwilling to relive that particular memory right now. "Just get to the point."

"That is the point. Sometimes things happen that mean nothing. Things that would be meaningless to bring up again because they were meaningless when they happened."

"I don't consider Fort Bennington to be one of those situations, but I think I get where you're going." He hated the way she was dancing around the subject. "It's gracious of you, really. But we're grown-ups now. You can cab home when you've had too much to drink, and I can be responsible for my behavior while intoxicated. I need to know what happened last night."

They studied one another for a long moment, and the minute she opened her mouth to speak Rex knew she was going to lie.

"You were a perfect gentlemen. You have nothing to apologize for."

He knew she was lying, but he also knew she had a stubborn streak as wide as the ocean was deep. "Damn, if you're not going to make me work for this."

"Rex—"

"Victoria, I have all sorts of things to apologize to you for: I'm sorry I wasn't strong enough to hang around and watch you drink yourself into oblivion the way your dear old daddy did. And I'm sorry I left you here to hook up with someone who didn't have the balls to hang around after the two of you had become friendly enough to make a baby. I'm sorry I wasn't around to watch you get strong enough to make this life for yourself. And I'm sorry I've come back into your life as a complication instead of a pleasure. I'm sorry for all of those things, I'm just trying to figure out if I have to add one more thing to the list." She opened her mouth when Rex took a breath, and he held up a finger for her to remain silent. "So, despite what half-truths you are trying to feed me, I'm sorry I got so drunk I didn't know my own name, and came back here and did whatever put that blush on your cheeks."

When he finished she looked at him. "Why did you come here at all? Last night, I mean."

"I don't know. I don't think it was a conscious decision at the time. You'd be a better judge. Was I lucid?" He raked a hand through his hair, ready to yank out a handful in self-induced aggravation.

"Relentlessly so, Major. I asked you how you got here and you gave me the entire route from helicopter to walking path."

She was watching him and Rex knew where Winnie got the piercing gaze thing from. He knew he needed to say something to make a difference, something she would hear that she could trust. God knew none of the men in her life had been dependable in any way, including him. He decided to try honesty. "I've wanted to talk to you since that first night at Jasper's, but we haven't exactly been in a time and place to discuss anything." He met her eyes. "Last night, I probably came over here thinking I had found the perfect time."

"Never know what you'll find in the bottom of a bottle of Jaeger," she agreed.

"I think I just wanted to ask you if we could find a way to put our missteps behind us and start over." Rex sat back, letting his hands fall into his lap. "That's all."

"You sure that's what you want?" Her eyes didn't leave his face, her expression unreadable. "To start over?"

"Pretty sure." His head and heart beat in unison and Rex didn't know if it was because of the previous night's alcohol consumption, or if it was because he was genuinely afraid of what she might say next.

"Because your teeth are all permanent now, and I'm fairly certain J.J. can break more than just your arm these days." She gave him the gamine wink from their youth and he finally exhaled. "Okay, maybe not that far back."

She smiled, but the expression didn't quite make it to her eyes. He knew her from old, knew her in's and out's and every variation in-between. The Victoria Hart he knew held nothing back, it was the quality that had made her so damn vulnerable. She wasn't that woman anymore. Rex was dealing with Queenie now. A woman that didn't wear her heart on her sleeve for the world to trample on.

"I'd like to, Rex." He heard the unspoken 'but' coming and raised a hand to stop it.

"Then do, Victoria. Let's you and I give ourselves the week to see if we can't work through our issues. Best case scenario: we're successful."

"And if we're not?" She asked.

"Then I sell you and Aaron back Jasper's portion of the business and go on my merry way."

"You going to be okay with that?"

Rex smiled at her. "Let's just say I like my odds."

\*\*\*

After Rex left, Queenie tried to focus on the accounts for all of the business she shared in the Heights, but failed. Rex was back and wanted to start over and she didn't know what to do. She sighed, closed the laptop and did what she should have done the day before.

The phone rang three times before Cece finally answered. "Well, look who's back from the dead."

"I know. I'm sorry." Queenie decided to get the groveling out of the way so she could jump straight into the mess her life had become.

"Of course you are, Queenie, but I'm probably still gonna yank your chain a little longer."

"Better get a good grip, there aren't many free links left."

"Oh, going for the 'Poor Baby' straight away?"

Queenie filled in the gaps of the last two days, leaving out the kiss from the previous evening, when she finished the other end of the line was silent. She waited.

"Wow." Cece finally spoke. "Sounds like the two of you have some unresolved issues."

"You do the Captain Obvious thing in court too, or is it all for me?" Queenie rolled her eyes.

"You know I save the best for you, honey."

Queenie could hear the smile in her friend's voice. "What's so funny?"

"Don't get bothered. I'm not laughing at you. But you have to admit there's a certain Shakespearean vibe to this entire conundrum. And what with you being the straightest shooter I've ever met, who would've thought?" Cece had a point. "What did he say when you told him about Winnie?"

Queenie remained silent.

"Dear god, Queenie. You didn't tell him, did you?" Cece asked. "Why not? Seems like he gave you the perfect opportunity."

He had. He'd sat right across from her at her own kitchen table and given her the chance she needed. Why hadn't she taken it?

"Girl, you've still got it so bad for that boy and it's killing you isn't it?"

"I tried, Cece. I had the words in my mouth and I don't know what stopped me."

"Colin Hart stopped you."

"I can't blame everything on my father, Cece."

"Maybe, maybe not. But this you certainly can. Angel Baby is always saying that a woman marries her father."

"I'm not marrying Rex."

"No, but you probably should. If anyone was a dead ringer for your poor old Pop, it's Aaron. Thank god you didn't marry him."

"He wasn't that bad."

"Of course he wasn't, but he wasn't that good either, was he? That was always Rex's place. And I bring up the point about marrying a father figure not because of your pop, but because of Whitey."

"What's Whitey got to do with it?"

"Girl, Whitey Montgomery was as much a father figure in your life as your real dad, maybe more so."

The thought should have cheered her, but had the opposite effect. "Cece, what if he wants to stay?"

"Sweet lord, Queenie, you are the only woman in the western hemisphere who would think that was a problem. Have you actually taken a good look at what you're trying to rid yourself of? Rex could melt a woman faster than a Vegas summer."

"I looked," she said, remembering the sight of him fresh from the shower.

"You left something out, didn't you?" Cece's talent for unearthing people's secrets was uncanny.

Queenie gave in and briefed her friend on the endless midnight kiss.

Cece whistled through the line. "What's the problem here exactly, then? Rex is obviously still burning a candle for you if the idea of Aaron referring to you in passing as 'his girl' upset him enough to come looking for you."

"But who is the candle burning for? The impulsive idiot girl he left behind for good? What use is that girl to anyone?" Queenie asked.

"Queenie, believe it or not, you are still the same person you were."

"Not a chance, Cece."

"It's true. The only difference between you and the person you were is that you've edited out all of the bullshit."

The idea was oddly comforting. "You think so?"

"Absolutely. You just had a lot more editing to do than most of us."

"Gee thanks."

"Bitch, it helped, didn't it?"

"It always does."

"So, what are you going to do now?"

"I think I'm going to give it a week."

"You're going to keep Winnie a secret from him for a whole week?"

"It's been quite a while already, in case you weren't paying attention."

"Sure, smartass, but he wasn't here trying to rekindle an old friendship then. He was off fighting the good fight somewhere."

*And getting holes shot through him for his trouble*, Queenie readily recalled.

"I'll manage somehow. I still don't understand how this could have happened."

"You haven't figured it out by now?" Cece's tone left little doubt that she had her suspicions.

"You have?"

"Queenie, there's only one person that would have edited the information you sent to Rex. I mean, obviously he got something of what you sent, because he never denied responding to your message. But what did the message he received from you actually say."

"Sounds like you've given this some thought."

"I'm a thinking machine, honey. You know that."

"True." Queenie wracked her brain trying to recall the awful day she wrote that letter to Rex. The last thing she had wanted was to derail him from his dreams, but Cece and Jasper had convinced her that he needed to know. So, she'd sat down and written to him about the baby that was on the way.

The child hadn't been planned, of course, but Queenie hadn't thought it would make any difference to Rex, not really. They'd been friends working on becoming more and had barely reached the stage of lovers when Winnie was conceived. Queenie had been making steady progress in putting her many faults behind her while Rex was off at boot camp, wanting to make him proud of her.

Their first night together she regressed, nerves encouraging her to lean on the Bacardi's familiar crutch. Just recalling the experience was enough to make her wince even now. But he had a short break before being shipped off, and they made the most of it.

Two months later her father finally succeeded in drinking himself to death. Rex tried to make it back for the funereal and Queenie had planned on telling him then. When he failed to show, she grew increasingly uncertain about what to do when Jasper and Angel Baby stepped in. Jasper had even forwarded along a photo of Cece and Queenie holding a piece of paper over her huge belly with a downward arrow and writing that said 'Guess what?'.

It took one long nerve-wracking week for the reply, and even though she knew some misunderstanding had to have taken place, the memory of reading Rex's correspondence still left her feeling hollow. Like an idiot, she dug it out the other night to steel her resolve and it had the undesirable effect of hurting her as much the last time as the first.

*Victoria,*

*Thanks for the letter and the picture. It's great to hear from you even if the choices you're making aren't what I would have wished for either of us. You'll always have a part of me, but I have to make my own way in the world now. My best to you.*
*Rex*

Seventeen years later and she was still stinging.
"Get there yet?" Cece dragged her into the present.
"It had to be Diana."
"And Bingo was her name-o, Queenie."

## ∽—Chapter Five—∽
☙

After leaving Victoria's, Rex headed to his sister's house. Deciding it was time to do something about his transportation situation, Rex stopped at a car dealership and drove off the lot an hour and a half later in a newish, serviceable pick-up he suspected would make Diana nuts.

Diana and Bradford Masterson lived in a gated secured complex that boasted its own country club and golf course, and as Rex approached the gate to register his new truck, he thought he recognized the hoodie clad form of his nephew Drake loitering in the park like area outside the neighborhood. Rex stored the info away, recalling Queenie's observations about the boy, and making a mental note to spend some time with Drake later.

He parked and went inside.

"Good evening, Major Montgomery," Lisette, his sister's personal assistant-housekeeper greeted him. Lisette was a twenty-something working her way through college. Why she'd chosen to add to her school burden by working for his sister was beyond him. Hopefully Diana paid well.

"Call me Rex, Lisette," he said. "Major Montgomery has left the building."

"Mrs. Masterson wouldn't like that, Rex." Lisette replied with a quick smile and a shy look that she let linger a little too long. She blushed and went back to putting the dishes away.

Flattered, but wise enough to know that an interlude with his sister's employee spelled certain doom for them both, Rex ignored her attempt at flirtation and put a finger over his mouth. "She doesn't have to know, it'll be our little secret," he promised, realizing as he said it how easy it was to unintentionally fall into a conversation fraught with double meanings. He changed the subject. "Since when do PA's wash dishes? I'd think my sister would have someone for that."

"Mrs. Masterson thinks people who have housekeepers are pretentious." She closed the cupboard and started to spray down the inside of the dishwasher with disinfectant spray.

*People who live in glass mansions...* he thought. "And assistants aren't?"

Lisette started to roll her eyes then caught herself, but not before Rex noticed. He chuckled and she blushed again. "I know I'm still a little off the rails today, but are you cleaning the inside of the dishwasher? I thought the idea of those things was that they were self-managing."

She wiped down the inside of the appliance and stood. "Mrs. Masterson likes it to look brand new when not in use." Her face was devoid of expression, and Rex marveled at her ability to keep the snark from her tone.

*OCD much, Diana?* "Whatever pays your bills, Lisette. Keep up the great work. She around?"

"If by she, you mean me, then yes." Diana answered them from the stairway of the great room.

Rex and Lisette exchanged a look, wondering how much of the conversation his sister had heard, but she sailed into the kitchen seemingly oblivious to anything but the earring she was trying to attach. "Where have you been?" She looked him over. "And aren't those your clothes from yesterday?" She finished warring with her jewelry and stood with her hands on her hips. "Well?"

Rex attempted to stem the flood of irritation that threatened to overflow onto his sister. "I've been away, and yes mother, these are my clothes from yesterday. Unless you prefer outright nudity to last night's re-do's, this was the only option available."

A sound like a mouse snickering came from Lisette's direction and Diana frowned, her gaze tracking to her assistant. "If you're finished with those, there's some laundry in the boys' room that needs attending. After that you should go."

Lisette avoided looking is Rex's direction and departed with a mumbled, "Yes, Mrs. Masterson."

When she'd gone, Diana turned a baleful eye on her brother. "Was that really necessary, Reggie?"

"I could ask you the same thing, Diana." Rex ignored the look and went to the massive fridge to grab a bottle of water. He closed the door and turned to find her standing behind him.

"Why do you insist on humiliating me?" She demanded.

Rex circled around her. "You come in here asking me about my whereabouts and my clothing as if I'm one of your sons, and I'm humiliating you? Diana, I'm a grown man. I've fought wars in other countries. I've been blown up and shot at on more than one occasion. I think I can manage myself for twenty-four hours without your supervision."

"Grown and matured are two separate things, Reginald." Diana replied stiffly.

"Oh, I definitely agree with you there, Diana," he stared her down, wondering if she'd even get his implication or if he needed to hold up a mirror for her.

"If you'd listened to me you never would have gone into the damn Army to begin with." She sighed abruptly, shifting gears. "But what's done is done, and we'll just have to make the best of things. Speaking of which, you need to get your haircut. You're starting to look like one of those bohemian hipster types. It won't do. I've made an appointment for you with my hairstylist for tomorrow."

It was the last straw for him. "It's my hair, Diana. And if I want to grow it out and join the cast of Duck Dynasty I think I've more than earned the right by now." Beyond frustrated, Rex raked a hand through the hair in question hair. "What part of this conversation are you hearing? Am I even here, or is this going on in your own head? Because if it is, then please feel free to continue without me." Rex headed out of the kitchen.

"You're behaving like an irrational child, Reginald," she called after him. "Bradford and I are going to the club for dinner. We can continue this conversation when I get back."

In the spirit of irrational children everywhere, Rex ignored her and headed upstairs to the guest room he was currently occupying. He closed the door to his temporary sanctuary and dropped on to the bed, counting to ten and hoping to dull the sharp edge of his sister's words. Realizing ten wasn't going to be nearly enough, Rex sat up and took a swig of water, trying to figure out what he was going to do next. *You can't stay here forever, boy-o.*

But, that had never been his intention anyway. He'd only meant to come in to town and stay long enough to visit with family and friends, clean up the loose ends Uncle Jasper left, and line up some sort of plan for the future. His departure from the service wasn't exactly premeditated, just needed. When she'd heard, Diana had insisted he take up a room with her family. God knew they had enough of them. Considering the size of the house he should've been able to come and go as he pleased without running into her every time he went downstairs. But that wasn't in the cards, apparently. They were averaging one argument a day, and that was one more than Rex needed. He'd had enough conflict to last a lifetime. And having it with Diana made it worse. She was his only family. No. He had to get his life on track. And soon.

He'd made some headway on his personal agenda, but seeing Victoria had been like taking two steps back straight into a tornado. And the Jaegermeister hadn't helped.

*Idiot.* He owed Aaron one.

For the life of him he couldn't recall what he'd said or done last night, but suspected it must have verged on inappropriate, which only made him want to remember it more. God knew he'd had nothing but inappropriate thoughts about her since seeing her in his uncle's house, but that was nothing new. *Face it, son: she's been your dream girl since you knew how to dream.* And though he'd tried to cut ties to her because he didn't want to witness her throwing herself away, when he knew he was coming back some tiny part of him had hoped against hope that he'd run into her again, and that she'd be a fraction of the girl he knew.

*Fraction, hell. She was the whole pie and then some these days.*

Julia Bidwell

Once he'd laid eyes on her again, he'd wanted to pick-up their relationship where it'd left off, but she'd been quick to remind him of the line he'd drawn in the sand between them. But fate was on his side, and Victoria had given him a foot in the door. *Now, all you have to figure out is how to bridge the distance and breach the defenses she's erected against you.*

Thank god for Jasper. He'd done most of the work already by leaving him his share of the Survivor's Hutt. *Right, there's work to be done.* Rex fished through his pockets until he located his cell phone, and made a call.

Three rings in a voice cut in. "Leonardo's Taxidermy. You snuff 'em, I stuff 'em. What can I stuff for you today?"

"Bet that goes over well with the ladies."

"Player's gotta play, Major."

"It's Rex, Leo. We're civilians now, remember?" Leonardo Jackman had been on his way out of the Rangers when Rex had been heading in. They'd spent the last six months of Leo's final tour together. More than enough time for Rex to realize that resourcefulness was a calling Leo had in spades. If you needed it he could get it, get it done, or get rid of it. And he could do it discreetly.

"Sure thing, Major. What's up?"

"You still in tight with that red-head from the pentagon?"

"Yvonne? Sure. You need intel on someone?"

"Background on one Matson, Aaron." Rex spelled out the name, read some vitals from the file Cece had given him and waited while Leo took it down.

"You been out what, two weeks, and you're already distrusting your fellow man? That's not very sporting, Major."

Rex explained the situation.

"Ah. Going into business with a jarhead-turned-mercenary. I never knew you had it in you."

"I might not, depends on what Yvonne turns up."

"Sure thing. I'll get back to you." Leo said. "Other than the imminent betrayal of an ex-marine, how's life on the outside treating you?"

Rex reviewed the last twenty-four hours of his life in his head. "Not bad at all, Leo. In fact, better than expected or deserved, actually."

"Glad to hear it, Major. If anyone deserves better than average, it's you."

Rex gave a short bark of laughter. "Thanks, Leo. Right back at ya."

Rex disconnected and felt his stomach rumble. The fries and Coke had done their best, but Rex's night was catching up with him. Deciding what he really needed was a good sweat, he changed into his running gear and hit the pavement relieved that his sister wasn't there. Bradford and Diana had their own gym and a personal trainer that babysat his sister's workouts three times a week. She probably thought her reputation as an upstanding pillar of the community would be irreparably tarnished if anyone saw her sweat. She'd encouraged Rex to use the workout room, and he had, but he'd spent so much of his life outdoors that he craved the fresh air.

He'd hit the five-mile mark, and slowed his pace to cool down. Approaching the meadow where he'd seen Drake on is way in, Rex detoured towards it, scanning the area for his nephew, catching sight of the back of his hoodie with a few other boys his age.

As Rex neared the group he smelled the drug of the day before he saw it, and like so many other things that day the heavy herbal scent of blunt took him back in time for a minute. Suddenly, he was fifteen and sitting in Cece's bedroom with Victoria, while J.J. schooled the three of them on the fine art of roach-toking without Bogarting the weed. Rex, fully aware of his uncle's viewpoint on smoking and drugs, passed on the experience, but the smell followed him home.

Uncle Jasper had taken one sniff and made him strip down in the yard, where he proceeded to hose the boy down. Mortified beyond belief, the experience had been enough to steer Rex clear of smoking in general and marijuana specifically.

Uncle Jasper, apparently, had been unable to service his great nephew in a similar capacity, or maybe he'd tried and it just hadn't stuck. It seemed up to Rex now.

"Any of you boys suffering from glaucoma?" Rex asked, approaching the group.

Two clean-cut faces stared up at him with the same expression he'd recently seen mirrored in a zombie flick. Drake stayed put, vainly attempting to disguise the contraband under his hand.

"Glau-whata?" Clean-cut number one asked.

Rex sighed. "I'm guessing that's not medical marijuana you're smoking, then."

"If you're a cop, you better just keep on moving. My dad's a judge. He'll burn your badge." Clean-cut number two informed Rex, smirking. *You're staying Number Two in my book, kiddo.*

"He's not a cop." Drake said in the eternal monotone of the doped. "He's my uncle." Drake turned bloodshot blue eyes on Rex. "Hey, Uncle Reggie."

Rex, deciding he'd reached his tolerance level for youthful indiscretion, reached down and dragged his nephew up by the neck of the hoodie. Drake made a weak strangling sound and dropped the weed. Before either of the other boys could grab the blunt, Rex stepped on it, crushing it into the impeccably kept lawn.

"Fuck, dude. Did ya have to?" Number Two whined.

"Sue me," Rex turned his back on the pair, never taking his hand off his nephew. "Nice friends, Drake." They walked home that way, Drake lagging occasionally, but not making any effort to put up a fight. Realizing he had no idea what he was doing, Rex stopped at the truck and opened the passenger door.

"Nice truck. I think the landscaper has one just like it."

*Right. You're lucky I already gave your name away, you little shit.* "Get in." He told Drake.

"Why? Where are we going?" Drake asked, doing as he was told.

Rex joined him from the driver's side, put the key in and revved the engine. "To get something to eat. You must be starved."

\*\*\*

Queenie sat in the booth at DeMarco's across from her daughter, wondering where to begin. She'd chosen DeMarco's because Antonia and Dante were the very first people she'd ever helped, and something about being in their kitschy Italian restaurant with its red-checked tablecloths and raffia covered

Chianti bottles made her feel like no problem was so big that it couldn't be fixed. Or at least forced into a food coma and ignored for a good long while.

*God knows you tried to ignore the Rex problem away. Food coma it is, then.*

"What is it, Mom?" Winnie took a sip from her iced tea, turning expectant blue eyes on Queenie.

"What do you mean?" Queenie faked pretense, humming along with the Frank Sinatra music in the background, directing her attention to the family photos dotting the walls. Vintage black and white portraits from another era merged into more recent shots of Antonia and Dante DeMarco along with their three strapping handsome Italian sons. Michelangelo's Davids, the trio of them. Dominic, Nicholas and Constantine were heartbreakers and Queenie counted herself lucky that she was too old for any of them. She never mixed business with pleasure, not after the Aaron fail, but that didn't stop her from appreciating the perks that proximity gave her when it came to the DeMarco boys.

"Is it my first day with a new mommy? I think not." Winnie drew her attention. "What I mean is, you're chewing the inside corner of your lip. Not a lot, but enough. That usually means you're thinking pretty hard about something."

Queenie froze mid-gnaw, Bandit's tale of tells coming to mind. She tapped the corner of her mouth with a finger, smiling. "You're a treasure, you know that? A tall, nosy, observant treasure. I may buy you a pony for that observation."

"The pony window has passed, Mom."

"The pony window never passes, Winnie." Queenie schooled, wondering at the same time why that was. She chalked it up to the White Knight cliché. In that scenario the horse was the only way out when the fairy tale fell apart and the Knight never learned to do his own laundry, or realize that dinner was something that happened every day and could be planned for. Not that she knew anything about cohabitation first hand. But she'd seen enough of it to know it wasn't always roses and sunshine. After all, someone had to pick up after the horse.

At that moment Antonia brought their order and they made room for the pizza. "Thanks Antonia."

Antonia winked and walked away, hips sashaying in a matronly yet sultry manner that still caught her husband's eye.

Winnie slid a slice of pepperoni and mushroom onto her plate, dosed it liberally with Parmesan and red pepper and bit into it. Queenie watched, shaking her head. "The pizza is nuclear. I still don't know how you can do that without melting your mouth."

Winnie swallowed. "The melting is part of the fun, Mom. Now, out with it. What's making that tiny Irish nose wrinkle? Is it the car? Is it Talin? Is it the fact that Cobra Bubbles is going to eat us out of house and home?"

"It's about your dad." Queenie blurted out. *Smooth, Queenie. Real smooth.*

"What about that loser?" Winnie bit into her pizza, unfazed.

Uncertain just how to proceed, Queenie opted for balls to the wall. "He may not exactly be the loser I assumed he was."

"What do you mean? He left you pregnant and alone. Of course he's a loser. He's probably their king by now. Sitting on a loser throne, with a sad, dented loser crown and loser minions to do his lame bidding."

Queenie winced at the visual. *She's your kid all right.* It was the exact same sentiment Queenie would have mirrored only two days earlier. "About that. He left me alone. Yes. Me." Queenie fiddled with her iced-tea spoon. "But certain circumstances have come to light that lead me to believe he had no idea about you."

"What gives? Now you sound like Aunt Cece," Winnie tilted her head and raised an exaggerated eyebrow, waggling it for effect. "Just spit it out, Mom. What circumstances? You mean you talked to him?"

Queenie nodded. "So, did you."

Winnie's face went blank and Queenie noticed with a certain satisfaction that her daughter shared her tell. Winnie worked the inside corner of her lower lip, then stopped abruptly. "The drunk with the hot bod is my dad?"

"Rex," Queenie confirmed, vainly trying not to recall the body. "And I don't think he's usually drunk." Queenie gave her daughter the rundown of what had transpired the past three days, ending with Rex coming to the door hammered the night before.

Winnie sat, her expression still thoughtful, pizza forgotten.

"Do you understand, Wee? I don't think he ever knew anything about you."

Winnie nodded vaguely, her eyes meeting her mother's. "Do we want him to?"

"I don't know," Queenie sat back against the booth. "There are a lot of things to consider. He's only committed to being here for a week. Let's talk about it."

"Talk fast, Mom, because he's coming this way."

\*\*\*

Rex and Drake pulled into the parking lot of an Italian bistro. He'd driven around his sister's neighborhood looking for a place to take his nephew where they'd be less identifiable, and failed. He was in his workout clothes, and Drake was high as a kite. No doubt, both socially unacceptable attributes where Diana's peers were concerned. So, he turned to more familiar stomping grounds, stopping at the first place that looked appetizing.

"Geez, Uncle Reggie. We're likely to get shot here."

"Might do you some good, Drake. I remember the first time I took a bullet with more fondness than you might expect." Rex got out of the car, not waiting for Drake to follow. He went inside, taking a moment to let his eyes adjust. By the time they had, Drake stood at his elbow and a friendly dark-haired woman waved them inside.

"Sit anywhere."

Rex scanned the room, eyes resting on a familiar young redheaded girl and her mother. "Come on." He threaded his way through the tables until he arrived at their booth. By the time he reached them, Victoria was already turning to look their way.

"Lost?" She asked him.

"No kidding," said Drake, looking from his uncle to the table's occupants. "Hey, you're Winnie Hart."

Winnie wrinkled her nose, scowling prettily. "And you're six kinds of Wednesday " She looked from Drake to Rex. "First you, now him. Is it substance abuse Saturday and nobody told me?"

"You should ask your mom," Drake said, his words slow and drawn out. "I hear she's got game."

"Dra—" Rex turned to silence his nephew, but Winnie waved it off. "It's getting old, Drake-y-pooh. Your insults, your emo and your angst. Get a cause already."

Rex felt his jaw clench. "Drake? Is she suggesting that you go around school telling people that her mother is some kind of substance abuser?" His nephew's face reddened and he said nothing. "I see."

"Oh, don't take it so personally, Rex. It has nothing to do with you." Queenie addressed Drake. "You caught me on a good day, Mr. Masterson. I happen to be substance free, but the day's still young and who knows what spending time in your company might drive me to do?" Victoria slid back towards the wall making room in the booth. "And if we're going to air my dirty laundry, let's try to keep everyone else out of it."

"Victoria, I don't think now is the tim—"

"Just sit, Rex." She patted the red vinyl upholstery with more friendliness than she felt. "The kid's baked to his eyeballs and is probably starving. Been there, as he so thoughtfully pointed out. And we have more than enough."

Rex looked at Winnie, who shrugged and slid over. Drake started to slide in next to her and Rex grabbed him by the hoodie and jerked. "This nice lady is offering to feed your stoned ass. That's fairly thoughtful considering your behavior so far. I think an apology may be in order, don't you?"

His nephew looked at him, saw the deadly stare and stammered an apology. "S-sorry."

"Ms. Hart," Rex prompted.

Queenie waved the introduction aside. "Oh, we don't stand on formalities this far north, Drake. You know Rex. That makes you almost family out here. You can call me Queenie from the Block," she gestured to Winnie, who was wearing a bright smile, "and I believe you and Little Red are already acquainted."

Even through his drug induced haze Drake froze, uncertainty piercing his cloak of arrogance.

"Mom," Winnie broke the spell.

"Great. Good. We're all friends now." Victoria said. "Hopefully, Angry Ranger Rex won't have to make another appearance and we'll all survive dinner without incident."

The men seated themselves and a fresh pitcher of iced tea materialized with two more glasses. "Thanks again, Antonia."

"Anything for you, Queenie." Antonia smiled at her. "And some bread for your boys, maybe?"

"So not my boys Antonia," Queenie corrected, before any notions could appeal to the older Italian woman's romantic nature. "These are Whitey's boys."

"I'm so sorry for your loss. Whitey, he will be missed." Antonia's first language was Italian and when she pronounced 'will' like 'wheel', Drake began a snicker that ended abruptly with him wincing and jerking in the booth suddenly, and looking around the table suspiciously.

"Thank you, Antonia," Rex replied. "He was a good man."

"Whitey, he loved the bread. Always with the butter." Antonia tsked sadly. "I will bring the bread in his memory."

She'd barely turned away before Drake dug in. Rex watched his nephew inhale his food, and caught Winnie doing the same.

"I once watched a lion take down a zebra on an Animal Planet documentary that was more civilized." She said to no one in particular.

Drake looked up, half a slice of pizza forming a cheesy beard that dangled from his mouth, to see everyone else at the table admiring his fine manners. "Sorry." He said over a mouthful of food, slowing his pace.

Now that his nephew was less of an embarrassment, Rex concentrated on his own food. Antonia brought the promised bread and Victoria and Winnie ate along with the boys, occasionally passing glances to one another that Rex couldn't quite define. Some of Drake's buzz seemed to have worn off. He sat, subdued, and to Rex's eyes, more than a little introverted.

"So, how do you know Drake, Rex?" Winnie asked.

"He's my nephew." Rex informed her. For some reason the response caused Winnie to look at her mother and give a nearly imperceptible head shake. He was just about to ferret out the cause of the reaction when Drake spoke.

"Who's Rex?" Drake asked, confused. "And Whitey for that matter?"

"You're uncle is, Drake." Victoria filled in. "That's his alias here in the hood. And Whitey was your great uncle."

"Wait. You've been here before?" Drake looked blankly at Rex. "And I have a great uncle?"

"Had." Victoria corrected, looking from Rex to Drake. "You never met Jasper, did you?"

Drake shook his head, waiting for Rex to make sense of things.

"I grew up here, in his house." Rex informed him. "About three blocks away."

"No way. Where was my mom?"

"Diana was there too," Victoria said.

"You know my mom?" Drake still hadn't lost his dazed expression, but Rex couldn't tell how much of that was the weed, and how much was just the boy's general detachment with the world around him.

"Yes, I do." Rex recognized the familiar undertone of hostility in Victoria's tone.

"But you *know* her? She really grew up here?" He looked to his uncle for confirmation. Rex nodded. "We can go by the house if you want. I have the keys."

"Is it safe?"

Winnie let out an exaggerated bark of laughter. "No. The bogeyman roams the streets, waiting to pick off entitled white boys in cashmere hoodies who ask stupid questions." Winnie rolled her eyes.

"How's Talin survived this long, I wonder?"

"Leave Talin out of this, Drake." Winnie warned.

"Who's Talin?" Rex asked Victoria, but Drake answered.

"Her loser grease-monkey boyfriend."

"He's not my boyfriend," Winnie shot back.

"He's not her boyfriend," Victoria sidelined to Rex, not taking her eyes off the kids. "He's a very well-mannered young man that likes to chauffeur her around in his project car."

"I can't blame him a bit," Rex nodded.

Drake ignored them. "Come to think of it, he probably fits right in around here," Drake looked around. "I can picture the pair of you at home together right here. I bet Antonia *weel* even put your picture up on the wall after the wedding."

"Drake—," Rex watched as the conversation car headed for the nearest cliff.

"—Drake Anthony Masterson," Winnie cut in, her tone dangerously low. "You can say what you want about my family. But if I go to school on Monday and a single whisper of gossip about Talin Reeves drifts my way, I will hunt you down and snap you like a twig. Everything you've ever heard about this neighborhood will seem like a fairy-tale after I get done raining grief down on you. And when I'm finished, your name will ring through the halls of West-Side Prep like a warning for generations to come. If you know what's good for you, you'll shut up and eat your pizza."

Silence descended over the table and all eyes were on Drake. Daunted, Drake backed down and did as he was told.

"Girl," Victoria cautioned. "That was a little too much for a Saturday afternoon. You don't usually go all dark-side until after nine."

"Sometimes exceptions need to be made, Victoria," Rex said. "Drake was out of line."

"Someone is always going to be out-of-line, Rex. The only thing you have control over in the world is yourself."

"Mom's right, Rex," Winnie caught her mother's warning and promptly pasted a pseudo-friendly smile on her face. "I'm sorry I lost my temper, Drake, but I live here. And while it probably isn't as pretty as your gated community, it's not exactly the barrio either."

"Not anymore, anyway," Rex barely caught Victoria's muttering.

"Wow." Impressed by Winnie's instant recovery, Rex looked from daughter to mother. "I remember being on the wrong side of that temper more than once. The resemblance is striking. Who would've guessed your knack for putting people in their place was an inheritable trait? You really are a parent," he said. "I couldn't have pictured it before now, but it suits you. "

"Sometimes," Victoria shrugged off his compliment, surveying what remained of the pizza situation. "She mostly parents herself."

"Was that an upgrade, or did the self-parenting come factory installed?" *C'mon Victoria, don't let my nimrod nephew ruin this afternoon,* Rex willed. Victoria smiled grudgingly and a wave of triumph washed over Rex. "I'm pretty sure she rolled off the assembly line fully equipped."

"Give yourself some credit, Mom." Rex was charmed by the sincere smile Winnie gave her mother. They were a complete family unit, just the two of them. "You've kept me finely tuned ever since."

"That's only because you don't require a lot of maintenance." Victoria waived off the compliment. "Kick the tires every ten-thousand miles, or so, change the wardrobe once a year and you're good to go."

"You're forgetting about the fuel costs," Rex said. "Keeping up with the rising cost of pizza these days is no laughing matter."

"Gotta keep the tank full," Winnie grinned in agreement. "You make it look effortless, Queenie from the Block. How about you, Rex?" Winnie leaned in and turned to him. "You have any kids?"

"Not me," he shook his head. "Never had the time, really."

"Been soldiering, you said." Winnie added.

"He was in Afghanistan," Drake offered up, done licking his wounds.

"With the bullet holes to prove it," Winnie recalled. "No G.I. Joe indiscretions you maybe just don't know about?"

"Winnie—" Victoria, obviously shocked at the turn the conversation had just taken cut off whatever Winnie was about to say next, but Drake was already defending Rex's honor. "—OMG, Hart. What the hell?" Drake shed his stoner-ennui and jumped in the fray. "Just because you don't know which dog in the yard father—"

"—This is going well, don't you think?" Victoria cut straight through Drake's tirade with no-nonsense. She tipped her head to Rex. "Only so much rudeness in one sitting, I always say. I hate to cut this short, but we have other vendettas to fan the flames of, and an elephant to feed at home."

"I'm sorry, Victoria." Frustrated, Rex stood to let her out, and used his nephew's convenient hoodie handle to jerk Drake out from his side to free Winnie. "I'll get this."

Victoria slid out from the booth, Winnie joining her. She offered him a finely tuned and completely false smile that he instantly hated down to his bones. "It's already taken care of, Rex. But thanks."

"Maybe we can do this again sometime?" Rex suggested.

"There's an idea. Uncle Jerome has a regulation octagon we can use." Winnie snorted delicately, grabbing her bag and giving Drake a withering look. "Try not to let the bogeyman get you, Burnout."

Victoria's wince silenced Winnie. "Good luck with Drake, Tex-Rex. I'll see you Monday."

\*\*\*

Rex and Drake didn't exchange words the entire way home, which exceeded Rex's expectations all around. His nephew's sulking suited his own frustration level with the boy. He'd spent the first ten minutes of the car ride just trying to keep from opening the door and leaving him on the side of the road. When they finally pulled in, the icing on the cake was Diana was laying in wait.

"There you are." She stood in the entryway, arms crossed over her chest.

"Here we are," Rex agreed, ignoring his sister and heading into the living room where David and Bradford sat watching a movie. David waved from the couch, and Rex waved back, pausing to shake hands with his brother-in-law.

"How's it, Reggie?" Bradford asked amiably, lounging on the oversized cream leather couch that took up most of the great-room.

"It's still hanging, Bradford." Rex said. "You?"

"Good enough, good enough." Bradford wasn't a man given to much conversation and Rex was a little overwhelmed at the level of chattiness his brother-in-law was employing. Before an awkward chasm of silence could develop between them Diana trailed into the room. "Where were you?"

"Are we doing this again?" Rex looked past his sister at Drake, who lounged against the doorjamb. The boy's body language practically broadcast his intention to stir the pot. *Well, that's what I get for not letting him smoke it.*

"It's okay, Mom. Uncle Rex took me out for pizza in your old neighborhood."

And that's the precise moment when Diana's head exploded. She whipped around to look at Drake so fast Rex was guessing she was going to need a chiropractor in the near future. Her head swiveled back to Rex in true Exorcist fashion, her eyes narrowing. "You did what?"

"You have an old neighborhood, Mom?" David asked from the couch.

"In North Town." Drake informed his twin. "The whole area is super sketchy, bro."

Rex shook his head more to himself than anything else. *You're not really anyone's problem but your own, buddy.*

"Reginald," his sister shortened the distance between them. "I demand some answers."

"Really, Diana. Don't you think you're overreacting a bit?" Bradford asked, clearly never having ever been in a firefight. Rex felt a bit sorry for his brother-in-law in that moment, but the scene was rapidly devolving into an everyman-for-himself moment. If Bradford didn't have enough sense not to make himself a target, the only thing Rex could hope to do now was draw the fire away.

"No, Bradford. I really don't." She bit out. "It's a dangerous place that neither he, nor our son, had any place being." She turned on Rex. "How could you? Why *would* you?"

"Ease up, Mom." Drake, displaying an ounce of discomfort at watching the emotional grenade he'd just lobbed into the room explode, tried to de-escalate his mother. "It was cool. We grabbed a pizza and hooked up with a girl from school and her mom." Unfortunately, his words had the opposite effect. Like a tanker of oil on a forest fire, Rex watched his sister's face turn bright red as her temper searched for an outlet. "And I can guess who that friend was. Shall I?"

"Do whatever you want, Di." Rex offered David and Bradford an apologetic shrug then went upstairs, his sister hot on his heels.

"Don't walk away from me, Reginald."

"I'm going to drive away in a minute, so talk fast." Rex headed into his room going straight to the closet and grabbing his duffle bag. He began packing his things.

"What do you think you're doing?" She demanded from the doorway, eyes bright with righteous indignation.

"I'm leaving. I'm grown," he reminded her, "I'm allowed."

"No," she jammed a hand on her hip and filled the doorframe. "I forbid it. I finally have my family back together, and you are not going to ruin it by leaving again."

Rex yanked the drawer out of the borrowed dresser with more force than necessary, and unceremoniously dumped the contents into his bag. He experienced a vague twinge of regret for the mess he was leaving behind for Lisette to straighten up, but it passed when his sister stamped her foot for his attention. *Lisette will have to get over it.* "We don't *belong* to you, Di."

"You know what I mean."

"I don't think *you* know what you mean." Rex continued, methodically emptying the drawers. "You didn't collect us. We are individuals, free to come and go as we please. And I'm exercising my right to do just that." He finished packing and looked around the room for anything he'd missed.

"Don't do this. Don't choose her over us."

"Choose her? Her who?" Rex looked at his sister, a wave of angry confusion washing over him. "You think this is about Victoria Hart?"

"Isn't it?" Diana demanded. "Who else has the power to wrap you around her finger and drag you back to that neighborhood?"

"First of all, why in the hell do you imagine she has anything at all to do with what's happening between you and I?" He wasn't sure if he imagined the flicker of relief in his sister's face. The Botox had somewhat limited her ability to display emotion, which Rex guessed was probably why she felt the need to describe her perceived slights in detail. "We have enough personality contrasts of our own without bringing other people into the mix." Rex grabbed his phone charger, tossed it onto his bag and zipped it closed.

"And secondly, as for being wrapped around her finger, that was almost twenty years ago. We've spent more time apart than we ever did together. I'm not leaving here to go to her. I'm leaving before you and I tear through each other."

"You're being ridiculous. We're just fine."

*We're just fine.* It was probably her mantra. How else could she walk past a son reeking of pot, with eyes so bloodshot they looked like a country roadmap unless she'd already brainwashed herself into believing everything was just fine.

"I'm being ridiculous?! You pick and choose your family based on how shiny they make you appear at the club. Your sons had a great uncle they never even met! A man who sacrificed for his country, and if that's too abstract for you, a man who sacrificed for you. He lived thirty minutes away and I bet you never even acknowledged him with a Christmas card, never mind sharing your sons with him." His sister's selfishness infuriated him. "And worse? You intentionally kept his illness from me! Christ! You knew what he meant to me and you never even told me he had cancer! Cancer, Di!" Rex felt his control slipping away. "What kind of reply do you have for that? You robbed me of a two-year window to come pay my respects to the man who made what I am today. Two years you waited? Why?!? What possible reason could you have for keeping that information from me? Out of some misguided notion of protecting me? You're not my mother, Diana Masterson. You're my sister, and if you and I are ever going to have any kind of relationship you're going to have to learn your place." He stopped talking and the whole house fell silent. Great, he'd just ranted at his sister in front of her whole family.

*I've got to get out of here.*

Diana stood in the hallway, head bowed, tears sliding off her chin onto the plush white carpet, refusing to even look at him. Suddenly he felt like a bully. Rex had no reason to burst his sister's bubble. Time would most likely do that on its own. He hefted his duffle and stepped past her. "I'll keep in touch."

# ∘—Chapter Six—∘

♕

"You sure this is the one you want?" Queenie asked Winnie, looking at the all too tiny pale blue Volkswagen Beetle they'd spent most of Sunday morning searching out. The car shopping was a welcome distraction from the subject raised the night before. Winnie hadn't brought Rex up, and Queenie was fine with leaving it alone for now.

"I love it! It's perfect! What's not to want?" Winnie walked around the car for the tenth time. "It has white wall tires Mom!"

"I don't know," Queenie shrugged. "It's just a little...small." The idea of Winnie driving around on her own was one thing, the reality was something else entirely. The car wasn't the issue. The independence that accompanied it was more the thing. That kid had been her lifeline for so long, Queenie already hated the distance the Beetle represented. Today the car, college around the corner..... *Guh. I'm going to blink and she'll have her own life complete with crazy friends and necrophilic animal companion.* But Queenie had no real complaints. *It's what you wanted.* Winnie was a much better daughter than she deserved considering her crappy parenting skills. *Did you think she'd never grow up, Queenie?*

"This model has some of the highest safety ratings in its class," Joe, the salesman, interrupted the train wreck of her thoughts.

"Do you have anything more..." Queenie studied the aggressively amiable bubble on wheels again as searched for the right word, "tank-like?"

"Mo-om." Winnie gave her crazy-face and stuck out her tongue across the roof of the car.

Queenie stopped fixating on das auto and took in her daughter's hopeful expression. She wished Cece were here. Cece would know exactly what to say. Most likely something along the lines of: *"Suck it up, Queenie"*.

"You're sure there's nothing else you want to see?" Queenie asked for the hundredth time.

"Motorcycle maybe?" Winnie shrugged casually. Queenie turned to Joe and caved. "We'll take it."

He grinned at Winnie then Queenie. "Come inside and we'll do the numbers."

After Queenie and Winnie survived the relatively pain-free process of buying a new car and Winnie was awarded the keys, the pair stood outside admiring Winnie's new Freedomobile.

"Thanks Mom. You're the best." Winnie bent down and kissed Queenie's cheek.

Queenie pinched her daughter's cheek lightly. "Try not to wreck yourself on your grand tour. I assume you're taking it visiting?"

"Of course. I've already texted Jon and Rachel. They can't wait!"

Now that the moment of doom arrived, Queenie felt her stomach seize with anxiety. "Winnie—" she stopped herself. What could she say that wasn't going to rain on the kiddo's parade? *She deserves this*, Queenie reminded herself.

"Yeah, Mom?"

"Have fun." She smiled through the sick feeling in her stomach.

"Always, Mom."

Despite the salesman's suggestion that Queenie could do with a newer vehicle herself, she headed home after Winnie drove off, pulling Jasper's old Crown Vic into her driveway. It wasn't the most reliable vehicle, but it was the one she'd brought Winnie home from the hospital in, and she wasn't ready to part with it just yet.

Cobra Bubbles barked a greeting from the front window, her blocky mug disappearing from view. When Queenie opened the door, the dog danced out, booty jiggling, excited to see her. Cobra Bubbles gave her the obligatory lick, before taking her mad dance moves out into the yard to perform her standard security check. Queenie headed inside to drop off her bag and new car paperwork, when she went back out to call the dog inside, she spotted the front gate standing wide open.

"The Great Houndini strikes again." Queenie hit the curb just in time to see Cobra Bubbles head into Jasper's open garage. She whistled for the dog, but was ignored.

Queenie trailed after her, pausing when she got to the garage. Both the inside and outside doors were left open, so someone was obviously working on the house. An unfamiliar truck parked at the curb lent weight to her theory. She heard Green Day coming from inside and guessed Rex and Diana probably hired someone to get the place ready for sale. *Thank the gods.* The sooner the Montgomery clan left the neighborhood, the sooner she could get a good night's rest.

She looked around the garage and saw the boxes Winnie had filled with stuff to go to Goodwill neatly labeled and lined up against the wall. "Hello?" She called through the open doorway. "I think my dog may have wandered inside." When no one replied Queenie got a little worried. She hadn't heard any screams or cries for help, but Cobra Bubbles could be a little intimidating and the last thing she wanted was for some freaked out house painter to call animal control. Or worse.

"Cobr—," she reconsidered the wisdom of calling out the dog's whole name, settling for the obviously harmless bit. "Bubbles?"

Queenie wandered inside and closed the door behind her, effectively closing off any means of doggy escape. She followed the odor of fresh paint and the sound of music down the hall to Jasper's bedroom. "Hello?"

"We're in here," Rex called from the bathroom.

Queenie's heart did the same stupid flip-flop thing that always happened when Rex was around. She sucked it up and stuck her head through the doorway to find the dog filling up most of the floor space in the tiny room. Rex stood in the shower, shirtless, barefoot and clad in worn denim jeans that had seen better days, but didn't miss them. A paint-splattered bandana covered the top of his head, leaving a few dark-gold curls to play peek-a-boo. He was holding a quart of paint and a brush. He smiled crookedly when he saw her and turned the music down. "Hey, you."

"Hey yourself," Queenie said trying to ignore Rex's washboard abs. "Sorry about Cobra Bubbles. She's used to having the run of the place. I'm glad it was you. I was half worried she'd cornered a handyman." Queenie looked around, noticing the new paint and hardware. "You've been busy. Nice work."

"I can be handy." He held up the paintbrush as proof.

Queenie entertained thoughts of his hands on her. *Stop it*, she chastised herself, feeling her face heat. "The bandana suits you. It's very Johnny Depp, or maybe Axl Rose circa nineteen-ninety."

"Bret Michaels?"

"Um, no," Queenie frowned and shook her head. "The blue guy-liner isn't my thing. Let's agree that it will never be yours either, shall we?"

"Done," he grinned. "I shudder to think what Uncle Jasper would make of this conversation." Rex scraped the paint off of the edge of his brush and into the can.

Queenie looked at Cobra Bubbles. "I'm guessing he wouldn't be a fan of the blue-guy-liner either. He'd probably recommend you stay with black."

"Can't go wrong with the basics," Rex agreed, chuckling.

"So, someone finally got around to painting over the naked lady murals in here, eh?" She admired his freshly painted walls.

"Were there some?"

"I wouldn't know. This was the only room Jasper wouldn't let me touch. I can only assume that was the reason. Don't spoil it for me, Tex-Rex. I have to have my dreams. Remodeling for potential neighbors?"

"Something like that." He finished the corner he was working on, dropped the brush in the sink and wiped his hands on his pants. Seeing he needed some space, Queenie backed out of the room, calling the dog after her. "Come on Cobra Bubbles."

The reaper trailed her obediently, Rex joining them. "How'd she end up with that name?"

In an effort to create some space between them, Queenie wandered over to the window, pausing to run her finger along the dusty sill. "Lilo and Stitch was Winnie's favorite movie when she was a kid. It's a character from there." She wiped the dust on her cutoffs. "And a strangely apt name for our Former Fiona." As if knowing the conversation was about her, Cobra Bubbles wagged her tail and lumbered over to Queenie for a pat.

"I don't think I've ever seen it," he reached for the shirt hanging on the back of the door and Queenie watched with both regret and gratitude as he pulled it on. *You could give Dwayne Johnson a run for his money.*

She dragged her mind out of the ab-laden gutter. "There's probably a copy in the garage in one of the boxes she packed. When she was little, it was always on. In fact, if you can't find one around, just ask Winnie. She'll be happy to act out the entire production for you. Complete with alien voices and ocean sound effects."

Rex dusted off his shirt. "Speaking of Winnie, she seems like a great kid."

"Um, thanks. She is, but like I said yesterday, that's all her." Queenie said not wanting to dwell on the topic.

"And let me apologize for Drake last night."

Queenie raised a hand to stop him. "Apologizing for other people is a step in the wrong direction. Drake can manage his own if he ever gets around to feeling the need."

"That's not likely." He closed up the paint can and wiped his hands on a rag hanging from his tool belt. Like Batman, Rex seemed to have a utility belt for every occasion. For a reason Queenie had yet to define, there was just something intangibly erotic about a man so obviously prepared. "He may surprise you yet." She caged her libido and re-joined the conversation. "Sometimes people do."

"A unicorn would surprise me. A changed Drake would shock me." He told her. "But then there's you."

"What do you mean?"

"His behavior was uncalled for, Victoria. The old you would have lit into him."

*And set his head on fire.* "Probably," she acknowledged, "but give the kid a break, Rex. To be fair, he didn't say anything about me that isn't common knowledge in this town, and wasn't true once upon a time. May be again one day. You never know. I certainly aimed myself in that direction the other night."

"I doubt it." Rex said, suppressing the memory of wanting to pop his nephew's head off the night before for how he'd treated Victoria. "Why are you cutting him so much slack, anyway?"

"I think he may need it," she grabbed a rag and finished the job of wiping the dust from the sill. "No offense to your sister, but I'd need a few breaks if she were my mom."

*And there it is again.* He'd almost convinced himself he was imagining the bite in Victoria's tone when she spoke of his sister, but this time her hostility piggybacked his own.

"Something happen between you two I should know about?" She turned his way, her expression exquisitely schooled to the same neutrality he'd seen his colonel wear on more than one occasion. *She is about to tell me a bald-faced lie.*

"Diana and me? Nothing at all." She added a smile that his colonel couldn't have pulled off on his best day and Rex knew whatever had gone on between Victoria and his sister must have been nuclear. "She has always just seemed a little high strung."

Fresh from his own Nagasaki with his sister, Rex filed away his discovery for later. After all, they had the whole week ahead of them in the Survivor's Hutt. "Electrical lines are a little high strung. Diana is a high wire on the moon."

Victoria laughed and Rex watched some of the tension drain out of her.

"So, you ran away from home for the day?" She tossed the rag she'd been using on to the pile he'd made already.

"I'm here for as long as you can tolerate me, neighborino." Rex tried to read her and failed when she turned to look at the dog. "Was this your idea?" She looked back at him. "Um, you're actually staying here now?" Her gaze tracked to the corner of the Spartan room where his duffel bag rested. "There's not a bed in this house big enough to fit you. What are you going to do, sleep on the floor?"

"Not the worst offer I've ever had, believe it or not. And I'm pretty sure they sell beds somewhere in the city." He'd been hoping for a warmer welcome, but she hadn't said no so far.

"Wow, you weren't kidding when you said you wanted to start again. How long do you plan on camping out here?"

"At least for the week. I figured I might as well do some work on it until I decide what's next for me." *C'mon, Victoria, throw me a bone.*

"I thought you were supposed to be enjoying the suburban hospitality of the palatial Masterson Estate. Your sister cannot be happy about this," Victoria said. "More like the opposite of whatever happy is, times infinity, plus one."

"Sounds about right."

"Made up your mind, have you?"

"I don't think it's up to just me. You said we could try again. Diana and I can't live together, so I'm here until you tell me to go. Apparently it's your neighborhood these days. What do you say?"

Rex waited while she studied him for a moment, eyes narrowed. She looked from Cobra Bubbles back to him, then shrugged. "I'll offer you the same caveats I give everyone else who is considering such a rash move. The gangs are all mostly east-side these days, but we still have our issues." She held up three fingers. "First: Bobby Vasquez from four houses down will egg your truck handles if you leave it parked in the street on Friday night."

"I have a whole week to worry about it then," Rex made a mental note to clear the garage before next Thursday. "Just Fridays?"

"Affirmative Major," Queenie shrugged. "Unless, of course he decides to expand his criminal repertoire and branch out. If that happens, you'll wake up to the memo just like everyone else." She explained. "His mom has taken a part-time job and he's acting out."

"How old is this punk?"

"Seven, so he's really more like a would-be punk, or a punk-in-training. He might even borrow the eggs from you first. The Vasquez's are vegans, so if you're barbequing or something and Bobby comes over to mooch a cheeseburger, don't give it to him or his mother will go medieval on your Ranger rear and you'll cry like a baby and ruin your street cred."

"Noted." Rex tried to keep his humor in check as she folded down a finger.

"Next is Morris White."

"Junior's dad?" It had been at least ten years since Rex thought of the Morrises. Junior was a few years older that the trio of misfits Rex was part of, so they never hung out, but when Junior went into the Army no one was prouder than the Senior Morris.

Victoria nodded. "Junior wasn't as fortunate as you. When he didn't make it back, Morris went on a bender. He's better these days, mostly because of Renee, his particular lady friend. But he does occasionally relapse. For that reason I recommend that you avoid painting anything close to the house yellow."

"Why yellow?" Rex asked.

"Because for some reason Morris can't see yellow. I'm talking like *at all*. It's your choice, of course, but the Domingos failed to heed the warning and their adorable birdhouse mailbox suffered the consequences. Be guided by their tragedy, Rex."

"Got it. No yellow. What's number three?"

She folded down the second finger, then frowned at the remaining digit. "Señor Pickles," she replied absently.

Rex shuddered for effect earning a small smile from Victoria. "Señor Pickles and I have an understanding."

She tsked in mock sadness. "Then you'll have to take it up with him when you get to the other side. Assuming you and that cat end up in the same place. Which would just be a shame."

"You're kidding?" The news caught him off guard. "I was convinced that cat was more demon than feline."

"We all were, so it has to be true. He must have been called home for some reason then. Demonic uprising that required his special skill set, perhaps."

"I'm ashamed to say the thought doesn't seem that far fetched." Rex admitted, hoping the idea wouldn't work its way into his nightmares where Cece's clown collection was currently holding court. "So, the neighborhood is truly free of his legendary reign of terror?"

"The end of an era," she smiled. "You're living the American dream now, Tex-Rex." Her blue eyes gleamed with genuine pleasure for the first time since he'd walked back into her life. "Welcome home."

\*\*\*

"There's my cup of white sugar," Queenie allowed herself to be swept into Angel Baby Woodson Weatherby's arms. Cece's mother was a darker, sultrier version of her daughter. Where Cece was lithe, Angel Baby was lush. Cece's dark hair had been tamed and lightened, while her mother left her curls wild and streaked with just the faintest bits of gray. The eyes were the same emerald green that could harden or soften as the moment demanded. Those eyes searched Queenie's face, and narrowed slightly. "Whatever it is won't seem so bad after some fried chicken and chocolate cake."

*Food coma therapy Round Two, here I come.* "I'm okay, Angel," Queenie lied.

"Let the girl be, Abby." Henry, Angel Baby's husband said from behind her. Henry Weatherby was a tall man in his early sixties with skin the color of bronzed caramel, and a distinguished greying at his temples that accentuated greenish-gold eyes.

"We'll talk later," Angel Baby said under her breath and turned her over to her husband's embrace. Henry indulged in a light embrace before releasing her with a comforting pat on the back. "How are things, Queenie?"

"Manageable Henry," Queenie said with a smile.

"Not exactly high praise, then?" He escorted the ladies down the hallway towards the living area that served as the central hub in their open floor plan.

"Let's just say there's room for improvement."

"Always a bright side, love," Henry readily agreed. "You never know when other people's lives will take a dump so you can feel better about your own."

Queenie choked on her own laughter, and Henry patted her back until she could breathe again. "Henry, stop it. You're terrible," Angel Baby berated him lightly, turning to Queenie, "No Winnie tonight, sugar?"

Queenie inhaled before answering, grateful to be breathing again. "She'll be along. You know how teenagers are."

"Don't I ever. The lot of you are lucky I didn't snatch you bald."

"Your hand would've gotten tired after Cece."

"Too true, honey love," Angel Baby agreed. "You all had your moments, but she was a terror from the day I brought her home from the hospital."

"Speaking of the terror, she here yet?"

"In the kitchen finishing the cake. Hopefully they'll be enough frosting for the cake. You know my baby and frosting." Angel Baby tsked.

"I heard that!" Cece called out from the kitchen.

Angel Baby ignored her daughter. "Henry, get Queenie a drink, love."

"Your usual?"

"Please," Queenie said and Henry wandered off to get her iced tea. Angel Baby tucked her arm through Queenie's and strolled with her towards the kitchen where they caught Cece licking the frosting knife.

"Baby, you aren't the only one eating that cake you know," the no-nonsense look Angel Baby gave her daughter would have frozen Queenie in her tracks, but Cece just took another feather lick of the frosted utensil, and rolled her eyes. "Oh please, mama. If you don't have my cooties by now then you haven't been trying hard enough."

Angel Baby looked pained. "Jerome is bringing a guest. He might not want your cooties."

"He will after he meets her, Angel." Queenie reassured her. It was a running bet with them. Without exception, every one of J.J.'s friends had propositioned Cece in one form or another. At this point she was twelve for twelve, and if she made it to fifteen without saying yes to any of them J.J. was going to have to fork over a season of ringside UFC fights. Not that Cece was all that into UFC, but the seats were expensive and the clientele she would be exposed to was even more so.

J.J. had been pulling out the stops all year long. Among the contenders so far there had been the fair share of fighters, of course, along with a Hollywood agent, Dwayne Johnson's stunt double, and the son of a Senator. Cece was a hard nut to crack in the love department.

"True. Besides all of Jerome's friends are built like brick outhouses. They're indestructible," Cece turned the frosting knife over and started on the other side.

"Speaking of brick outhouses," Angel Baby gave up on her offspring and looked around. "Where's my puppy?"

"In doggy detention," Queenie answered. "She needed some alone time." After retrieving Cobra Bubbles from Rex's, Queenie had brought her home thinking she would finish her accounting before taking Cobra Bubbles out for a walk. When she went in search of her to deliver on her promise, Queenie found the dog in Winnie's room patiently chewing her way through her daughter's textbooks. Cobra Bubbles was still a puppy in her own mind and chewing accidents were bound to happen, but Queenie didn't want to take a chance with Angel Baby's fine furniture. Not that Angel Baby would have cared if Cobra Bubbles chewed through her sofa. The dog could eat the wall and Angel Baby would just smile and say it could be fixed. But Queenie would have minded.

"Shame. Next week, then. I miss the pitter patter of little feet." Angel Baby started to look in Cece's direction, but her meaningful glance was redirected by male voices coming through the front door and she headed off.

Cece pointed a finger at Queenie. "I don't care who he is. He saved me from mama's lecture about grandchildren so you better have sex with him to show my appreciation."

"Me?" Queenie snorted. "It's your mama."

"But it's your fault. If you hadn't had Winnie, then my mother wouldn't be pressing me to follow in your footsteps."

"Your argument has some huge holes in it, counselor." Queenie dipped a finger in the frosting bowl and waggled back it at her friend before licking it clean. "Besides, I'm sure this is another contender for your affections, and I'm not even current in the sex department. He'd have to tell me what to do."

"Men like that. Especially Jerome's friends." She finished frosting the cake and put it aside. "This could be your chance to get current. I'm starting to worry about you."

"Why are we worrying about you now, Queenie?" Henry rejoined them and passed Queenie a tall glass of tea artfully decorated with an orange slice.

"Because she hasn't had a booty call in this decade, Henry," Cece answered.

Queenie ignored Cece and took a swallow of tea.

"I think they're probably booty texts these days, hon." Henry replied, prompting Queenie to choke on her drink. "Or maybe that's sexting. I'm not sure. Your mother surely would know."

Cece laughed out loud while Queenie tried to stop drowning in Angel Baby's kitchen. She finally recovered to the point of being able to draw breath. "Let's please not ask her."

At that moment Angel Baby entered the kitchen, flanked by Jerome and Rex.

Henry took one look at Rex and arched an eyebrow at Queenie. "I'm certainly no judge, Queenie, but this one doesn't appear to be too poor a prospect for texting."

Cece swallowed her laughter, slapping a hand over her mouth. Henry caught the reaction, nodding knowingly. "Ah." He patted Queenie's hand. "He must be from the last decade, I'm assuming."

Oblivious to the exchange, Angel Baby waded in to the conversation, "Henry, this is Reginald Montgomery, my lost boy. Finally home again." She reached up and patted Rex on the cheek. Henry and Rex shook hands. "Break out the champagne!"

"I brought some, ma'am," Rex produced a bottle, shooting Queenie an apologetic look.

"Lord, you're a thoughtful young man," Angel Baby swept the bottle from his hand, delivering it neatly to Henry.

"Let me get the glasses, Mama," Cece offered.

"You all just go on and sit." Angel Baby fussed. "Dinner is ready for the table anyway. Henry and I can manage." She shooed them away.

Displaced, the four of them obediently migrated into the dining room, Cece leading the way. They began to take their usual places, and Rex moved to sit next to Queenie. "That's Wee's spot, Rex. You've been replaced." Jerome stopped him, gesturing to another seat.

"Wee to you, J.J." Queenie said.

"Wee?" Rex asked. "Who are we missing?"

"He means Winnie." Cece clarified as Henry entered with a bottle of champagne on ice.

"Ah, Wonder Winnie," Rex commented. Queenie shot him a pained look. "Please don't indulge her. She's grandiose enough as it is."

"You're acquainted with our little charmer then?" Henry asked, setting out the champagne glasses.

"On two separate occasions already. And she's had the upper hand both times."

"That's Winnie," Jerome grinned. "Just like her mama."

"And her Gran," Angel Baby added, laying out a huge platter of fried chicken and mashed potatoes."

"She coming, Queenie?" J.J. asked, helping himself to the potatoes.

"She said so, but you know that girl and time." Queenie took a biscuit from the plate that passed her way. "She could be standing on a sundial at noon and guess it was midnight."

"I was the same way," Rex said, and Queenie suddenly remembered Rex and his wristwatches.

"Ha, I'd forgotten all about your beep-bands," Cece appeared to be cruising the same wavelength. "Which one was which again?"

"Beep-band?" Henry inquired.

"Watches, Henry." Queenie supplied.

"Rex never quite got the hang of knowing the time of day, so Whitey had the bright idea to put a watch on each wrist. They made this high pitched beeping noise when the alarm went off."

"How clever," Henry nodded.

"Uncle Jasper was solution oriented," Rex said.

"I remember one was G.I. Joe," Cece tapped a finger to her lip, a sure sign to Queenie that Cece was reaching for a memory. "The other one is escaping me. The dinner alarm." She groaned, "this is gonna make me crazy."

"It was the Lone Ranger and Silver," Queenie supplied.

"How could I forget that?" Cece shook her head. "It had that recording in it."

"High ho, Silver! Away," Rex laughed.

"Except that it sounded like an electric chipmunk," J.J. added. "To this day I get hungry whenever I hear an electric chipmunk," J.J. said, shoving a forkful of mashed potatoes into his mouth.

Henry chuckled. "You seem to have overcome your chronological disability, my boy. Must have, I assume, to have survived in the Army."

"Not really, sir. I just adapted." Rex held up one arm, displaying a stainless-steel wristwatch with a massive face and three dials.

"Does that come in rose gold? We need to get Winnie one of those," Angel Baby glanced at the clock on the wall. "That raptor boy dropping her off?"

"I believe the boy's name was Talin, love." Henry offered helpfully.

"What a peculiar name for someone to give their child." Angel Baby's comment prompted an eye roll from her daughter. "Well, we'd know, wouldn't we, Mama?"

"Some boy sniffing around Little Red?" At the mention of Talin's name, J.J. lost all interest in his dinner, pinning Queenie with a look.

"Not sniffing, exactly," Queenie answered, uncertain how, or even if, she should field questions about her daughter's possibly-non-existent love life.

"Leave her alone, J.J.. It's what boys do best," Angel Baby passed the gravy down the table, laid out the salad bowl and let Henry tuck her chair in behind her. "You remember how you were at that age." Jerome opened his mouth as if to argue, but Cece cut him off. "Do not make me bring up the Lister sisters, J.J."

"The Lister girls?" Queenie turned to J.J., but he was suddenly unwilling to meet her gaze. "Elaine *and* Jillian?"

"Now, see what you've done, boy?" Henry admonished good-naturedly.

"Didn't Elaine have a wandering eye?" Cece asked.

"In more ways than one," Rex said.

"Traitor," J.J. gave Rex a look that was more hang-dog than threatening.

"Leave him alone, Cece." Angel Baby waved off her daughter.

"She did," Jerome answered. "And that's the point I'm trying to make. Boys are dogs. And they grow into men that are dogs."

"Speak for yourself, Jerome." Angel Baby served herself a piece of chicken and handed the platter down the table. "Rex was a perfect gentleman in high school."

Rex served himself a healthy portion of potatoes, chuckling. "I didn't have much choice in the matter, ma'am. Between Cece and Victoria my lady friends were pretty much decided."

"Victoria?" Henry asked, looking around the table.

"That's my given name, Henry." Queenie spoke up.

"I've never heard anyone ever call you that, Queenie. I feel a little ashamed that I didn't know it before today."

"Don't bother, Henry. Only her papa and Rex ever called her that." Cece added, delicately arranging food on her plate.

"So, wherever did 'Queenie' come from?" Henry asked, working the champagne cork. The pop reverberated through the room, but no injuries followed and he began to pour out a measure for everyone but Queenie.

"She picked it up working the tables, honey," Angel Baby said. "You know how it is in the casinos. Nobody can be bothered to remember your name, so they just call you whatever dances off the tongue, and sometimes it sticks."

And considering most of the things she'd been called in her life, Queenie considered herself lucky. *It could've been worse.*

"I'm guessing that's how Jasper became Whitey?" Henry finished pouring and took his place at Angel Baby's side.

"You'd think, wouldn't you?" Angel Baby shook her head. "But no. When he moved into the neighborhood there were no whites." She looked at Queenie. "Your parents didn't move in until a few years later. Lord knows what he was thinking when he bought that house." She sighed. "Anyway, it only took him about a week to figure out that he was a bit lighter than most folks were comfortable with in that area. We were taking bets on how long it would be before the moving van pulled in. About ten days after he moved in he went out to the yard and pulled up his mailbox. We all thought for sure that was it. He was done. White flight had begun. But he showed us. The next morning when I went to work, that old mailbox was back up, and you can guess what he'd added to the side of it."

Cece burst out laughing. "You mean he gave *himself* the name Whitey?"

Angel Baby smiled at the memory, nodding. "Later, he said he knew that's probably what we were calling him anyway, so why not embrace it?"

"Never met one like him," J.J. offered.

"That's because there isn't one, sugar." Angel Baby raised her glass. "To Jasper Montgomery. You were a crusty old treasure who will be remembered for your color blindness—

"—and for showing me there are many kinds of strength by not beating my ass, or calling the cops when he caught me boosting his car." J.J. said, raising his glass.

Cece raised hers to his, eyes tearing up. "For convincing me that success wasn't something a skinny Jamaican girl from north town was just meant to dream about, and driving me to my LSAT so I wouldn't chicken out."

Rex hugged Cece to him and took his turn. "For being an unrelenting do-er and taking on the thankless jobs of serving both his country and his family."

When it was her turn, Queenie swallowed the lump of emotion in her throat, and held up her iced tea glass. "For being there, without fail, or judgment."

All eyes turned to Henry, who looked apologetic, but raised his glass. "For sharing fine company and your cornbread recipe."

Angel Baby sniffled, but carried on. "Whitey, you'll surely be missed, but remembered. Cheers."

Cheers echoed around the table and they toasted. During the meal they shared Whitey stories until J.J. couldn't eat another bite. Cece and Queenie cleared the table while the men sat around the table holding court for Angel Baby.

"One more admirer for the table," Cece observed from the kitchen. "Thank god it's just Rex. Saves Theo from having to field any awkward calls this week. I can leave the line open for you."

Queenie filled up the coffee reservoir with water and set the beans to grind. "Your mother is just leading by example. That'll be you one day."

"True," Cece set out dessert plates while Queenie retrieved the forks. "So?"

It was a loaded question; one word that managed to ask twenty questions only a best friend could get away with.

Queenie shrugged. "He's moved in across the street for the week, and will be standing in for Aaron this week while he's away."

Cece gave a low whistle. "You work fast."

"I didn't work at all. We saw him at dinner last night and he didn't say a word about moving in to Jasper's, then next thing I know he's parked across the street this morning."

"You saw him last night too?"

Queenie gave Cece the breakdown of what happened the night before and Cece just shook her head. "Diana," she summed up. "Did you tell him about—" she glanced in the other room, then back at Queenie, "— you know?"

Queenie dug around in the cupboard under the island until she found the serving tray, set it down and began loading it with the coffee cups. "Nope. But I told her about him."

Cece's eyes widened. "How'd that go?"

"Better than expected. But that's how everything with Winnie goes." Queenie fished the creamer out of the refrigerator.

"You're actually planning on keeping everything from him for a whole week, then just dropping it on him?"

Cece had a point. The plan had its drawbacks. When she'd worked it out, it hadn't felt so much like, well, lying. But he hadn't been living across the street from her then. She'd assumed that they'd run into each other, maybe make some arrangements to hang out, not be thrown together by circumstances. He'd managed to cross her path every day since coming home and in seventy-two hours he'd moved into her neighborhood and her business life. *At the rate things are going I'll probably see him in the poker room any day now.*

To her annoyance, Queenie realized she was chewing the inside of her cheek again and stopped. "Maybe not. Let's just play it as it lays."

"Sorry, I'm late!" A familiar voice came through the door, followed by a familiar face. "Hi, Mom." Winnie deposited a kiss on Queenie's cheek and gave Cece a quick hug as she surveyed the leftovers. "Wow, enough food here to feed India."

"You hungry, baby girl?" Cece added another plate to her pile.

"Nah, I ate. But I could go for some dessert." She spied the towering chocolate cake. "I think that should just about do."

"Then grab it." Cece picked up the tray she'd prepared, and Queenie retrieved the carafe of freshly brewed coffee.

"I'm on it, Aunt Cece."

"Is that my Winnie?" Angel Baby called out.

"I'm here, Gran." She led the dessert parade into the next room, eyes lighting on Rex almost immediately. "You again."

"Guilty." He laughed, his face settling into the same crooked smile Winnie was wearing and Queenie was suddenly paranoid that she was about to be outed.

"You're an alien life form using us for our food supply, aren't you?" Winnie laid the cake down.

"You have cake. Would you blame me?"

"Where have you been, baby girl?" Angel Baby opened her arms and Winnie went into them. Queenie and Cece distributed plates and poured coffee while Winnie made her rounds from Angel Baby to Henry, then to J.J. before settling in to her regular seat. "I was bowling with Talin and lost track of the time."

"Bowling?" J.J. raised an eyebrow. "Is that what the kids are calling it now?"

"Don't make me kill you, Uncle Jerome. It would embarrass both of us." She stuck out her tongue playfully. "And anyway, his mom was there."

"Since when do you bowl?" Cece asked, serving up rich slices of buttery chocolate cake. "I remember... a birthday party—? Wasn't it Queenie?" Cece settled down with her own cake. "I think you were maybe eight."

"Nine," Queenie supplied. "Bratton Holmes."

"That was it." Cece added cream to her coffee and stirred. "His momma had the brat part right."

"That bad?" Rex asked.

"That the boy that pushed her into the boys room and kissed her?" J.J. stabbed his cake with more force than necessary.

"Please tell me that's not the end of the story, my dears." Henry frowned.

"Whitey was about ready to turn that boy inside out." Cece remembered.

"My uncle was there?" Rex wanted to know.

Cece nodded. "Queenie was working nights back then, so he and I offered to chaperone Wonder Winnie on that occasion while Queenie slept." She sat back, remembering. "And to think, at the time I thought it was going to be a complete waste of a Saturday afternoon. But you,' she pointed her fork across the table at Winnie, "never fail to entertain."

"I did handle it," Winnie grinned.

"Yes, you did." Cece acknowledged with sass and a wink. "And I'm certain that to this day Bratton doesn't look at a bowling ball without feeling a twinge in his man parts."

J.J., Rex and Henry cringed in sympathy. "Boy had it coming."

"They always do, Henry," Angel Baby nodded sagely. "And my girls are just the ones to give it to them."

"Talin was spared the same fate, I hope?" Queenie delved into her own dessert.

"Talin is a perfect gentleman, so far." Winnie informed the table. "The bowling is his mom's thing. Talin says it's like a religious thing for her. She gets together with some other people every Sunday."

"Like a league?"

"I assumed it was, but Talin says no. His mom is some kind of Buddhist priest. So, on Sunday she and her peeps gather to drink White Russians and bowl."

"I've never heard of a priest that does that." J.J. voiced his suspicions. "Priests are supposed to speak in Latin and carry incense. Not bowl."

"So not Buddhist, Wonder Winnie," Rex said.

"Ex-squeeze me? I think I know what my would-be-loser-grease-monkey-boy-toy's mother is." Winnie forked a piece of cake into her mouth.

"Big Lebowski?" Queenie raised an eyebrow in Rex's direction. "Do people do that?"

"You live in Vegas. You tell me." Rex said.

"That Jeff Bridges movie?" Henry asked.

"Are we still talking about Irene?" Winnie asked.

"Talin's mother, it would appear, is a *Dudeist* Priest, princess." Henry informed Winnie. "And I believe that the cocktail in question is referred to as a Caucasian among the devout."

"I'd almost forgotten about that," Cece finished her cake. "I could go for one of those about now."

Winnie checked the table. "You're not making this up? His mom practices a religion based on a movie?"

"Not just a movie. More like a cult classic."

"Hmm," Winnie tilted her head in amused contemplation. "I think Irene just leveled up."

"I don't even know her and she's a little cooler than average." Cece agreed.

"This Talin boy kept his hands off you on the ride home? I don't need to find him and familiarize him with the octagon, do I?"

Winnie made a crazy cringing face and Angel Baby laughed. "Please don't. I drove myself. Mom bought me a car this morning."

"You did what?" All heads turned to Queenie.

"What?" Queenie raised her hands in defense. "She'll be seventeen in two months. She has a driver's license and a life."

"My lord, how time flies," Angle Baby tsked. "It seems like just yesterday Whitey drove you home from the hospital."

"Man, kid, you were a peanut." J.J. held out a massive forearm. "I could hold you right here."

"You could hold the Bellagio there," Winnie observed. "And before this lapses into embarrassing stories I've heard before, who wants to see my new ride?"

The table rose almost as one. "I do love that new car smell," Cece said.

Queenie started collecting the dishes as the rest of the party exited. "You coming, Rex?" J.J. asked.

"I'll see it later. I'm going to help Vict—," Rex caught himself. "—Queenie with the dishes."

J.J. gave the pair of them a pointed look, but Angel Baby tucked an arm through his elbow before he could say anything. "You leave them alone, boy. Nothing wrong with a man who wants to wash dishes."

Queenie had the sink filled with hot soapy water, while Rex finished clearing the table. He scraped food remnants into the trash and stacked the dirty plates while Queenie sponged off the plates and loaded them into the dishwasher.

"Henry seems nice," Rex said.

"Henry is perfect." Queenie confirmed.

"How did they meet?"

"He was one of her George's," Queenie said, and must've read his confusion. "When you cocktail, you tend to collect your own groupies. Like Rockstars, except without the hair, money, fame or drug addictions. They won't sit in anyone else's station if you're there."

"Those are Georges?" Rex tried to keep up.

"No. Those are fanboys." She rinsed a fork and dropped it in the cage. "The fat tippers are Georges. Don't ask me where the name came from, they've just always been called that. Anyway, a George is like a non-stalking, super-fan who likes you for whatever reason and over-tips on a grand scale to show appreciation."

"Are we talking fifty-dollars for the powder room, over-tipping?" Rex asked.

"Breakfast at Tiffany's, Fred, Darling?" Queenie paused and Rex nodded. "Wait 'til I tell Cece the Army failed to cleanse you of her Hepburn teachings. She'll have you roped into an Audrey film festival before you can say 'Cat'."

"Bring it." He grinned.

"Consider it brought."

"If she asks nicely I'll bring along my pirated copy of My Fair Lady."

"Hmmm, what would a nice boy like you be doing with a pirated copy of anything?"

"It was a gift," Rex briefly thought about trying to explain Leo, but decided against it. "And it's dubbed in Korean."

"All of it? Even the songs?"

"Oh yeah," he nodded. "Especially the songs. You haven't lived until you've seen it."

"Tempting."

"But I digress," Rex backtracked. "So, Henry was a George. Got it."

"I think even Henry would agree that he's probably less interesting than Audrey Hepburn dubbed in Korean. But yes, he was a George. Not for too long, to his credit. I think Winnie was two when he came on the scene and swept Angel Baby off her feet." She smiled at the memory. "No one deserved it more than she did."

"He take good care of her?"

"The best." Queenie drained the water out of the sink and searched for any stray utensils that may have evaded her. "He was a widower with no kids from Florida when they met. He retired from investment banking just last year. So, if you need a guy to manage your euros he's your man. I don't know the specifics, but he and Angel Baby have a house in Florida and one in Santa Barbara, so I think he must know what he's doing."

Rex whistled. "Seems like it. Do they spend much time here?"

"Less and less lately. But we're all here, so when they are here we do Sunday dinners." Satisfied, she rinsed out the sink then looked at him. "So, better pencil yourself in for the duration." Queenie grabbed a washcloth and wiped her hands.

"Did Whitey come to dinner?"

"Of course," Queenie tilted her head at him. "Every Sunday like clockwork. Sat where you're sitting, in fact. He used to bring the best cornbread. Why do you ask?"

"No reason. I just can't picture what his life looked like." *Making cornbread and bowling with nine year-olds wasn't the Whitey you knew.*

Rex realized he'd opened himself up the minute the words left his mouth, but she didn't take the shot.

"He was okay." She said after a pause. "He had a makeshift family, and a place to go during the day to relive old times and share his area of expertise with the world."

"Sounds better than okay."

"Don't kid yourself, Tex-Rex." Queenie admonished. "He missed you, and worried along with the rest of us. But I'm guessing he knew you had your reasons for staying away."

"He brought me back in the end."

"He was a crafty bastard." She agreed.

"Queenie, thanks a—"

"None of that." She cut him off. "I owed him more than I was ever able to repay. What little I did, I did for him. Not you. You're going to have to face your own demons from the past."

"The gloves are off, eh?" Rex leaned back against the counter.

Queenie laughed. "I stopped wearing them a long time ago. I could never get the bloodstains out afterwards."

*That, I can believe.* Rex chuckled to himself as he watched her walk away. One week to get back in her good graces where he belonged. Suddenly, he couldn't wait to get started. *Come on, Monday.*

# ๑—Chapter Seven—๑
♕

Monday morning Rex trailed Queenie around the Survivor's Hutt while she acquainted him with the inventory.

"Pretty standard set up for an arsenal," Rex commented after he'd seen the inventory.

"I wouldn't know," Queenie said, handing him a set of keys she'd had duplicated before coming in. "They're all labeled for your convenience, Tex-Rex."

"And the safes?"

Queenie copied down the combination and passed it to him. "That's for the first one. The rest are all one number forward for each turn." They stood in front of the computer screen that functioned as the register. "It's also the password for the store. Aaron changes it every ten days."

"That seems like overkill," Rex said.

Queenie shrugged petite shoulders. "I don't interfere with his paranoia and he doesn't try to keep the accounting. It works. If you decide to stay on, I'm sure the pair of you can come to an arrangement regarding password protection."

Rex chuckled at the comment. "And the accounting?"

"Your request is being processed for the early stuff. I have this fiscal year available, but don't come crying to me when you can't figure out Aaron's chicken scratchings," she shook her head, "he really should've been a doctor."

Rex gestured to the screen. "He doesn't put everything on this?"

Queenie shook her head and fished some receipt paper out of a drawer. "Not hardly. For weapons purchases, yes. Always. The paper trail is a must."

"What else is there?"

"We're not licensed to resell weapons, only new inventory." Queenie loaded the printer and shut it. When it lit to her satisfaction she turned her attention back to him.

"But?" Rex prompted.

"But, as I'm sure you noticed, Aaron deals with a lot of former military."

Rex had. The zombie guys were all either current, or former, members of some kind of armed forces. Guys like that were bound to have weapons that they were ready to move. "He deals in used weapons on the side? Isn't that illegal?"

"That would be. And if I catch him doing it the law will be the least of his worries." She pulled up a contact file and opened it. Rex noticed the notes next to each person's name. "Sometimes guys are looking for something specific that we don't stock, or you can't buy anymore."

"Sure."

"So, Aaron will sometimes put people together."

Rex gave a low whistle. "He's an arms broker on the side?"

"I think he prefers to think of himself as a consultant."

"I bet." Rex said.

"Jasper cleaned his clock when he found out about it. Hence the file. To make it into the file you have to have been a former customer with a clean record. Nothing shady."

"Still, hard to be sure," Rex commented, wondering if this were the time to voice his suspicions about their partner, deciding to hold off until he knew something more.

"No kidding. But Aaron is his own man. I'm not in a position to tell him how to behave, only to keep him on the right side of the law. He knows that I will be the first one to call the authorities on him should he depart the shady confines of his gray area for obviously darker waters." She looked at him, blue eyes holding him. "And the same goes for you."

"I—

She raised a hand and he stopped. "I know, I know. I'm not saying you will. I'm just saying that the Survivor's Hutt operates as a piece of the whole and everyone has to toe the line. If you cross over, then you're out."

Rex raised his hands in mock surrender, knowing she was serious. "I'm buying what you're selling, Vict-, Queenie." In the Rangers there was always a guy looking to score a little extra by offering just the facilitation services Queenie had described. Apparently, Aaron had been that guy, and still was.

By Aaron's own account he knew what was at stake, and he still walked the line a little too close for comfort. It made Rex want to strangle him. But just a little. "How'd the two of you ever get together anyway?" The look she gave him was guarded and he realized how the question sounded, so he tried again. "As business partners, I mean."

She grimaced. "I think the answer is the same for both questions. I needed a change and Aaron manufactures it." She headed up to the front door and unlocked it, turned off the alarm and headed back. "Sometimes you just have to stir the pot and see what comes up, you know?"

"So, you tried dating each other, but that didn't work?" Rex watched her expression turn wary. "Winnie mentioned it. I'm not stalking you, I'm just curious, Queenie. Allow me that, will you? It's been seventeen years."

She exhaled and smiled. "It has been. I'm sorry, I'm just not used to people asking questions, you know?"

"Am I just 'people' now?" His question prompted her to nibble at the inside of her cheek, she saw him catch her and stopped. "We went to juvie together, Queenie."

"That was your fault," she reminded him. "I told you to run. You were an idiot to stay."

"Your personal idiot," he agreed remembering. "You used to sneak into my room and leave jelly beans in the pockets of my ROTC uniform, how was I supposed to leave you hanging?" As soon as he'd said it, he wished he hadn't. To her credit she left the opportunity alone.

"You had first lunch, you needed the sugar rush."

Rex remembered the grind of summer soldiering in his junior year and the sugary sweetness of Queenie's offerings pressed against the roof of his mouth so the commander would never know Rex was violating the no eating rule. "Also true. I don't think I ever thanked you for that. Or for taking the blame with Whitey when the Taylor's five pound poodle turned up with a military cut instead of that stupid teddy bear thing he usually had."

She finally laughed aloud and Rex felt himself relax a little.

"They had it coming when they named him Tank," she rolled her eyes, relenting. "No. You are not just 'people', Tex-Rex."

"Then let's catch up. Together. The right way." Rex said giving her his corniest smolder and grinning when she rolled her eyes at him. "I'll buy you dinner tonight after closing and we'll talk about old times, new times, whatever you want. What do you say?"

"I say okay."

\*\*\*

Cobra Bubbles' bark alerted Queenie to Rex's presence on the doorstep at precisely seven thirty.

"I'll get it, Mom!" Winnie called from the hallway. A thread of apprehension wormed through Queenie. Winnie was obviously excited by the thought of having a father near. Who wouldn't be after years of believing she'd been all but abandoned by him?

*What if this all falls apart in a week? What are you going to do then, Queenie Hart? Who will be there to put the pieces of Winnie back together if Rex decides to pull his vanishing act on you again?*

As much as she wanted to believe his departure from her life had been self-preservation on his part, she hesitated. Recovering from him had taken her longer than she wanted to admit. And seeing him in the flesh, *tasting him in the flesh*, brought back a flood of broken dreams she thought she'd put behind her. Cece was right; Queenie still wanted him.

*We want things that aren't good for us,* she rationalized. *Like cheesecake for breakfast. Wanting is normal. It's just a week,* she reminded herself. *You can do this.*

Resolved, she headed out to the living room and was greeted with the sight of Rex and Winnie laughing together at some shared amusement. They looked at her when she entered, heads turning simultaneously, appearing more like siblings than father and daughter in that instant.

"Hey Mom, did you know Rex is a gamer?" Winnie's smile widened into a grin.

Cobra Bubbles lumbered over to greet her, giving her hand a lick and thrusting her head under it for some loving. Queenie absently scratched behind the dog's ears. "I had no idea actually. Finally, someone to go on a zombie killing spree with you."

"You're not a fan, Queenie?" Rex asked, looking scruffy and delicious in a pressed shirt and worn jeans. She made a concerted effort to ignore the allure of his cologne. *Not strong enough to be cologne,* she thought. *Must be some kind of manly body wash with a ridiculous name like Slayer, or Spartan.* She tried, but failed, to banish the thought of Rex as the latter; shirtless and armed, ready to rain death to tyranny in all forms. *You really are your own worst enemy, Queenie.*

"The graphics make her want to hurl," Winnie commented. "She plays, but she's only good for twenty minutes at a time without Dramamine. You want to take a crack at my Left for Dead score before dinner?"

Rex turned a questioning glance at Queenie, oblivious to her historically inaccurate erotic montage.

"Be my guest. Literally. I thought we'd stay in, if it's all the same to you." She explained. "I have a lasagna in the oven, and half of Angel Baby's chocolate cake leftover from yesterday. It will take someone with a strapping appetite to dent it. Up for the job, soldier?"

"You cooked for me?" He seemed genuinely touched, and she held up a hand to prevent any preconceived domestic notions he might be entertaining.

"If by cook, you mean reheat Antonia DeMarco's incomprehensibly tasty food, then yes. I will also be showcasing my culinary skills by reheating her garlic bread, and dumping her salad in a bowl for your pleasure."

"It's okay Mom, you have other gifts," Winnie bolstered her ego from the couch, focus on getting her zombies on-line.

"Thanks for noticing, Wee," Queenie said.

"You shouldn't have gone to so much trouble," Rex said.

"Did you hear anything I just said?" Queenie rolled her eyes at him. "It wasn't trouble, more like community service. Dante and Antonia don't feel comfortable unless they're feeding me. I'm hopeless in the kitchen as far as Antonia is concerned. Come to think of it, she's right." She shrugged. "I stopped by there on my way home to pick up their end-of-month figures, and they plowed me with enough food to feed the Army. That, of course, immediately made me think of you. I was going to bring it over for you to put in your freezer, but then thought: why not eat in instead?" She glanced at him. "We can go out if you want."

"No, I'm good with this, but I would have brought something if I'd have known."

"You brought yourself," she reminded him. "It was quite a journey, and included traversing most of the continents as nearly as I can tell. That will have to do." Queenie gestured to Winnie, Cobra Bubbles, and the waiting couch. "You have thirty minutes before dinner is ready. Better get busy saving what's left of humanity or she'll wipe the floor with you."

"Truth," Winnie said from the couch, her attention already in the game, the extra controller resting invitingly on the coffee table. "In fact the wiping has already begun and the loser is the evening's dishwasher."

Rex looked at Queenie for reassurance. It was a look straight from their childhood. "Go. The zombies threaten our very survival!"

While Rex joined Winnie in slaughter, Queenie set the table and fed the dog. Having Antonia as her semi-personal chef took all the work out of dinner. When everything was ready, she sat down and watched them play. Cobra finished her kibble and joined them, her blockhead tilted at the television screen as if attempting to figure out why bits of human remains kept splattering the screen.

"Mo-om," Winnie wailed uncharacteristically, "he's beating me!"

"You have five minutes to catch up, kiddo." Queenie rose and headed to the kitchen.

"Not a chance, Wonder Winnie." Rex tsked, laughing as his upper body moved in sync with the game. "Unlike you, I've actually used all the weapons on the screen."

"No fair!" Winnie called out, eyes on the screen, thumbs mashing controller buttons like a fiend.

"Don't play, if you can't pay, kidlet," Rex replied, equally intent on the game, his focus never wavering. "Behind you. Zombie Witch on your six, Winnie."

"Gah," Winnie ground out, stamping her foot in frustration. "Why won't she stay dead?!?"

"Grenade, girl." Rex advised.

Queenie put all the food on the table and rejoined them in time to watch her daughter's character run from the recently deployed grenade.

"Take cover," Rex said, positioning his own avatar in front of Winnie's. The gesture wasn't lost on Queenie, although Rex probably didn't even notice it. Sacrifice was second nature to him. Even in a fictional pixelated universe he was ready to be the meat shield.

"Yes!" Winnie cried out, arms raised in victory as the unfortunate undead in question was blown to bits, and the scene rolled into save mode.

"Good job, slayer," Rex grinned, sharing a fist bump with her.

"I'm calling it, kids," Queenie announced. "Dinner is ready. The undead will have to wait for a rematch." She looked at the numbers on the screen and tsked. "He smoked you, girl."

"Indeed he did." They settled in at the table and began serving themselves. "Shut me out like a noob," Winnie grinned over at him. "School me in the ways, Jedi Master."

Rex took the serving spoon from her and helped himself to some pasta. "You've got all the moves, you just need more practice at finding the right tool for the job." He replaced the dish. "Anything magical needs a grenade or better. Everything else you can get by with hack and slash."

"And the mobs?" Winnie asked before filling her mouth.

"Bob and weave, kiddo. Just bob and weave," Rex supplied. "The trick is to stay on the edges picking them off as they peel away from the group. And be prepared. More than three on you is almost certain death unless you have med pacs."

Queenie listened to the pair of them bond through dinner over the finer points of game slaying. When they finished eating she cleared the table.

"So, you really know your way around an armory then?" Winnie asked.

Rex nodded. "Misspent youth."

"Someone's already claimed that, Tex-Rex." Queenie snorted, running the hot water and filling up the sink to allow the dishes to soak.

"Tex-Rex?" Winnie asked, getting dessert plates out of the cupboard. "What's that moniker about?"

"It's about a boy who wouldn't step out of his house without his regulation Lone Ranger holster and genuine plastic pearl handled shoot-em ups." Queenie supplied.

"You remember that?" Rex blanched, then shrugged it off. "What can I say, little lady? It was a dangerous neighborhood back then. Never knew what trouble you might come across back in the day." Rex caught Queenie's gaze and his smile deepened. Her core went all melty and she forced herself to turn his look aside, busying herself with retrieving the dessert forks.

"Did you have a cowboy hat too?" Winnie wanted to know.

"I did indeed," Rex nodded, taking over cake cutting duty. "But Whitey never let me wear it. It was white, of course, and he thought I would get it dirty. Which I would have, because that's what boys do. I suppose it's still around somewhere. Not that it would fit anymore. My lost childhood..." He sighed with the pretense of longing and Winnie rolled her eyes at him.

"Uncle Whitey gave me one when I was little too." Winnie said, getting two glasses and the milk from the fridge.

"Make that three please." Rex said and Winnie obliged.

"It was Rex's hat, Winnie." Queenie put the forks on the table.

"Way?" She finished pouring the milk and looked to Queenie.

"Way."

"Well, it was choice, Tex-Rex. Thanks for the anonymous hand-me-down." She brought the milk to the table.

"Anytime, kiddo." He tipped the imaginary hat in her direction. "Just tell me you tamed the Old West with it."

"Look around, man." She grinned. "Of course, Mom helped. And she didn't even need the hat."

"So, I keep hearing," Rex looked Queenie's way again, his expression interested. "Tell me about the elevation to royalty, if you don't mind."

Queenie raised a hand and waived it in a manner befitting the queen. "I rarely speak of it with commoners."

Rex grinned. "I'm a commoner, then, am I?" *Not hardly*, Queenie thought, trying to ignore the way his shirt stretched across his chest. "Beats peasant." Cobra Bubbles, having sniffed out every available crumb on the kitchen tile, came to sit at Rex's side looking every inch more like the faithful steed than loyal hound.

"Not by much," Queenie sniffed delicately and Winnie giggled. "Mo-om."

"Angel Baby said you worked the tables, and Winnie mentioned that you cocktailed for a while," Rex prompted. "But that doesn't really explain how you became the resident Fairy Godmother around here."

"Well, I am half-Irish."

Rex snorted. "I've seen it in action. You're going to tell me that you charmed a leprechaun out on his pot of gold?"

"Charmed nothing," Winnie said. "She tricked him out of it fair-and-square."

"Now, I have to know."

"Fine, but I'm warning you, it's not much of a story."

"Liar," Winnie said around a mouthful of cake. Queenie shot her a look and her daughter swallowed before speaking again. "Liar, Liar." She looked at Rex, "It's a great story."

"Queenie?" Hazel eyes captured hers, and she had to look away.

"Winnie was only about six months old, and we were living here. Or trying to, anyway. You remember what it was like?" He nodded. "I didn't have a job, and Whitey was trying to support me. He felt sorry for me, I guess."

Whitey's charity went over like a lead balloon, Queenie recalled. Between the pair of them it was impossible to determine who was the bull and who was the bulldozer. "So, Angel Baby got me a job cocktailing," she said.

"And she wasn't even twenty-one," Winnie said, scraping the chocolate frosting off her cake and licking the fork.

"Vegas was different back then. Angel Baby's word was enough, and god knows I was no stranger to the bar scene." She smiled ruefully. "If the heels are high enough and the cleavage is low enough the customers don't complain." Queenie caught the telltale clenching of Rex's jaw. *You did ask, after all.*

She shook her head. "It wasn't that bad. Angel Baby threw her Georges my way, and the money was steady. Whitey watched Winnie at night and Angel Baby took her on her days off. By then she had met Henry and was only cocktailing two days a week, so it worked out."

"But you're not working tables now?" He prompted. "Aaron says you have a piece of most of the businesses in the area."

"Aaron says a lot of things," Queenie sighed.

"She's working different tables," Winnie said, taking her plate to the sink. "Mom is a professional poker player."

"You're kidding." Rex looked from Winnie to Queenie, who shrugged. "It's a living."

"How did that happen?"

Before Queenie could explain, Winnie jumped in. "One night, some jack-hole groped her butt and stuffed a grand down her top," Winnie said, wanting to get to the good stuff.

"Pardon?" Rex's expression drained of humor.

"That would be the gist of it." Queenie admitted. "In his defense, he was celebrating a big win at the tables, and he was *really* drunk, so I could sympathize."

"Please tell me something bad happened to him," Rex said darkly.

"Yes and no." As badly as she'd wanted to smack the fool, she'd needed the job more than she wanted the satisfaction of physically assaulting him. It was a growth moment for her. Much later, after she'd washed off the feeling of being violated, Queenie decided if she couldn't beat him literally, then she would join him and do her best to teach him some better manners. "I used the money to buy in to my first poker game and the rest is pretty much history."

"And the jack-hole?"

"Since he seemed intent on giving me his money, I let him."

"Mom cleaned his clock at the WSOP a year later," Winnie grinned. "It was her first major pot! Almost a million dollars! I still remember that day." She shot her hands up in the air like she was announcing a field goal. "You picked us up and you were so shocked you hardly said anything. I was little and thought something was wrong, but Aunt Cece told me you had been playing a game and won and you were happy. We picked up Jasper and went to the Bellagio for dinner and I ate two desserts. It was the most exciting day of my life!"

"WeeSoP?" Rex asked.

"World Series of Poker," she answered. "I entered as a lark. Henry actually sponsored me that first time. Not because he thought I would win, but because he has money to burn and was looking for excuses to be around Angel Baby." She smiled at the memory. Darling Henry was so crushed on Cece's mom. *Like you were on the cowboy kid across the street*, she reminded herself.

"We *looove* Henry," Winnie told Rex, grinning.

"I can see why."

Winnie looked at the clock on the wall and frowned. "What I wouldn't give for an actual Tardis, or at the very least a Time-Turner." She sighed with the dramatic flair of a teenager headed for the bright lights of Broadway. "If you'll excuse me, I have Spanish homework to decipher," she gave Cobra Bubbles a pointed look, "and you, *perro*, are going to be my able bodied assistant since you ate most of the pages." The dog rose, cast a backward glance at the dinner table, and followed her. "I'll be back for the dishes later," she called as she disappeared down the hall.

"A million dollars?" Rex whistled, still obviously shocked.

"It wasn't my money. Without Henry I never would've made the game." She shrugged. "It was mostly just luck, and a fierce yearning to beat Cowboy."

"Cowboy the jack-hole?"

"He was," she was still able to recall Cowboy's shocked expression when he realized who she was that first time. "He's cleaned up his act since then."

"Given up groping cocktail waitresses?"

"Oh, yeah," Queenie said. "God knows it cost him enough."

"That's unbelievable," he leaned in. "You must be amazing."

"I'm not bad," she shrugged, uncomfortable about discussing it. Poker was just a thing she could do well. She'd always been able to spot a losing hand, whether it was hers or someone else's. *Drawn from real life, thanks dad.*

"And you built Queen's Heights from poker winnings?"

Queenie moved a crumb of cake around her plate. "It's probably more accurate to say that the residents built the Heights from my winnings," she answered, putting her fork down.

"Is that why you stayed here?"

"Think I should've picked up and joined your sister on the west side? Traded in my Crown Vic for a new Mercedes?"

"Maybe, maybe not. There are other sides to this city that aren't here."

"Here isn't here anymore." Queenie nodded. "Honestly, yes. I've thought about it, but it was never for the right reasons."

There's a question she'd never been able to answer. Queenie dusted a stray crumb off the tabletop. "I stayed because it was the only thing I knew. I'm not like you and Cece. You've been everywhere. You had a plan." She shrugged. "You remember what it was like. What I was like; another tweaker dropout with no family and no future. I was nothing, and I had nothing. Then I had Winnie." She pushed her plate away, the topic of conversation robbing her of her appetite. *Just spit it out, Girl. 'Actually WE had Winnie.'*

Queenie chickened out. "The house was paid for and Whitey seemed to like having Winnie around, so I guess I just sort of got stuck." *Jeez, coward much, Queenie?* "I didn't really have anything to do with the rest. Antonia and Dante, you met her," Rex nodded and Queenie continued, "they had a food truck before the restaurant. Nothing big, just pizza and whatever the take out of the day was. But the take-out was always amazing. Melt in your mouth, authentic Italian fare. All Antonia's grandmother's recipes. I took Winnie out to get a couple of slices one day and Dante was talking about opening a restaurant, but didn't want to over-extend himself because their boys were young. And there I was, flush with more cash than I knew what to do with. Whitey told me to invest it in something, and I thought, why not invest in Dante and

Antonia?" She shrugged. "Things kind of took off from there. After that it was more of the same. I'd bring home a big pot, and one of Dante's friends would drop by to chat about a business idea."

"And you'd what? Have them kiss your ring and write a check?" He grinned.

"You joke at your own peril," Queenie narrowed an eye at him. "A lot of people owe me favors in this neighborhood."

"I'm shaking in my combat boots, Your Majesty."

Queenie stacked her fork on her plate and started to rise, but Rex grabbed her wrist and pulled her back down. "You're not going anywhere until I hear the end of this story. It's just getting good." He prompted her. "You'd write a check and someone would go build a monument to your generosity. Go on."

The heat of Rex's hand on her was making her insides do funny things, but she persevered. "Fine, but if you fall asleep during the story because of it's utter lack of high points Winnie and I will do you over in drag make-up, take your picture, and post it to my Facebook page."

"Understood," Rex nodded. "Just stay away from red lipstick. It contrasts with my skin tone and makes me look trashy."

"It does that to everyone. Making you look trashy and available is pretty much the point of red lipstick." Queenie informed him, wondering how he'd made this self-discovery. "And this is your lucky day, because I don't own any. Some ghastly frosted pink is probably the worst we could manage."

"That's fine then. The pink will accentuate my golden undertones."

*Yes, it will,* she realized, finally giving in to the laugh she'd been holding back. Rex just grinned. "C'mon, I'm dying to hear how a skinny kid from the mean streets of Vegas managed to achieve the glory that has become Queenie's Heights."

"I feel like an idiot talking about it like this," Queenie said. "I didn't do anything."

"You gave your money away. In this day and age that's a miracle. If you're not careful, they might try to canonize you as a Saint after you die." Rex crossed himself jokingly. "I mean, I remember when we couldn't walk to the gas and go without Jasper as an escort. Now, you can stumble blind drunk down the street at midnight and make it home in one piece. You did that."

"No, I didn't," Queenie disagreed. "People don't want to live like that—" Rex opened his mouth and she cut him off. "—Not most of them. They want friends and neighbors they can trust. They want a place to go to earn a decent living and to feel useful."

"Does living here and doing this make you feel useful?" Rex asked. "I mean, let's face it, you could help the neighborhood from anywhere."

*Is that why she stayed? Because being the girl from the hood who'd made it gave her an identity?* Queenie didn't know and didn't want to. "Let's save the psychoanalyzing for another time."

"Fair enough." Rex nodded. "So, you made a little dough and decided to start funding other people's dreams?"

"I guess." Queenie agreed. "I mean, what was I going to do with all of it? Let piles of it sit in an account somewhere and get rich off the interest?"

"Isn't that the American Dream? I'm pretty sure it was in the citizenship handbook."

"If it is, then it's a dream that needs an upgrade." She slipped her hand out of his. "Money is like air, or water. It has it's own life and energy. It doesn't start out as mine, and it won't end up as mine. I only control what I can do with it during our brief encounter together."

"Hmm, I think the Government warned me about people like you. People with *ideas*."

Queenie waived aside his words. "Not me. I'm not political. I don't even vote."

Rex whistled. "Heretic."

"You're telling me. Cece hates it. Says it's the only way to change things."

"Not so. It would seem you've found another way. You're a Money Whisperer."

"More like a Money Channeler. The way I figure it, when a High Roller sits down across the table from me that's his way of saying he's ready to give back to the community."

Rex chuckled. "Do you issue receipts for tax deduction purposes? Or maybe send a little note a year, or so, later thanking the donor for their contribution and sending a photo of the changing community."

"You're making fun of me."

"I'm making fun with you. Get used to it." Rex retired his fork and looked around. "You, this house, Jasper's house, the neighborhood. All of things are better because of you. Few enough people actually do anything in their life, Queenie. Let alone change things up like this."

"Stop it." Queenie couldn't take any more praise from a man she was lying to. She stood and took her plate to the trash to scraped away the remnants of her dessert. "As a friend of ours is fond of saying: it wasn't so much change, as it was editing out the mess."

"Sounds like Cece."

"Yep. She was talking about me, but I think the same thing applies to the Heights." Queenie pointed her fork at him, then the cake. "You better eat that or I'll tell Angel Baby."

"Believe me I wish I could," he sat back. "I'm trying to find some room in my stomach that isn't taken up with lasagna. Can I get it to go and still keep my reputation in tact? I'm stuffed."

"You? Full? That's got to be a first." She some foil from a drawer and tore off a piece before taking his cake away. "When did that start happening?"

"When I went in the Army. Eating the food is almost worse than going hungry sometimes. Maybe I shrunk my stomach down to a normal size."

"Pfft," Queenie deposited his wrapped dessert on the table. "Angel Baby will fix that in no time. She loves a challenge." On impulse, she reached out to toy with his hair, catching a golden curl. "I like this. Who knew you were such a pretty boy?"

"How pretty am I?" He grabbed her hand again before she could pull it away.

Queenie's heart flip-flopped, and she froze. "What is it?"

"Nothing," broad shoulders shrugged lightly. "Everything. The same thing it's been since I was fourteen and you held hands with Rick Gonthier. The same thing it was when you came to visit me at Fort Bennington, and the other night when Aaron was yanking my chain."

"Rex—"

"—Queenie," he interrupted her, using his hold on her hand to draw her closer. She didn't stop him. "Is the thing between you and Aaron over, I mean really over? No lingering doubts? No second chances?"

She nodded without hesitation, and Rex smiled. "Are there any other contenders for your affections that I should be aware of? Winnie's dad, maybe?"

This time it took her longer to answer. *Tell him now,* she told herself sternly. "Not in the way you're thinking," was all she could manage. "Why? Clearing the field?"

"Because this is my time. Yours and mine."

"Rex, we tried this already."

"Did we?" She looked into his eyes reacquainting herself with all of the tiny gold flecks she'd missed over the years. *I remember you.* "Maybe what we had was simply a taste of a possible future." He said, his free hand gliding up her back and setting butterflies free in her spine.

"Maybe you watch too many episodes of Doctor Who," Queenie replied, willing herself not to lean into his touch.

"You can't watch too many episodes, sugar," his smile sent a heat though parts of her that she'd forgotten she had.

"Winnie would agree with you," Queenie said, trying to divert him, realizing for the first time that she was standing between his legs. The posture was ridiculously intimate for a woman claiming she didn't want what he was offering. *Geez, red lipstick, here I come.*

"She's an amazing child. Just like her mother." He sat up straighter, lessening the distance between their faces until they were inches apart. Queenie's pulse raced, her heart beating to a soundtrack she hadn't heard in seventeen years. *Queenie, what are you doing?* "Rex, I don't think this is a go—"

"I've moved past thinking, Queenie. On to wanting."

His thumb was making small circles in the palm of her hand; the sensation was maddening and delicious all at once. She swallowed. "Wanting?"

"Oh yes," hazel eyes tangled with hers, his hand coming to rest on her hip. "You said we could start again. I'm just rewinding our relationship a bit and revisiting some of my favorite parts."

"Can we do that?" *No, you idiot, you can't. This is going to screw up everything and you know it.*

"We can do anything we want, Queenie." Rex said, his smile deepening. "What do you want?" *An Army Ranger with a side of golden curls and a crooked grin,* her subconscious answered, and her pulse fluttered in agreement. She wrestled with the truth, deciding a lie was the only path open to her now. "Um, I'm not—"

"—Liar." He pulled her close, mouth melting against him, deceit drowning in the passion between them.

## —Chapter Eight—

The next morning Queenie tried to get her day together with limited success.

"So. You and dad...," Winnie let the sentence linger, taking a bite of her bagel and nonchalantly perusing the open page of her textbook.

*He's 'dad' now?* Queenie thought as she grabbed Cobra Bubble's water dish and hunted down her leash in the coat closet. "Saw that did you?"

"I came out of my room because I was thirsty, but not as thirsty as you, apparently." Winnie looked up at her mother, waggling her eyebrows suggestively and earning a laugh.

"He wants to try again," Queenie said, for lack of a better way to explain something she didn't understand herself.

"Mm-hmm, I gathered that from the intense seal of the lip-lock you two were sharing last night." She took a final bite of her bagel, offered the rest to the dog, and tidied up her breakfast mess.

"How do you feel about the idea, kiddo?"

"Since you asked, I'm selfish enough to admit to being less than thrilled to find out that Burnout Drake of the Perpetual Hoodie and I are cousins." She pushed out her lower lip in a thoughtful pout, but shrugged it off. "David I can manage, but Emo-boy? Guh." Winnie grabbed her messenger bag and rifled

143

through it until she found her phone. "But, it's not how I feel about it, Mom. It's how your tens of fans feel about the idea. Let's see what comments last night's Snap Chat of your tender moment has collected."

"You took a picture of us?" Queenie briefly wanted to strangle her only child. Winnie read her mother's expression and flashed her a grin.

"Of course I did," she scrolled through her phone. "Ah, here we go! The Counselor says it's about time. George's Girl adds kisses of her own. King George says you must have figured out the texting thing." Winnie gave her mother an inquisitive look. "What's that mean?"

"I'll tell you when I'm older," Queenie said. "I can't believe you did that without asking me, Winnie. Or Rex, for that matter. He might not want his personal life headlining your social network." Cobra Bubbles having finished her bagel bite, wandered over to Queenie, saw the leash and started nosing her hand. "Cobra Bubbles, stop please." When the dog refused, Queenie just dropped the leash. Cobra Bubbles grabbed it and ran through the doggie door with it, where Queenie knew she would be running in mad circles waiting for someone to come get her.

"That's a negative, Mamacita," Winnie flashed the phone towards her mother. "Hella Jalapeny, a.k.a. Rex, says the pic doesn't do it justice." She looked at her Queenie. "Aww, that's so sweet."

"Rex is Hella Jalapeny?" Queenie asked, confused. "When did that happen?"

"I'm fairly certain that like me, he was born with his hotness. But the Snap Chat thing happened last night. I texted him to see if he wanted to come over tonight for a Netflix marathon of the Lone Ranger. One thing led to another and poof! He's in this century with a Twitter account and everything."

"You invited him over *tonight*?" Queenie tried to sort through the weeds of her daughter's train of thought. Winnie had one setting: Light Speed.

"Yes. It's Tuesday. You usually Double Down at the Plaza on Tuesdays. So, I thought since you and he were obviously getting along so well, he and I should bond. That's why I suggested the

Lone Ranger. But he said he's jonesing for the last season of Supernatural, which is even better because we haven't seen it yet." Winnie took a breath, then looked at her mother, blue-grey eyes gleaming with youthful innocence. "You don't mind, do you?"

"Not at all," Queenie answered, unsure if she was being completely truthful. She was the Oprah of Deception all of a sudden: *You get a lie, and you get a lie... everybody gets a lie.* The idea depressed her.

"To answer your original question: neither do I."

Queenie tried to follow her daughter's sentence and gave up. "Did I have an original question? That must've been so five minutes ago."

Winnie giggled. "I don't mind. About the two of you." She put her phone away and laid her bag down on the table so she could put her shoes on. "I'm princess enough to admit that I harbored all sorts of silly fantasies about my dad coming home one day and sweeping us off of our feet."

"I never knew that," Queenie said, feeling guilty that she'd never known Winnie experienced father envy. *Your mediocre mothering skills slip yet another notch.* She picked up the dishes from the table and took them to the sink.

"You weren't supposed to," Winnie said to Queenie's back. "They were just daydreams really. I got older and realized how crappy dads can actually be, and how amazing my Franken-family truly is. How amazing you are." Queenie swallowed the lump of emotion suddenly welling in her throat. *I don't deserve you, kiddo.* She turned around to see Winnie finish with her shoes.

Her kid straightened and sat up, smiling her father's smile. "I outgrew the dream. But when I saw the two of you last night— *Wow.* I realized that maybe you hadn't. And I can't begin to tell you how cool that is." Winnie rose and shortened the distance between them, coming to stand at Queenie's side and tucking her arm through her mother's. "I'll tell you what you've been telling me for as long as I can remember: the things that pass your way are meant for you. No one else. Ranger Rex must be passing your way for a reason, yes?"

Emotion clogged Queenie's throat again, and for a long minute she couldn't speak. *The kid makes sense.* Queenie had been so wrapped around the emotional axle since Rex dropped onto the scene that she hadn't been able to get a clear view of opportunity the moment was offering. She'd been angry with him for almost twenty years because he'd left them behind. Turns out he hadn't left them. Only her. And she couldn't really blame him for that. *Let it go, Queenie.*

"Mom?"

"I'm here," Queenie tugged her daughter into an embrace. "How'd you get so smart?"

Winnie dropped a light kiss on her mother's cheek. "It's all in the genes, Mom."

***

"Cobra Bubbles! Come here girl," J.J. said as Queenie pushed open the door to the store.

"Thanks for coming in early, J.J.," she unleashed her canine companion and Cobra Bubbles took off like a hurricane in J.J.'s direction. He was one of a handful of people that could weather her unbridled attention. "I had some errands to run."

"Never a problem, Queenie," J.J. said, kneeling to subdue the oncoming force of nature. "Who's my girl?" He ruffled the dog's ears. "You are, aren't you sweetheart?" J.J. submitted to Cobra's licky enthusiasm before standing. "Gave me a chance to hang with my boy."

"Where is your boy?" Queenie studiously avoided looking around, uncertain of what she'd do if she saw him. *Awkward much? You knew this was a bad idea.*

"Running through the finer points of a Ruger with a customer on the range."

Some of the tension left her as the telltale sound of shots fired in the distance echoed her way. "Buy, or try?"

"Buy." He dusted the dog hair off of his black cargo pants. Cobra Bubbles, recognizing an end to their interlude headed off to the office and her pillow there. "It's a pick up from last week." Queenie and J.J. followed behind. "You playing tonight?"

"Yes," Queenie deposited her laptop on top of Aaron's perpetual mess. She'd tried to clean it up a few times, but the Pile, as it was known, must've had a life-force of it's own because it always returned with a vengeance. "But Winnie's made other arrangements, so you're off the hook tonight."

J.J. lifted a menacing brow, dark eyes suspicious. "These arrangements don't include a male of the species, do they?"

*A prime specimen, as a matter of fact.* "Why yes. Yes, they do."

"Um, that's a hard no, then." He crossed ripped mocha arms over a massive chest, square jaw set and radiating disapproval. "I don't mean to question your parenting skills, but teenage boys are not to be trusted in the company of the Wee."

"Relax, Papa Bear. Rex has the comm tonight." Queenie reached up and patted J.J.'s cheek. "Chanel know how cute you are when you get all protective?" Chanel was J.J.'s on again, off again girlfriend and a co-worker of Cece's.

"She knows," he grumbled. "Cute wasn't exactly the word she used."

She searched around the desk looking for the power cord to the laptop. "Come to think of it, you're probably a huge pain in the as—"

"—Take your mouth to church, girl. Your vocabulary needs Jesus." J.J. cut her off. "Worse than a sailor." He tsked. "Hopefully, Rex can show you better things to do with it than curse."

Queenie whipped her head around. "Jerome Jermaine Woodson!" Heat rushed to her face and she scowled as effectively as she could manage considering he was three times her mass and towered over her. "You did not just say that." *Winnie can kiss her phone goodbye.*

He grinned, taking advantage of his height to give her a patronizing pat on the head. "I'm sure I just did, Queenie. You think I can't see what's going on between you two? He washed dishes with you, girl."

"It was dishes, not a marriage proposal, J.J.," Queenie tried to reign him in.

"It's about time you washed dishes with someone," J.J. ignored her. "If I remember correctly, the last man you washed dishes with was Aaro—"

"—I'm so not talking about this with you." Queenie raised a hand to pre-empt anymore unwelcome speculation on her non-lovelife.

"What aren't we talking about?" Rex asked from the doorway.

Queenie gave J.J. her most menacing look. His grin just widened as he turned to Rex. "Dishes, bro. Just dishes."

Queenie answered Rex's questioning look with a fake smile and a nod. *Please don't ask, please don't ask, please don't ask*, she chanted silently to herself.

"Um, I'm not going to ask." Cobra Bubbles abandoned the comfort of her bed to offer up a doggie hello. Rex ignored them to greet the dog. "Hola Perro, long-time no see." He ruffled her ears and straightened, looking from J.J. to Queenie. "Can I get a little help from one of you with the ammo drawer. I must have zigged when I should've zagged on the combination."

"I got this," Rex headed out, J.J. following. He gave Queenie a last look. "We'll talk about this later."

"No, we won't," Queenie called after him, Cobra Bubbles waffling in agreement.

The day passed quickly for Queenie. The store maintained a steady stream of customers until late afternoon. She was able to slog through her company accounts, sending them off to her accountant to be logged, while she was at it she isolated the Survivor's Hutt file from the others and emailed it to Rex. Despite her intention to avoid managing the Pile in any way, Queenie did battle with the mess of paperwork until some of the actual desktop was visible.

"I think that's a wrap, girl." Finished, she looked at Cobra Bubbles, who met her mistress's gaze with soulful eyes. Cobra's head swiveled to the door, and Rex knocked lightly on the frame before entering. "Hey, stranger."

"Hey yourself," she sat back and stretched.

"Nice work in here," he came over and sat on the cleared corner of her desk. "For some reason, when I took this gig, I imagined we'd be spending more time together."

Queenie tried not to notice the way his t-shirt flexed across his bicep, the tail of his tattoo playing peek-a-boo under the hem of his sleeve. He was sporting a black range vest and jeans and smelled like leather and gunpowder *Women all over the country would build me a shrine if only I could figure out how to bottle the scent of him right now.*

"Civilian life interfering with a player's moves?" She asked, leaning back in her chair.

"As a matter of fact," he followed the arc of the chair and leaned in to steal a quick kiss.

"What was that for?" Queenie asked, surprised she was still able to form sentences with her insides melting.

He braced his hands on the arms of her chair, the intimacy of the gesture fanning the desire his kiss had sparked. Queenie wanted to reach out and slide her fingers into his curling mass of golden hair, but forced herself not to, she was barely hanging on to her good sense where he was concerned.

Hazel eyes warmed her and his smile deepened. "J.J. says I need to give you something to do with your mouth besides curse."

"Oh, did he?" She asked, unable to move.

"Oh, yeah," Rex nodded playfully. "Apparently, you have a mouth that could make a sailor blush."

"Too bad you're not a sailor, Tex-Rex." Queenie hadn't meant to go there, but the innuendo floated between them and she watched his eyes darken with desire.

"Take pity on a poor soldier boy?" He asked, the timbre of his voice heavy.

"I have standards, you know," Queenie informed him, her tone mirroring his. "High standards."

Rex hooked the bottom of her chair with a foot and pulled her to him. "You'll have to acquaint me with them, Queenie." Before she could formulate a reply, his mouth was on hers again and her good sense was out the window. When he drew back to end the kiss, she grabbed a hearty handful of his shirt and pulled him back, her teeth nipping at his full lower lip, punishing him for his liberties. He groaned and strong arms slid around her, drawing the kiss out.

Breathless, they finally broke apart. Queenie forced aside the cloud of desire confusing her thoughts. *Down girl, you've been kissed before*, she reminded herself. *But never like that*, her libido answered back.

"Mmm," Rex stroked the side of her face and she betrayed herself by tilting her head towards his hand. "There might just be something to this standards thing."

"I may just make a sailor out of you yet," Queenie said, trying to get right with herself and failing.

"Jasper would love you for it." Rex said. "But, like me, he always had a soft spot for you."

"It doesn't feel very soft at the moment," Queenie remarked. *I'm an innuendo machine all of a sudden. I need help.* Rex's answering laughter was immediate, her body shaking with the rhythm of his.

"J.J. was right about you," he grinned. "I do believe I'm actually blushing."

Rex resumed his perch on the desk, and Queenie pulled back. "You're easy then."

"Only when it comes to you."

She refused to walk down that road and changed the subject. "How's your second day on the job going?"

"I'm getting the hang of it." He let go of her chair, giving her the much-needed space she didn't want anymore. "I do have one question, before it slips my mind. Aaron has 'Tommy's' on the schedule for tomorrow."

Queenie nodded, grateful to have a safe topic of conversation. "Those are tourist groups who come in to shoot the machine gun."

"You have a machine gun?" His head tilted at the revelation.

"We have two, in case one is feeling under the weather," she informed him. "It's Vegas. We have everything. Sometimes we have showgirls and Tommy guns. When the porn awards are in town we have a Topless Tommygun night. The Tommies get more action than most guys I know." She checked the time and realized she was going to be late for her game if she didn't hustle. "Ask J.J. about it. He can show you the ropes," at his reproachful look she laughed and help up her hands, "not that you'll need it, Tex-Rex." She started to pack her laptop up, looking around for Cobra's leash.

Rex's gaze followed hers around the room. He read her mind and slid the lead off the doorknob. Seeing one of her favorite things deployed, Cobra Bubbles levered her massive frame from her bed and waddled over to him, nosing her head into his hand. "Is this yours?" He asked the dog. She let loose a resonating bark. "I'll take that as a yes," he looked at Queenie. "I can take her home later, if you want."

"You sure?" Queenie asked.

"Of course," he nodded giving Cobra Bubbles a scratch behind the ears. "Winnie says your game starts at six," he looked at his watch. "It's almost that now."

"You don't have to do this," she questioned the sanity of letting him take over her domestic duties. *Face it, after that kiss, you don't have much sanity left.*

He took her bag from the desk and hung it on her shoulder, leading her out the door. "I want to. I'll take care of your girls. Go. Win lots of money." Rex dropped a kiss on her forehead and patted her butt out the door. "Good luck."

***

Queenie rested a single finger on her cards and waited for the flop. She was sitting pretty with two kings in the pocket and one on the flop, now all she had to do was wait for the river to christen her hand.

Double down nights at the Plaza was entertaining its usual high stakes rounders. Cowboy sat in his customary place across the table from her, eyes flicking over Queenie every few seconds trying to read her. She ignored him. Thanks to Winnie, she knew what he was looking for and kept her mouth set like stone.

Tuesday at the Plaza wasn't for the faint of heart. Double down nights could shake down the boldest of them. The hands and the pots were progressive, with a five thousand dollar buy in to start. A few bad rounds would set you back a month's earnings. Cowboy was holding his own, but had yet to win a large pot. Queenie couldn't complain, but the stakes were getting a bit high for her comfort zone. She'd had to call at one hundred thousand, an amount she could easily afford, but still made her feel light-headed.

*Like Rex's kisses.*

The dealer flipped over the final card and Queenie barely registered the fourth king, closing her eyes in an attempt to banish the image of his chiseled features bearing down on hers.

"I call you, Queenie," Cowboy said.

Queenie opened her eyes in time to see him tip his Stetson back and push what was left of his stack into the pot.

"You're dragging light there, Cowboy," Gypsy, one of the other players pointed out. Gypsy was a regular, and a transvestite. Initially, Queenie had some trouble figuring out how to sort out the gender bending issue, opting in favor of referring to the sex Gypsy worked hardest at emulating. God knew Gypsy pulled off her femininity better than Queenie. As nearly as Queenie could figure, Gypsy was probably in her mid to late forties, but her slim build made it hard to tell. Tonight she was wearing a black off the shoulder cocktail dress adorned with a rhinestone replication of the Queen of Diamonds and sporting her blonde Marilyn wig. Currently, she was amusing herself by annoying Cowboy.

Cowboy's conservatism seemed to war with Gypsy's nature. A conflict that Gypsy used to her advantage, sitting next to him when she could, flirting with him and blowing him glossy, red-lipped kisses across the table when she couldn't.

Cowboy scowled in Gypsy's general direction, "I'm good for it."

"I'm sure you're good for a lot of things, lover," Gypsy drawled in a perfect imitation of Cowboy's Georgia accent, "but rules are rules."

Cowboy looked at the dealer, who shrugged, but nodded. "Another two-thousand to call."

"Really?" He asked Queenie.

She shrugged back. "I don't make the rules." The flop was sitting with a pair of kings and an ace. If someone had offered Queenie a side bet on the hand, she'd guess Cowboy was sitting with a pair of aces. *A very nice full house, but not nice enough to beat my king quartet.*

"Fine," Cowboy pulled out his billfold: a long, leather-tooled monster obviously handcrafted by the same man who'd designed his boots.

"Oh, honey," Gypsy laughed in falsetto, laying a manicured hand on her bosom. "Your handbag matches your heels."

A round of good-humored chuckles floated around the table, but Cowboy ignored them. He pulled two-tickets out of his billfold and dropped them on the table. "A pair of VIP tickets for Lady Gaga's sold-out show Saturday night. Easily fifteen hundred a piece."

"I wish I'd have known those were going to make an appearance," Bandit sighed. "I missed my anniversary this week."

Gypsy agreed with a low-whistle. "If I'd have known those were going to be here I would've paid more attention to the hand."

"Queenie?" The dealer waited for her to reply.

"Sure," Queenie said, guessing Winnie would probably get a kick out of the concert. "Why not."

With all the deliberate arrogance he could muster, Cowboy turned his cards over, revealing his flush for all to see.

"Tsk," Gypsy gave Queenie a look of sympathy. "Easy come, easy go."

Cowboy reached for the pot, but Queenie raised an eyebrow at the dealer, who laid a pre-emptive hand on Cowboy's arm. He sat back, eyebrows narrowed. "You were bluffing. I know you were."

*He knew I was bluffing?* She racked her brain trying to figure out what her body was doing while her head was in La-La land, but it was useless. He sounded so sure of himself, Queenie almost felt sorry for him. "Was I?" She flipped her cards revealing her king parade, and Gypsy bounced in her seat, applauding. "Oooh!"

"Son of a bi—" Cowboy cut himself off, stood abruptly and marched off, leaving a half lit cigar behind.

"Girl, you had us all fooled with that long blink." Gypsy said, patting Queenie on the knee. "Good for you!"

*Long blink?* She recalled closing her eyes to get a better visual memory of Rex, but hadn't realized it was a thing. "Thanks Gypsy," Queenie said. "I could really kiss you right now."

"Darlin', those days are long gone for me." Gypsy grinned. "You really didn't know?"

"Not a clue." Queenie slid a modest stack of chips in Gypsy's direction as thanks.

Gypsy fanned herself at the gift. "I don't normally accept charity, young lady."

"Think of it as a consulting fee," Queenie said.

"In that case, I'm not sure it's enough. I may have created a monster." Gypsy gave the rest of the table an apologetic look and brushed an imaginary piece of lint from her dress. "I noticed you'd given up the mouth chewing, so I just assumed you knew about the long blink bluff and you were doing it to fake Cowboy out."

"Honestly, my mind had wandered off," Queenie confessed.

"I'm guessing this is about a man," Gypsy's said knowingly. "He could've been an expensive mistake, honey," she warned in a stage whisper, tipping her head to Queenie's hoard. "It takes more than a holiday weekend on a good corner to pull down that kind of dough. And Gaga tickets to boot."

"An expensive mistake sums him up quite nicely," Queenie said. "I promise to be more careful."

"Oh, please, not on my account," Gypsy waived an airy hand. "It'll be more fun to watch you now that I know sometimes you're flying blind. And life's all about finding joy where you can, girl." She shrugged bare shoulders and dazzled Queenie with her smile. "It's not completely hopeless for the rest of us anyway. There's still that thing you do with your fingers that I haven't figured out yet." Gypsy wiggled her fingers at Queenie. "And if it's man trouble you need help with, I'm all ears."

"I'll keep that in mind, Gypsy," Queenie promised.

## —Chapter Nine—

It was almost two in the morning by the time Queenie made it home and the house was dark. She let herself in, hushing Cobra Bubbles at the door when she came to greet her.

"Go back to bed, girl," Queenie whispered, not wanting to disturb the prone form on her sofa. Queenie stepped gingerly through the living room in the darkness, feeling her way down the hall, pausing to look in on Winnie, before making her way to her own bedroom. She closed the door behind her before turning on her bedside night lamp.

Queenie reeked of smoke from the casino, and stripped off her clothes for a quick shower before bed. She cranked the water to hot and stepped in, making short work of shampooing her hair and shedding the grime of the evening. After toweling off and getting her short curls mostly dry, she pulled on the ratty oversized tee shirt she slept in and walked into her room, stopping dead at finding Rex sitting at the foot of her bed.

His hair was rumpled, his smile sleepy, and he was still dressed in the clothes he'd worn earlier that day. *It should be illegal for a man to look that sexy at two in the morning.* But, she acknowledged, it was Rex, and she already knew what he was rocking under his shirt. "Hey," Queenie attacked the silence with awkwardness.

"Hey, yourself," he yawned, running a hand through his hair. "I heard noises and came to check. Thank god it wasn't a burglar in your shower."

"That would've made it a tight fit," she agreed. *Geez, Queenie, random much?* "I didn't mean to wake you."

"You didn't. I'm a light sleeper." He looked her over, taking in her state of undress. "Lions fan?"

"They are the mightiest of all the cats," she replied automatically, wondering where the question came from.

A deep chuckle from Rex accompanied her statement. "Either you're really on right now, or I'm really off." He pointed at her shirt. "You're wearing a Lions jersey, Queenie," his smile tilted in her direction. "Or what's left of one."

She confirmed his observation with a downward glance. *Oh, that.* Feeling like an idiot, Queenie shrugged. "I stand by my position."

"On the cats?" He asked. When she nodded, he agreed. "Seems solid. You have one on the team?"

She racked her brain trying to figure out what sport they even played. The team thing had been J.J.'s attempt at educating the women in his life on the pursuits that men enjoyed. Oddly, Cece took to the sporting world like Columbus questing for the new world. In retrospect it probably wasn't much of a leap, considering how competitive she was, Queenie realized. No one loved consoling a loser more than her best friend.

"Hockey?" Queenie guessed.

"Close," Rex said, his approval bordering on mockery to her ears. "But in Detroit the team would be the Redwings."

She tried again. "Baseball."

"Tigers," Rex supplied. "Third time's a charm. I believe in you."

"That should count. They're both cats," she said. "How many teams does one city need?" She asked no one in particular. *What's left?* "Basketball?"

"Pistons," he said holding out a hand. "I'm afraid I'll have to take the jersey back."

Queenie smacked his hand away. He chuckled and she stuck her tongue out at him, entertaining the thought of stripping in front of him for a millisecond before discarding it. *Mostly.* "What sport do they play?"

He offered her an exaggerated pout, then ruined it by grinning. "Football."

She rolled her eyes. "I could've guessed that if you'd only offered me fifteen more tries."

"Not very sporting of me," Rex agreed, lying back on her bed.

"Also, I just worked, for like, four hours," she reminded him. "You could've given me a hint."

The bed vibrated under him as he laughed. "I gave you plenty of hints. You're just an NFL poser."

"Guilty," Queenie sat on the edge of the bed. "You were never sporty. When did that happen?"

"It still hasn't," Rex answered, tilting his face to hers. "I'm a poser too. You have to be it to see it."

"Punk," she laughed. "Then why the Two A.M. Team Trivia?"

"Well, first off, who in their right mind says 'no' to Two A.M. Team Trivia? Not me. And not you. We're never gonna be those people, Queenie."

"Wow," Queenie shook her head, guessing Rex was one of those people that needed at least two hours of uninterrupted sleep to operate at a basic level. "I can't believe I verged on suggesting either of us were capable of that. Is there another reason?"

"You had the look of a deer in the headlights." His eyes widened, his mouth forming a perfect 'o'. Queenie choked back a laugh, and he broke character, his mouth widening back into a smile again. "Not used to having a man in your bedroom?"

"As a matter of fact, no." Even with Aaron, Queenie had always gone to his house, and only when Winnie was over at a friend's or spending the weekend with Angel Baby and Henry. She'd resolved early on not to be the mother that paraded a line of uncles through her daughter's life.

Oddly, letting Aaron stay over never even crossed her mind. *But Rex.* Having him splayed across her bed— Well, that invited dark and delicious temptations better left alone.

"Can't say I mind hearing that," he leered and patted the bed next to him playfully.

"I'm sure you had game back in New Arabistan, soldier," Queenie couldn't help but laugh. "But, I told you—"

"—you have high standards," he nodded lazily. "I remember."

He reached out and tugged her to him. The heat of his body bled into her, sending a thrill up her spine. Queenie's heart hammered in her chest at his close proximity and she hoped he couldn't tell.

"Tell me about your night," he said. "Lady Luck play hard to get?"

"If you must know, the wanton trollop left her lipstick on my collar," Queenie said, surprising herself by sounding relatively normal.

"Let me make sure you got it all off," Rex said, sliding a hand into her hair, and drawing her to him. In a breathless instant the heat of his mouth on her flesh seared a path straight to her loins. She sucked in a breath, trying to steal back her senses, only to lose them again when he nipped his way down her neck, lips and teeth forging a path to the hollow of her throat and back up the other side. She arched her neck, blindly giving him access to the sensitive space below her earlobe, an infinity of pleasure coursing through her when the heat of his mouth settled there.

Queenie heard herself gasp, the breathless sound more animal than human.

He paused in his attentions, his face hovering inches from hers, smiling, hazel eyes dark with desire. "Mmm, that sounds encouraging."

"I like a man to feel he's doing well," Queenie said, wishing he would stop talking and go back to using his mouth for other things.

"Queenie?"

"Hmm?" She reluctantly banked her desire, wondering if he could hear the echoing of her heartbeat or if it was only deafening her. She met his stare, the heat in his eyes broadcasting an invitation.

"Now, would be the moment for objections if you have any."

Queenie realized what he was asking, and desire morphed into anxiety. "I—" She stopped, then started again. "You want to—. Right now?"

Amusement warred with desire in her would-be-lover's eyes. "Yes, I very much want to." He stroked her lower lip with his finger. "But whether we do or not, well, that's up to you."

A flash of annoyance raced through her at Rex's interruption of their lovemaking to ask her a question she didn't want to be forced to answer.

*Interrupted our lovemaking? Dear god, Queenie, what are you doing? You hated him for seventeen years. He's been in town for three days and he's already in your bed.*

She placed a hand on his chest, more to stop her world from spinning any further out of control than anything else.

"Queenie?" He trapped her hand under his own, frowned and drew back. "Your hand is shaking."

*Well, at least some part of her body was trying to send her brain a mayday signal.* "I have no idea what I'm doing," she blurted out, fingers clutching the fabric of his shirt, unable to figure out if she was trying to hold him off, or pull him close. *Geez, make up your mind, Queenie.* She let go, and would've pulled away, but Rex prevented her from backing away entirely.

"Stop for a minute." he let his arm slide down and rest on her bare hip, and Queenie suddenly realized how intimate their positions had become. He slipped an arm under his head and they lay on her bed, side-by-side and face-to-face. "You're trembling, and I'm guessing it's not from the awesome power of my kisses." Most of the passion melted had out of his eyes, replaced with concern. "You know I'd never hurt you."

*Not intentionally,* Queenie thought, *but accidents happen, and then they grow up and get driver's licenses. Here we are again, one wrong turn shy of the road to Hell.*

"I'm not afraid of you." She closed her eyes, held his hand and ran her fingers over his knuckles trying to unknot the mess she'd just made. She opted for honesty. "I could never be afraid of you." *After all,* she realized, *you've done the worst thing you can to me, whether by accident or design, and I'm still here.* "But this—" she couldn't find the words to describe what she was feeling. "We've tried this before—," *and it was a dismal catastrophic failure.*

"Ah, you must be thinking of Fort Bennington?"

*I haven't stopped since I laid eyes on you in Whitey's,* Queenie thought, managing a nod. "Aren't you?"

"I have to admit, it was memorable." She felt the bed vibrate lightly when he chuckled. "But judging from your reaction, I probably remember it a bit differently than you."

Queenie winced; glad she still had her eyes closed so she didn't have to see the mocking glint she could hear in his tone. Still, if he wanted to try again, it couldn't have been as bad as she remembered. *Could it?* "I only recall bits and pieces of it," she confessed, thinking back. *Like the vomiting, and the cracked tile on the cold floor of the hotel bathroom.*

"And none of them were good? I'm hurt," he said. "You weren't charmed by the prison-orange of the walls, or the cold and cold running water?"

She laughed despite herself, and opened her eyes to see him smiling her way. "Can't say that I was. My mind was somewhere else at the time." She felt him tuck a piece of hair behind her ear.

"Oh? Like where?"

Queenie remembered their clumsy first attempt at lovemaking, comparing the sinewy, gangly boy he'd been to the man lying across the bed from her now, knowing if they tried again it would be very different. Just the though of him putting his hands on her made her insides all melty again.

"Is it wandering now, Queenie?" Rex asked, drawing her back to the moment.

"I was just thinking that maybe one or two of my memories were exceptional before the Southern Comfort kicked in." He laughed lightly, tilted smile deepening. "Those are some of my favorite moments of all-time, woman. I was hoping we might be able to relive our greatest hits."

"It was the ones that came after...." She covered her face in mortification, groaning, trying to obliterate the youthful memory of running to the bathroom to loose her cookies right after she and Rex had technically completed their first and final act of lovemaking.

Strong hands gripped her hips and pulled her close, their bodies aligning, the heat of him bleeding into hers. "Admittedly, it wasn't a strong finish," he said, the warmth of his breath caressing her face. "But I think I've gotten better."

He drew lazy circles on her back with one hand, the act creating a ripple effect of tingling throughout her body. She bit her lip to keep from moaning. "You were never the problem and you know it."

He stopped stroking her and pulled her hands away from her face, forcing her to look at him. "Let's make some new memories, Queenie. I believe in us." Green-gold eyes sparkled in the dim light, the passion returning and bringing challenge with it.

"Are you mocking me and trying to get me into bed at the same time, Tex-Rex?" She asked, feeling herself smile and knowing she shouldn't. *Queenie, don't do this.*

"Maybe just a little," he grinned, his thumb stroking the back of the hand he held. "Is it working?"

*It's magical.* "I think it may be a little." *You're losing it. Stay strong.*

"Good, because after tonight there won't be any more room for that memory between either of us."

She gave up arguing with herself as the bed shifted when he rolled them over, his body weight coming to rest over her, his long legs lying between hers. She parted them slightly to accommodate him, quivering as a strong hand slipped up her thigh to cup her bottom. She felt the warmth of his breath against the side of her face. "Maybe a lo—"

He kissed her into silence, teasing her lower lip lightly with his teeth before abandoning her mouth all together and drifting lower. Queenie let her head fall back in pleasure as Rex lingered on the sensitive spot beneath her ear again and she moaned, giving in to the hot and sweet feel of him.

"That's nice," he whispered, the heat of his breath warming the sensitive curve of her neck, "but I think we can do better."

She tried to make sense of what he'd said, but his affections had rattled her brains. Before she could formulate a reply Queenie felt Rex take her nipple into his mouth, gasping as he lavished the tightness through the thin cotton of her t-shirt. A current of desire shot through her. When he'd aroused her bud to his satisfaction, Rex moved on to its twin. *Dear god, he has gotten better*, she managed to string the thought together.

Amidst his attentions she felt a hand slide under her shirt and catch the edge. Rex drew back, tugging the shirt up and over her head, leaving her naked except for her panties. She pulled her arms in to cover herself, but Rex stopped her. "You know, I think the Lions may be my all-time favorite team." He covered one breast with his hand, thumb roaming over her tightness.

"Mine too," Queenie melted again and gave up trying to hide from him. Rex rewarded her by tracking kisses down her midriff. She arched against him, wanting more, barely registering him sliding her panties off until his tongue dipped lower, finding her pleasure center. "Rex—" A hot, wet wave of wonderful broke over her taking her ability to form words with it.

A part of her registered his hands on her, sliding over her, making every nerve ending cry out. She was wound so tight she could register everything and nothing at the same time. The cool linen of her duvet cradled her overheated body. She struggled against the passion building inside her.

Rex intensified the rhythm of his attentions, and when he slipped a finger inside her Queenie cried out, feeling herself fall over the edge and making no attempt to save herself. Ecstasy pulsed through her for one long minute, before settling and restoring her senses.

She lay panting on the bed, and opened her eyes to find him watching her. "I can't argue with your notion of better, Tex-Rex."

He chuckled, the familiar sound distinctly male in the darkness. "Oh, I'm not quite done yet, Queenie." Rex rose up onto his knees and pulled off his shirt in one fluid movement. The light from the bathroom cast a golden glow over his fit form, shadows accenting broad shoulders and lean abs. *Those abs,* Queenie almost drooled wanting to reach out and touch them.

"You like?" He asked and she realized she must've made a sound.

"You could sell tickets," she informed him thinking: *between Cece and Angel Baby you could earn enough money for a house in the hills.*

"I only have one, and it has your name on it," he told her, hands unbuckling his belt. The gesture was so overtly manly, Queenie thought, feeling a second round of heat begin to build. *Tramp.*

"But you have to return the favor," he said, disrobing and resuming his place between her legs again, this time naked and beautiful. He stroked her thigh, his eyes drifting over her body, finally meeting her eyes. "God, you're more spectacular than I remember."

"Then your brains must have been rattled." She reached for the edge of the cover, but Rex caught her hand.

"Let's not have any of that, Queenie." His other hand caressed her, and she wanted to moan, but stopped herself. "That moment has passed," he continued. "And I, for one, am glad to see it go." He leaned over and kissed her hard. She returned it, losing herself in the rightness of the moment. When he pulled away, she made one last effort to slow their combined descent into disaster.

"Rex," despite the thundering of her pulse, she forced herself to speak normally. "This is too much."

"Not yet," he answered, dipping his head to her breast and licking the tightness there, dragging a sigh of pleasure from her. He grinned at her. "But soon." The simple sight of his arousal unleashed another flood of desire in Queenie, and she wanted to feel him, all of him, against her. *Inside her.* As if hearing her silent wish, Rex knelt over her. Queenie's hands slid down his back to grip the delicious tightness of his backside. He laughed lightly, mouth dipping to sample her flesh again, the heat of his mouth enough to shut all reason down.

"Rex," she moaned, her hips rising to tell him what she couldn't say aloud. He rewarded her by sliding a finger deep inside her and Queenie groaned.

As before, he took his time, pacing himself and drawing out her pleasure until she thought she was going to burst with it.

"Oh, my god," His voice was heavy with his own need. "Queenie you're beautiful like this."

"Stop talking," she begged. "Start—" His fingers abandoned her and she cried out then she felt him surge into her, filling her. Rex's hips took over where hers had left off, driving her to the edge again. Just when she was about to leave her senses, he deepened his rhythm, taking long intense strokes. Dizzy with pleasure, she began to move with him, catching his rhythm and riding the edge of passion until the only she felt was all of them.

"I think it might be too much now," he said rasping, intensifying his need.

"Rex!" Queenie gasped his name as every nerve in her body came alive for the second time that night. His hands pulled her to him as he thrust through her, shuddering, spasming helplessly and crying out her name. He rested against her until their pulses slowed, then rolled over, dragging Queenie with him. He sat up long enough to grab the edge of the bedding and pull it over them before collapsing again.

"My god, woman," he said, when he'd caught his breath. "You might be on to something with this having standards thing."

"I'll have to raise the bar, now," Queenie stroked his chest, feeling like the human version of melted caramel. She let her fingers wander over his abs, fingertips straying over his collection of scars. "You weren't supposed to let people shoot you, fool."

"Yeah, that was poorly thought out." His hand found her hair and began absently stroking it away from her face. "If it's any consolation they let me shoot them back."

"No. No, I don't think it is." Queenie had never understood war and decided a long time ago that it was generally a man's pursuit. Not that she begrudged women their due; the Survivor's Hutt had its fair share of lady shooters. Rolanda Sweet, one of their best customers, was a die-hard champion marksman, but Rolanda wasn't a killer, and war wasn't about accuracy. War had a distinctly random quality to it that Queenie mistrusted. Bullets lacked consciousness and the news was full of stories about unfortunate victims being in the wrong place at the wrong time. The idea that Rex could have ended up like Junior Morris…

*Let it go, girl.* Queenie shuddered.

"Hey," Rex pulled her closer. "That part of my life is done now."

"Think you'll miss it?" She tilted her face towards his.

His light chuckle reverberated through his chest into her. "Not really much to miss."

"That bad?" She asked, the damn of curiosity breaking.

"Where to begin?" Rex's fingertips danced lightly over her bare shoulder. "The food was awful, so that's off the list."

"Probably why you're rocking these lean abs," she stroked the muscles in question and he shuddered. "Mmm, I'm glad you like them. And you're probably right. In the army even eating can be an endurance test."

"C'mon," she chided. "Bad food is pretty universal, isn't it?"

"Have you ever eaten a powdered egg before?" He raised an eyebrow at her.

"Can't say that I've had that particular pleasure, no."

"Think congealed chemical custard with a grainy finish," he blanched for her benefit.

"The grainy part sounds intriguing." She tried for a positive spin.

"That would be sand," he informed her.

"Stop, you're ruining the culinary odyssey for me."

"My apologies, Julia Child. I'll get you a shaker filled with sand and you can experience it first-hand if you'd like."

"I do like a solution oriented man, Tex-Rex." Queenie smiled against him. "So, I guess it's safe to say you won't miss the sand either?"

"Oh, I don't know," he stretched one arm and folded it under his head. "We had about a hundred different kinds out there."

"Edible sand," Queenie started him off.

"All of it was edible at one point or another," he said. "Then there was the washable sand. The fine silty stuff was the easiest to manage. And the wearable sand, which you never really noticed you were coated in until a monsoon came along and ten minutes afterwards you were scraping a thin film of mud off everything."

"Sounds awful," Queenie said, trying to imagine it and failing.

"Not really. The really grainy stuff was the worst. Even sheltered in a windstorm it was in your eyes and ears. Other places I won't mention."

"Ouch."

Rex just shrugged. "That's the stuff that the scorpions and snakes called home."

"No thanks," it was Queenie's turn to shudder. "So, that's it? No regrets? No looking back?"

"I needed to do it and I did." He shrugged. "It feels finished. Know what I mean?" He asked.

*I did once*, she thought, *then you came back*.

"The longer I was there, the less I understood why," he continued. "When Jasper died I felt like my appetite for that life died with him."

"No one left to be disappointed?" She asked.

"Partly," Rex answered, his voice blanketing her in the darkness. "Also, because staying past your tolerance level tends to bend a man in a way that's hard to fix."

"Like Aaron."

"Worse than Aaron. I don't really know him very well, but I'm guessing he's always been a little out there."

"Your powers of perception are frightening."

He grinned, his teeth gleaming in the moonlight. "Aren't they, though?"

"Creeper," she smacked his chest, playfully, then let her fingers tangle softly in the pale drift of hair covering his chest. "I envy you."

"What do you mean?" His hand caressed her hair.

"Your ability to walk away back then. I always wished I'd had the strength to leave my dad behind. But I couldn't, you know?"

He tipped her face to meet his. "Don't envy my weakness, woman. I look around here and see what you've done and I'm ashamed. It took so much more strength to stay." He stroked her face. "And I may have walked away, but I still missed you."

"Rex, don't." She started to pull back, but he drew her close.

"No way," his tone was steady and firm, his stare never wavering. "I'm going to say this and you're going to listen." She started to object, but Rex put a finger over her mouth. "I missed you," he began. "The old you, the old *us*. And please believe me when I say I tried not to. I know I was the one who walked away, but don't think I didn't second guess that decision at least once a day."

"Rex—" she objected, but his finger stayed put.

"Listen to me for a second. Every Thanksgiving no matter where I was I was tempted to send you a Happy Birthday card as a joke." Her own father couldn't recall her actual birthday, but he knew it was late in November. So, every year while he was alive, Colin would leave her a card on turkey day. Even now, she and her friends and family celebrated her birthday on the holiday as a weird form of memorial. Queenie swallowed the lump of emotion in her throat.

"There wasn't a day that went by that I didn't think of you or see something that made me want to reach out to you across space and time." She giggled, an obnoxious sound even to her ears.

"I meant what I said before about this being our time if we want it."

"What was the time before?"

"Hmm, a practice try." His fingers traced the curve of her breast. "An experimental drop in the well of the universal time span. A preview of a window of opportunity for improvement." He was caressing her nipple now, teasing it into a hard peak that sent tremors of pleasure through her.

"Mmm, I'd say that was a significant improvement, Tex-Rex."

"I'd say that was just Act One, Woman." Rex rolled above her and she felt the hard evidence of his desire against her hip. "You and I have some lost time to make up for." Rex covered her mouth with his own.

\*\*\*

Rex's internal clock woke him at the crack of yawn as usual. Even as a kid he'd never managed to figure out how to sleep past six am. He looked at Queenie, her petite form barely visible under the covers. He stroked her hair and climbed out of bed, careful not to wake her, hoping to sneak out of the bedroom ahead of Winnie waking so Queenie wouldn't be forced to answer any complicated questions this soon.

As he stood by her dresser a glint of something golden caught his eye and Rex stopped to investigate. Her modest jewelry box lay open, revealing two of the largest and ugliest bracelets Rex had ever laid eyes on. He picked one up, catching sight of the letters WSOP encrusted in diamonds across the top. It's partner was only slightly less extravagant, a gold monstrosity that must have dwarfed Queenie's wrist.

"I'll be damned," he said under his breath, leaving the jewelry where he'd found it. *Not once, but twice.*

He pulled on his clothes, combed a hand through his hair to right it and crept out in to the hall, shutting the door quietly behind him. With no sign of Cobra Bubbles to give him away, Rex grabbed his shoes and headed to the front door when a gentle throat clearing stopped him in his tracks. He turned his head to find Winnie's pajama laden person sitting at the table, a half-chewed textbook open in front of her, the chewer resting at her feet. She turned his way, treating him to her patented stare, which disarmed him more than it should've considering the bearer was shoveling cereal into her mouth and sporting a comical case of spikey bed-head.

"You're up early," Rex observed, hoping he'd managed to put his clothes on right-side out.

She leaned back in her chair to get a better look at him. "I've always been an early bird. Mom says it must be hard-wired into me. But that's enough about me." Winnie gave a sweeping head-to-toe gesture in his direction. "Look at you, doing the walk of shame on a Wednesday morning. What exactly do you have to say for yourself, young man?" She raised a red brow, clearly expecting an explanation. Rex looked at the dog, but Cobra Bubbles' expression mirrored Winnie's.

*Face it. You're busted, buddy.*

"What do you want to hear?" He changed direction and headed to the table, taking the chair across from her.

Winnie tsked and giggled, shaking her head in mock sadness. "Don't leave yourself open like that. It's a poor position to negotiate from."

Rex found himself wishing he'd had half her composure at that age. "Sounds like you've been there."

Winnie winked at him and smiled easily. "I'm sixteen. I've built my house at the intersection of Poor Decisions and Bad Judgment. It's expected of me. What's your excuse?"

Rex shook his head, chuckling. "You're so much like your mother, it's scary."

"I'll take that as a compliment, sir." Winnie gave him a quick grin, looked at the clock and back at him. "Hurry up and explain yourself. Mom's alarm clock will start going off soonish. I need to have you blackmailed and on your way before that."

"A little mercenary, aren't we?"

"I'm always crabby before breakfast. Live with it." She said airily. "Now spill. What the hell do you think you're doing with my precious Mommykins?"

*As much as she'll let me, kiddo.* Rex thought silently, and decided to answer truthfully. "I love her."

His admission gave Winnie pause. Cobra Bubbles used the opportunity to sidle up to Rex, who obligingly stroked her blocky black head.

"She's lovable, I'll admit." Winnie said finally, drawing out her words. "But you've really only known her for three days. Think you're being a bit forward with the devotion?"

"Not at all," Rex said seriously, giving Winnie her due. "I think I loved her before I even knew what love was."

"That's really sweet, Tex-Rex," Winnie crossed her hands in front of her and smiled at him. "And kind of unexpected, I'll admit. So, let's say I believe you," Winnie narrowed her eyes at him. "Others have loved her before you. My dad. JP. What's your love have to offer that theirs lacked?"

*She's got you there, Old Son,* Rex realized. "She'll have to figure that out for herself."

Winnie nodded approvingly. "Good answer. The judges would also have accepted 'A pony'. Because, as Mom pointed out to me the other day, a girl never outgrows a pony."

He laughed, but she hushed him. "Now, get out of here before she wakes up." Rex rose and Winnie followed him to the door letting him out. "Rex?"

He turned, "Yes?"

"As my mom is fond of saying: Play for real, or don't play at all."

Rex took the warning in her stormy blue eyes to heart and ruffled her spikey sleep-tousled locks on his way out. "Understood, kiddo."

# ◦—Chapter Ten—◦

Queenie woke for the second time that day, looked at the clock and tried to remember falling asleep. She'd gotten up and seen Winnie off to school, but if Cobra Bubbles' insistent snuffling in her face was any indication, she'd neglected to feed the dog. "Sorry, sweetie." Queenie sat up, scrubbed the sleep from her eyes and scratched the dog's head. Glossy black eyes closed at the pleasure of Queenie's touch.

"C'mon, girl."

Queenie fed the dog and hurried through her morning routine, relentlessly avoiding any thought about the night before. It wasn't that she regretted it, *yet.* More like the topic was too complicated to be able to resolve with random morning musings. It needed input from people wiser than she. People like Cece and Winnie. After all, it was a subject that had been sidelining for seventeen years. A few more hours wasn't going to hurt.

She and Cobra Bubbles pulled in to the Survivor's Hutt with time to kill before opening. Since she wasn't expecting Rex for a little while, she took her Beretta and two ammo clips out of the safe, grabbed her coffee and headed to the back where the gun range waited. Despite her partial ownership of the store, she'd never have classified herself as a gun enthusiast. Initially, the store had been a chance to help the failing area. Aaron needed a backer, and Queenie just happened to fit the bill. Later, it had helped with Whitey. It augmented his cash flow, offered him insurance, and gave him a place to talk shop in his old age.

Cobra Bubbles dislike the noise of the range, but padded after Queenie anyway. She flipped on the lights and looked around, realizing not much had changed. Until this week she hadn't lingered longer than the hour a week necessary to manage the financials. Spending too much time in Aaron's company led to awkward feelings on her part. Aaron made no attempt to hide his ongoing affections for her. Rebuffing his persistent attentions wore her down, and before Rex showed up, she was woman enough to admit she'd thought about giving in on more than one occasion.

*He would've made one heck of a booty call, but Aaron was no Rex*. He'd always been an enthusiastic and attentive lover, but his nature was too destructive for anything long-term. Aaron drank too much, fought too much, and swore too much. And Queenie had no idea what he did when he wasn't in the store, but she wouldn't be surprised if it came back to bite him one day. *And me, come to think of it.*

She thought back to their final date. They'd gone to a music festival downtown. It was a three-day event, but Aaron barely made it through the first two hours of day one before starting a fight with a house of a man who was blocking Queenie's view of one of the bands. She was five-foot-four. *Everyone* blocked her view and she'd had a lifetime to get used to it. But Aaron had imbibed one too many that day, as usual, and was spoiling for a knuckle up.

It was that day, after watching a brief tussle that ended up with some bruised faces on both sides, and Queenie watching security escort him out, that she realized her relationship with Aaron probably stemmed more from the need to pay back what her own friends had done for her, rather than anything else.

To give herself some credit, she did like Aaron. It was almost impossible not to. He was funny, occasionally thoughtful as need demanded, and didn't ask for much in return. But being with him was like riding a roller coaster with no safety harness; it was a blast until you got to the loop-de-loops and had to hold on for dear life. *Sound like anyone else you know, Queenie?*

"Good thing I ain't about that life, no mo' ," she said to Cobra Bubbles. Shiny black eyes met hers, reminding her that she wasn't gansta enough to rock that line. "No," Queenie agreed, giving the dog a scratch behind the ears. "You're right." Reminding herself that she'd come in the range to clear her head, not fill it with the past, Queenie slipped a magazine into her pistol, loaded a fresh target sheet, and sent it down to the fifty-foot mark.

She cleared her head, locked onto her target and put Aaron out of her mind. She'd worked halfway through the clip before thoughts of Rex took Aaron's place. Queenie resisted the invasion, managing to draw down on her paper assailant a few more times.

*'After tonight there won't be any more room for that memory between either of us.'*

Her shot went wide as Rex's promise from the night before bobbed to the surface of her consciousness. *Holy geez, he hadn't been kidding.* He'd banished it all right. *Mission accomplished, Tex-Rex.*

"Leave me alone," she said aloud. "I'm not thinking about you right now." She looked around for the dog for support, but Cobra Bubbles had abandoned her at some point. "Great, now I'm talking to myself. Get it together, Queenie."

The task would've been easier to manage if Rex had proven to be a mediocre lover, but he couldn't even give her that. The mind-blowing sex just made everything worse. *Wow, did you really just think that?* Queenie paused, trying to sort herself. *What am I resisting besides telling him about Winnie?*

Cece was right. Rex was like catnip. When they were kids, before her dad went on his terminal bender, Queenie would sometimes imagine what her life would be like when she was older. Like most kids, her imagination resembled the typical sitcom family where Rex was always the dad and Queenie was the mom and Cece was the friend that popped in an out getting Queenie out of trouble when the occasion arose. *Strictly speaking, you're living the dream*, she realized ruefully. *Your fairy godmother just got the details wrong. Really wrong.*

"Stupid fairies," Queenie muttered under her breath. *Your real problem is that you want him too much. You always did.* Her subconscious was right. She'd never imagined that he could have left, and when he did... *You're afraid it's going to be Fort Bennington all over again. Admit it. You won't be enough for him and he'll leave again.* And that would be awful, Queenie knew, really awful, because although on a rational level she knew his first departure had been planned, if he left a second time he would be leaving her. *For real.*

Her follow-up thought was that if that happened she was going to end up featured on an episode of Snapped and there would be nothing Cece could do about it.

*But maybe he won't go.*

She fired again, her shot sailing through the center hole.

*What you need is a sign, Queenie. A good old fashioned, burning-bush, dove-with-a-twig, neon marquee sign.* Not that she would've classified herself as a woman who looked for, or even believed in, such things. *But one sure would be nice right about now.*

"Mmm, nothing like a woman with a nine-millimeter first thing in the morning." Rex's voice carried through the range as she pulled off another shot. "Bull's-eye." Queenie turned to see him narrowing the distance between them. He'd showered and donned new clothes. He joined her, the smell of fresh Rex and manly body wash going straight to her head and drifting to other parts.

*Stop it*, she told herself. The admonition ruined when Rex bent down to kiss her and she automatically tilted her face to receive it. His face lingered after the kiss, full mouth melting into an intimate smile. Queenie blushed and Rex grinned, straightening. "You taste like coffee."

"Want some?" She gestured to her cup, resting below the posted sign that read: NO FOOD OR DRINK ON THE RANGE. EVER. SINCERELY, THE BOSS.

"Depends, what's the penalty for being caught on the range with food?"

"I've no idea. No one's been brave enough to defy the rule, yet."

"Except you," he pointed out. "Does that mean I get to punish you, Queenie?" Rex's suggestion melted parts of Queenie that had only reawakened from a long sleep the night before. "Catch me if you can, boy-o." She'd opened her mouth to tell him that technically Aaron was the boss, but the dare popped out. *You're flirting with him now? Make up your freaking mind already!*

He smiled at her knowingly, a blanket of shared intimacy settling over them. *When did that happen,* she wondered. *It was always happening, fool.*

"You always were a fan of the chase."

"I can be a little competitive sometimes," she admitted, remembering the time he'd beaten her at Operation and she refused to talk to him for the rest of the day.

"But always fair," he acknowledged, turning to study her target. "Nice. How many shots?"

Queenie, relieved to have something else to talk about, checked the chamber of the weapon. "The whole clip, so fifteen." The Beretta could take a clip that held more shots, but Queenie liked it light.

He whistled appreciatively. "Fifteen shots in two holes? You're a ringer, sweetheart. Shoot here often?"

Queenie snorted indelicately. "Is that your line, Major?"

"Do I need one?" He asked, brows arching.

She ignored the innuendo. "A man always needs a line, even if it's just for back up."

"I favor honesty."

Queenie tsked. "What if one of your boys calls and needs a wingman?"

"Thankfully, my boys have more sense." He took the Beretta out of her hand and tested the weight absently. "What about you, do you have a line?"

"I don't need a what comes with a line. I'm not available." As the words left her mouth she realized the potential for disaster in what she'd implied. "Even when I was available, I wasn't available," she clarified badly. *Still failing, Queenie.*

"Am I supposed to be able to follow that, or are you trying to talk about last night without talking about last night?"

"I'm most definitely not trying to talk about last night." She took her pistol back and slid the magazine out, replacing it with the full one in one smooth motion. "I'm trying to shoot. What about you? Forget how?"

Rex laughed. "I see where Winnie get's her edge."

"Yes, that would be all me." Queenie replaced the target.

"I don't see anybody but you in her," Rex commented, setting up a target next to Queenie. "She much like her dad?"

She wanted to tell him to get a mirror, but held back. *Tell him! Tell him she has her dad's broken smile and his weird taste in bad sci-fi shows! Tell him she'll only eat bologna sandwiches with mustard just like another boy she knows! For god's sake, Queenie!*

"A little," was all she managed.

"I'll understand if you don't want to talk about it."

"Would you?" Queenie asked, *because I'd be curious as hell if you showed up with a kid in tow.* She almost grabbed the out, but stopped herself. "Tell you what. You go choose your weapon and come back here. We'll do one round with our own picks, then switch. For every shot you beat me on I'll answer any question about Winnie's dad you want to know. Sound fair?"

"I don't want to make you uncomfortable by bringing up the past, Victoria. I just want to know what I've missed, and it seems like a lot."

"It was a lot, Rex," she agreed. "And we're starting over, right?" Queenie asked. "I don't have anything to hide from you." *Just some really big things loitering in plain sight.*

They matched off, and after two rounds Queenie had lost one shot when Cobra Bubbles reappeared long enough to shark against her leg for attention.

"You did that on purpose, dog," Queenie admonished, passing Rex back his pistol. Rex knelt down to scratch Cobra Bubble's monstrous head. "That's my girl."

"Well, go ahead and ask." Queenie prompted, her heart beating erratically, waiting for Rex to ask the question that would change everything.

"Did you love him?" He didn't look up from the dog. "Winnie's dad, I mean."

Queenie tried to sort out if she'd just been spared, or if this was worse. *Don't play if you don't want to pay,* she reminded herself. "He was my whole world when we were together."

"But he didn't stay." Rex looked up at her and for the briefest instant she thought he'd made the connection, but then she realized he was sympathizing.

*Great,* Queenie thought. *Now, he's feeling sorry for me because he left me.* She felt like going crazy. If it were an actual place she would have booked a ticket and stayed a week. She settled for shrugging off his empathy. "Sometimes people don't. And it really was his loss. I had Winnie."

"No joke. She's a great kid," he agreed. "Isn't she, girl?" He asked Cobra Bubbled in a high-pitched tone that earned a doggie wuffle in reply.

"She likes you."

"Which she? Winnie, or this young lady?" Rex asked.

"Both," Queenie answered.

Rex straightened and smiled, taking Queenie by the waist and drawing her towards him. "I'm going for the hat trick. What about you? Do you like me?"

"What's a 'hat trick'?" She asked, trying to ignore the red lipstick-wearing wanton inside her trying to claw her way out.

"A sports term for three-in-a-row," Rex informed her bringing his head to nose-to-nose with hers.

"Guh. More sports trivia," Queenie said.

"You didn't seem to mind it much last night," he reminded her, trapping her body against him.

Queenie rolled her eyes, but couldn't keep from smiling. "Maybe. But only a little."

"I'll take what I can get, woman." Rex captured her lips in a hot, sweet kiss that melted her insides and made her forget her troubles. When he finally broke the kiss she had to hold on to him to stay upright. Rex grinned at her sudden instability, but said nothing.

"Don't you have work to do?" Queenie asked.

"This *is* work," Rex said, capturing her lower lip between his and sucking it softly. He released in, only to imprison it between his teeth, an action he'd performed on other parts of her body only hours earlier. Traitor that it was, Queenie's body came alive at his touch.

Cobra Bubbles' warning bark at something in the other room made Queenie jerk, but Rex kept calm, chuckling under his breath. "Maybe we should start opening later."

*Or never*, Queenie thought before reigning herself in. When the voices in the distance grew closer, Rex pulled back with obvious regret.

"I'll talk to the boss." Queenie promised.

\*\*\*

"Hey, boss." Jimmy acknowledged her as she walked in, before turning his attention back to his customer. Queenie spied Rex leading a group of four men towards the range. *Tommys*, she remembered.

Her phone rang and Queenie caught it just as she hit the office.

"Hey, Cece. What's up?" Queenie asked, dropping her paperwork on Aaron's desk.

"Well, my best friends are apparently carrying on a torrid affair, and no one has seen fit to tell me about it."

*That was fast, even for Winnie*, Queenie thought, trying to come up with something that would appease Cece. "Um…" Queenie scrambled for a reply.

"Oh, Lord, it's true?" Cece's voice rose an octave, and Queenie winced. "I was fishing based on the Darling's Snap Chats, but your silence is tattling on you."

"What did she post this time?" *I really have to talk to that girl.*

"Nothing too damning. Just Rex's boots next to an empty couch. I had to read between the lines a little."

"I bet," Queenie sighed. *Nice and subtle, kiddo.*

"Girl," Cece continued. "Start talking, and I'm hoping to heaven that this convo is going to begin with: 'After I told him about Winnie,'."

Queenie cringed. It hadn't even occurred to her to bring it up until this morning.

"More damning silence," Cece sighed audibly. "What am I going to do with you?"

"There wasn't really time," Queenie explained. *Liar.*

"Liar. You need to make time, honey. It's hump day in more ways than one apparently and the end of the week is right around the corner."

"I will." Her mind raced, trying to find a spot in her calendar where she could force her cowardice to stay put.

"When?" Cece pressed.

"You want to go see Lady Gaga on Saturday night?"

"Not that I don't understand your urgent desire to change the subject, but don't you think it's time you put your big girl pantie—"

"I have two tickets to Gaga. You take Winnie, and I'll have a clear window to tell Rex."

Cece was silent on the other end, no doubt looking for a loophole in Queenie's suggestion. "Her concert has been sold out for months. How did you score tickets last minute?"

Queenie ran down the adventures of the previous evening and Cece was partially mollified. "Well, no one deserves to lose his ass more than that pompous twit. Poor Cowboy."

"What do you say?" The idea had come to her out of nowhere, but in the face of Cece's scorn, Queenie had to act.

"I'm in, of course," Cece said. "And Winnie? You'll let her know what's going on with you and our boy, just in case things don't go as planned and he bails?"

"You think we're working off an actual plan? I thought you knew me." Queenie looked at the dog and rolled her eyes. Cobra Bubbles just lowered her head. *Even the dog thinks you're hopeless.*

"Nu-uh, white girl, there is no 'we' now," Cece chastised. "I warned you to come clean. This mess is all you."

"I know, I know," Queenie paused, remembering Rex's words from the night before and hoping against hope that just this once things would work out. For Winnie if no one else. "I think it will be okay, Cece."

"Define 'okay'," Cece said. "'Okay' like winning the lottery, but having to split it fifteen ways, 'okay'? Or 'okay' like getting home and finding out that you got screwed in the drive-thru and they forgot your fries again, but you convinced yourself that you didn't need the carbs anyway, 'okay'? Because that is *not* 'okay'. Let's face it. You only went there for the fries to begin with."

"Um, how about okay like the drive-thru people delivered new fries, along with a pint of Haagen-Dazs Chocolate ice cream and a DVD copy of Guardians of the Galaxy, along with a lottery ticket."

Cece thought about it for a minute. "A leather-clad Chris Pratt, hmm? That would be pretty okay. But why are we waiting until Saturday if things are swimming along at such a high level of okay-ness?"

"Because I'm a lily-livered coward, if you want the truth."

"Ah," Cece sighed. "At least you can finally admit it. So, that's progress."

"Pfft, progress is overrated."

## ⌒Chapter Eleven⌒
🐚

Queenie locked up while Rex waited. Winnie had come by after school and picked up Cobra Bubbles, and it was eerily quiet in the store. She set the alarm and he took her hand walking her out to the parking lot like they were sixteen-year-old sweethearts. *Except when you were sixteen you'd already dropped out of high school and were spending your days tweaking in Colin's garage,* she reminded herself.

"You headed to Whitey's?" She asked, feeling like ten kinds of awkward all of a sudden.

"In that direction, but I thought I might plague you with my company if you think you can stand it. I owe Winnie a rematch."

"We've already spent ten hours in the same building," she said. "You must be a glutton for punishment."

"Was it really ten hours?" He asked. "If that's punishment, then sign me up for ten more." Rex walked her to her car and waited while she jiggled her key in the ancient lock. It finally gave and she slid inside.

"I'll follow you," Rex closed the door behind her.

They drove the short route home, and as she pulled in Queenie caught sight of an unfamiliar Mercedes parked in Rex's driveway. As they parked, an unwelcome memory let herself out of the car.

*Well, well. If it isn't Diana Masterson looking every inch the Stepford-wife.* Queenie hadn't seen Diana in a while, but there was no mistaking the air of distaste in Mrs. Masterson's stance. *And this day held such promise,* Queenie thought, wondering what the chances of a drive by were these days. There hadn't been one in years, she reasoned. It could happen anytime. *Stop it,* she chided herself.

Rex's sister wasted no time eyeing Queenie up and down, her gaze traveling accusingly to Rex, but she said nothing, her body language radiating more disapproval than mere words could manage.

*You have no power here,* Queenie thought, channeling her inner Gandalf as she exited her car.

"Diana?" Rex closed the door to his truck. "What are you doing here?"

Diana looked over at Queenie. "Do you mind?"

*As a matter of fact...* Queenie debated the level of white trash she was willing to throw down at the moment, but was saved by Rex.

"If you've come to be rude, then you know the way home." He shoved his keys in his pocket, turned his back on his sister and started across the street towards Queenie. Something in Diana's rigid expression finally broke. *She's afraid,* Queenie realized. Only fear would be motivating enough to get Diana into this neighborhood after dark.

"Something's wrong, Rex," Queenie said under her breath.

"Reginal—" Diana called out, but Rex ignored her, taking Queenie's arm. "Something's always wrong in her world. It's her personal setting." Rex answered and Queenie laid a hand on his chest. "No. Something's really wrong. She wouldn't come down here otherwise."

"I'm surprised she still knows the way," Rex exhaled roughly, dragging a hand through his hair and turned back to his waiting sister. "Well?"

She perched a hand on her hip. "Are you going to make me shout across the street?"

"Only if you want to tell me something, Di," Rex started to turn back.

"—It's Drake." She called out hurriedly.

Queenie felt Rex freeze, his face swiveling in his sister's direction. "What do you mean? What happened to him?"

"He's gone, Reggie," her voice broke, and for the first time in her life Queenie's heart went out to Diana. "Drake is gone."

\*\*\*

*Poor Diana*, Queenie thought, closing the front door behind her.

"Hey, Mom," Winnie called from the couch.

"Hey, honey," Queenie answered, the sound of her daughter's voice easing some of the tension Diana had left behind. Cobra Bubbles lumbered in Queenie's direction, and rubbed the side of her big body against her mistress until Queenie bent over to stroke her. "How's my Hellhound? Unearth any history-altering skeletal remains today?" Cobra Bubbles wuffled an unintelligible reply and gave Queenie's downturned face a lick before wandering back to Winnie and the bowl of Cheeze Doodles on the couch.

"Rex coming over?" Winnie asked, her attention still on her game. "I've been upping my game for the last hour."

"No," Queenie hung her bag on the hook near the door and joined her daughter. "I'm sure he'd rather be here, but he's got some pressing family matters to look after."

Winnie paused the game and looked at her mother. "I'm his family and I'm here. How pressing can they be?"

"You'll remember that he doesn't exactly know that you're family yet?" Queenie pointed out.

"Details," she waved her mother's point aside.

"You think?" Queenie picked a Cheeze Doodle out of the bowl, then realized she had no appetite and offered it to the dog, who made it disappear.

"You don't?" With fierce determination, Winnie maneuvered her blood-spattered avatar across the television screen, hacking and slashing the whole way. "He's clearly got it bad where you're concerned," she paused to change weapons. "And I'm adorable. What's not to want?"

Wishing she had her daughter's confidence, Queenie dropped onto the couch next to Winnie. "You don't think the fact that he hasn't known about you all these years might get in the way?"

"Hmm, I have given that some thought."

"And?"

"And I decided that this is like winning the lottery for him."

Queenie choked out a short laugh. "Um? Some 'splaining, please, Lucy."

"Obviously there's a chance the he'll be shocked when he finds out, but, much like a lottery winner, realistically he couldn't want more than us." She continued. "You heard him: he's a man without connections. He has no woman, no children, and no family really unless you count the Masterson's. And the drawbacks of such an association are painfully obvious. C'mon, Mom."

Queenie processed her daughter's line of thinking. "Some people might not be able to get past the unexpected thrill of learning they've been an absent parent all this time," she pointed out.

"Those people end up on Maury Povich, Mommykins," Winnie said. "Which is fine. I can do that if the need arises. I've wanted to unleash my inner teenage angst monster on a random for a while now, but something tells me things won't roll out that way in the end. Ranger Rex is not *those people*. Ranger Rex adapts and overcomes." She paused her game to pop a Cheeze Doodle in her mouth. "Speaking of which, when are we breaking the good news to Dear Old Daddio?"

"Uh, soon," Queenie answered vaguely. "Something's come up for him."

Winnie tilted her head at her mother, nodding. "You said a family matter? What's the deal?"

"Drake is missing, honey," Queenie said, reaching out to stroke Cobra Bubble's head for comfort. The canine laid her blocky head on the couch near Queenie's knee.

"Since when? He was in third period today. He can't have gone too far," Winnie read Queenie's expression and laid her controller aside, forehead wrinkling prettily. "Is it serious? Like kidnapped serious?"

"Let's hope not," Queenie tried not to imagine the worst-case scenario. "Let's hope he's just taking a self-directed vacation and forgot to tell his parents."

"And his brother?" Winnie looked unsure.

Queenie shrugged. "It's too early to know anything for sure. Rex has gone to help out."

"Should we be doing something? Like making flyers, or canvassing the city, or something?" Winnie asked.

"I have no idea." Queenie replied. *If it were you, kiddo, I'd have called out the National Guard by now.* Just the thought of Winnie not coming home was enough to spike Queenie's adrenalin. "Do you know any of his friends?"

Winnie went into thinking mode, laying her head on her mother's lap and letting her feet dangle over the edge of the sofa. "A few. But they're all burnouts, like Drake." Winnie absently took a Cheeze-Doodle out of the bowl and offered it to Cobra Bubbles, who took it gingerly. "Maybe it's Weed Wednesday and he just lost track of time. Maybe he's home already, rooting through the fridge trying to quell the munchies."

"Maybe." Queenie willed the idea to be true and stroked the hair from her daughter's forehead.

"Mom?" Queenie detected the thread of fear in Winnie's question, and would've done or said anything to make it go away. *Goddamn you Drake, you better not be in any serious trouble.* "It'll be okay, honey," Queenie promised, hoping she wasn't lying.

\*\*\*

Rex pulled his truck into the driveway of the Masterson home. It was past three in the morning and he'd driven all over town looking for his nephew with nothing to show for it. *When I get my hands on that boy...*

*If you get your hands on him*, he reminded himself.

There was no question Drake was an epic pain, but the kid had yet to display the kind of poor judgment that would have the police looking for him. Not that the police would, not yet anyway. Drake hadn't been missing long enough, and no matter what Diana said,

Rex wasn't sure his nephew hadn't just run away. *Following in your footsteps, boy-o?*

The porch light shone across the lawn and Diana came out the front door towards tugging a robe over her nightgown. "Anything?" She asked.

Rex gave a hard shake, settling an arm around his sister. "We'll find him, Di."

She nodded. "Come inside, Reggie. It's chilly out."

"I'm going home," he gave her a light squeeze. "I've done all I can tonight."

"Home? Home where?" Diana stepped back and glared up at him. "This is your home. You mean you're going back to her, Reggie? I need you here." Diana bit out. "Surely, you can do without your piece of a—"

"—Diana," Rex cut her off and struggled to keep from rationalizing the energy expenditure it would take to strangle her. "You're about to make a scene."

"I don't care! My son is missing and all you can think about is running back to your piece of ta—"

"—Diana! That's enough." Upstairs lights from nearby houses illuminated the neighborhood and Bradford made an appearance, coming to stand by Diana.

"You're not being reasonable," Rex said, keeping his voice low. "All my things are at Jasper's. My phone-charger too. If Drake tries to call me, or come to visit, how will I know?"

"He's right, sweetie," Bradford agreed in low tones. "Drake might reach out to him. We don't know."

"He wouldn't even know about Jasper's if you hadn't taken him there," she glared at Rex accusingly.

"Let it go, Di," Rex tried reasoning with her. "I'll call you in the morning."

She gave him a last look, her mouth thinned in repressed rage, before turning her back on him and walking off without a another word. Bradford sighed at the departing silhouette. "She's just worried, you know? Drake's never been one to toe the line, but she's managed to turn a blind eye to it, until now."

Rex was suddenly seeing his brother-in-law in a new light. "I didn't realize his, er, more anti-social behaviors were that obvious."

"Oh, he makes it hard to miss. He's a lot like his mother in that way," Bradford shoved his hands into the pockets of his robe. "He steals, just little things, but I notice. I can only assume he's trading them, or pawning them for cash to feed his drug hobby." He shook his head. "There's money all over the house, so I'm guessing he's stealing from us so he can be caught in the act."

"If you think he wants you catch him, why don't you get him some help?" Rex was flabbergasted.

"I've tried, believe me. In the early days I wanted to straighten him out. Pressed for counseling, that sort of thing." Bradford shrugged, "Diana wouldn't have it. Said I was damaging his self-esteem by implying there were things about him that needed fixing. Now, things are just getting worse."

*God forbid other people think there was something wrong with one of her sons.*

Rex marveled at his sister's ability to keep her head buried in the sand where her son was concerned. *No wonder the kid was so jacked up.* "We all need fixing in one way or another. Jasper fixed me plenty of times growing up," Rex couldn't help but think of his hosing down on the lawn.

Bradford nodded. "My dad fixed me a few times as well."

Rex heard the regret in his brother-in-law's voice, but was at a loss for how to help the man. "We'll take up the search again tomorrow, Bradford."

Bradford nodded up at him, "I appreciate everything you've done, Reggie. But I have a feeling Drake will be found when he wants to be and not a minute before."

"You think he's a runaway? Gone off with a friend for an extended stay maybe?"

"Be my guess," Bradford shrugged.

"Diana doesn't seem to think so."

"Well, she wouldn't, would she?" The revelation dawn on Rex that Bradford put up a naïve front, but understood far more about his family than anyone gave him credit for.

"She's lucky to have you, Bradford."

His brother-in-law gave him a sad smile. "Your sister is a good woman, once you get past the crazy."

Rex pulled in to his own driveway and the neighborhood was dark. Inside he plugged his phone in and was rewarded with the stirring of electrical life and chirps alerting him to a message and a text.

He read the text first:

Missed you tonight. Call me if you need me. Anytime. Sleep in if you ever figured out how, J.J. has you covered. Q.

Rex dropped into Jasper's old armchair and stared at the dial pad, talking himself out of pressing the call button. Talking to Queenie would make him feel better, it always had. But three-thirty in the morning wasn't the time. He distracted himself by listening to the voice message that had appeared. He didn't recognize the number, but the area code was D.C. so he suspected it was Leo.

'Major, I have the lowdown on your jarhead. I suspect you won't be pleased. Hit me up when you can and I'll give you the rundown. In the meantime, try to stay out of collateral range.'

*Well, shit,* Rex thought with a sinking feeling. Leo was always short and to the point, so that meant that on top of Drake missing, and his sister going crazy, Rex was going to have to deal with Aaron. At that moment Rex was reminded of one of his Ranger buddy's sayings: *When it rains acid, Major, it usually pours salt.*

## ❍—Chapter Twelve—❍
❦

Cobra Bubbles looked up from her pillow on the floor, shiny doggie gaze drifting hopefully from Queenie to the drawer that held the peanut butter treats she would do anything for.

"How can you eat at a time like this?" Queenie berated gently, obligingly retrieving two paw-shaped doggy cookies and tossing them, one after the other, for Cobra Bubbles to catch. The dog inhaled the goodies, giving Queenie a satisfied blink. "You are one spoiled pooch, you know that?"

Cobra Bubbles wuffled agreeably, rolling on to her back to continue her nap.

It wasn't the first time Queenie had occasion to envy the dog. The thought of being able to go back to bed and forget all of her troubles was tempting, but her troubles would still be there when she awoke, and the bed... *The bed just hasn't been the same since Rex.*

After indulging in hour after hour of reliving the night before, Queenie had finally given up on sleep entirely and gone into the living room to watch TV hoping the boob tube would numb her brain asleep. It must've worked, because she woke around four to the sound of Rex's truck. She'd wanted to go to him and find out what was happening, but stopped herself. It was a family affair, and as far as Diana was concerned, no matter how many illegitimate children she gave Rex, Queenie would never be family. So, instead of reaching out, Queenie had lain back down, one ear to her cell phone in case Rex decided to finally text her back.

When she'd risen that morning, his truck was gone again. She'd spent the whole day trying not to imagine what might have happened to Drake.

Anything?

Winnie's single word text held more optimism than Queenie felt.

Not yet. Try not to worry. She replied, reminding herself to do the same. Worrying didn't change anything. Home now?

Student Council, then a few errands. Winnie replied. I'll txt u when I'm done. Love you.

Love you back.

The office phone rang and the sound was so unfamiliar that Queenie startled. No one called the office line. All of the store calls went to the front and everything else was transferred to the back with a quiet beep. *Aaron*, she realized, feeling suddenly guilty because she hadn't really thought of him once the entire time he'd been gone.

Queenie picked up. "Boss's office, boss speaking."

The deep chuckle on the other end confirmed the caller's identity. "Babe, it's only been four days."

"A lot can happen in four days," she said.

There was a pause. "Not too much, I hope." Queenie heard the longing in his tone and changed the subject. "What's up Aaron? Calling to extend your vacation?"

He snorted over the line. "This isn't a vacation. The Keys were a vacation. Remember that trip?"

"I remember it," Queenie replied. "It was five years ago."

"We ate in that little tapas place." He continued. "You loved it so much we had to go back two more times."

"Santiago's Bodega," Queenie supplied, wondering where the conversation was headed.

"That was it," Aaron agreed. "They had some short-rib dish you talked about for weeks afterwards. Remember?"

*Remember?* She still dreamt about those ribs. Her mouth was watering just thinking about it. "I remember. Why do you? What's with the stroll down memory lane all of a sudden?"

"And Better-Than-Sex, remember that little spot?" He ignored her question. "That chocolate cheesecake thing that went on forever."

"It was red-velvet," she corrected and Aaron chuckled over the line. "You do remember."

"Of course I do, that cake was almost a religious experience," she said. "Why ask? Why now?"

"I was thinking when I get back, we should go back there. You know, just the two of us."

Queenie rolled her eyes at Cobra Bubbles, but the dog ignored her and continued snoring softly from her bed. "Aaron, there is no two of us."

"C'mon, Queenie, you know you're still my girl."

*Guh. Not this again.* "Aaron, we've been over this." *And you have the worst timing,* Queenie realized. A week earlier and things might be different right now. "And now we're over it," Queenie said, changing the subject. "Where did you leave the extra ammo for the Tommy? Jerome can't find it and we're booked."

He chuckled again, but this time with less humor. "Tell Jerome it's being delivered tomorrow. And you sidelined me, Queenie. Did I hit a nerve?"

*With a blunt instrument, as usual,* she thought. He still knew her. He always had. Behind his lax façade worked a mind of keen intelligence. Intelligence that he often chose to blunt with a bottle of Glenmoranghie.

"It's Dogface, isn't it?"

Queenie looked at Cobra Bubbles guessing he wasn't talking about her. "I can't translate that, Aaron."

"Rex. It's Rex, isn't it? I've seen the kid's posts. Your old flame has blown into town and you're enjoying the heat."

"It's not anything," she said firmly, not willing to discuss Rex with Aaron under any circumstances. Aaron was a good guy most of the time, but she was always aware that his potential for violence brimmed just beneath the surface of his ruggedly handsome exterior. "Or rather, it's everything." Knowing he wouldn't let go of the bone he had unless she gave him something else to gnaw on Queenie filled him in on the recent happenings with Drake.

"Damn, that's a tough break." He said when she finished. "They've got to be going out of their minds. I know I would be if it was Winnie."

And there it was again. Sure Aaron might be a volatile, functioning alcoholic, but you could count on him to do the right thing assuming he agreed with your interpretation of what the right thing was. *Just like Colin Hart,* she realized.

"When are you coming back?"

"You've got your new lover boy and you still miss little old me?" Aaron flirted. "I think there's still something between us, babe. Even you can't deny it."

"I miss you like I miss the chicken pox," she told him.

"I'm an itch that you love to scratch? You say the sweetest things, babe."

Queenie rolled her eyes and tried not to laugh because she knew he'd take it and run with it. "You're an idiot."

"Truth," he agreed. "I'll be back tomorrow, but I might have to pull a quick turn around and I want to talk to you before I do. I'll let you know."

"Do that," Queenie replied. "I have a life to lead, you know."

"I try not to think about it."

"Be safe, Aaron."

"Not a chance, babe."

***

Queenie finished up the remains of Antonia's lasagna, scraping off her plate into Cobra Bubble's dish. The dog inhaled her after dinner treat, and padded silently after her mistress into the living room where they both tucked themselves onto the couch and restarted Supernatural where Rex and Winnie had left off the other night.

Queenie woke with a start to the sound of a car door closing, realizing she must have dropped off sometime during Sam and Dean's adventure. Cobra Bubbles woofed lightly and left the couch to sit by the door, where her wagging tail advertised her affections.

"I know how you feel, girl." Queenie said, guessing the door would soon produce Rex. Less than a minute passed before she heard a soft knock.

Cobra Bubbles stood, but didn't bark, her whole body resonating the need to display affection. Queenie backed her up, opening the door to reveal a tired Rex. The dog performed her Mata Hari doggie dance for him as he entered. He dropped a quick kiss on Queenie's lips and pressed a pink bakery box into her hands. "Hey."

"Hey." She felt her face widen into a smile. "What's this?"

"Can I come in?"

"Of course." She let him pass, closing the door behind him.

"It's pie. I figured you already had dinner and might be in the mood for dessert."

"Pie, huh?" She'd almost forgotten Rex's childhood penchant for pie. It'd been his cure-all. As far as drugs of choice went, he could certainly do worse. Some people took an aspirin when they got a headache. Not Rex. When things went south, he headed to Marie Callendar's. "That bad?"

"It could be better," he shrugged. "No day is so bad that it can't be fixed with pie, right? No Winnie?" He dropped onto the couch, taking over the spot Queenie had just abandoned. "I didn't see the Blue Beetle."

"She had some things to do after school." Queenie said, taking the box into the kitchen. "What time is it?"

"Almost nine, I think." Rex paused to give formerly Fiona a proper greeting.

Queenie checked her phone to see if Winnie had texted, but there was nothing. "She must have lost track of the time." *Which would surprise no one.* Nine was later than Winnie usually stayed out on a school night. *Calm down,* she told herself. *So, the kiddo was a little late, that didn't mean it was time to call a red alert.* The whole thing with Drake must have shaken her up more than she realized.

"Any word on Drake?"

"No," he raked a frustrated hand through his hair leaving behind a trail of golden spikes. "Between Bradford and I, no part of the city has been untouched. And some of it really didn't want to be disturbed."

"I can imagine. It is Vegas, after all." She was still full from dinner and left the pie on the counter. "You talking about the Naked City?" She slid onto the couch next to him.

"Mmm-hmm," he nodded, making room for her. The Naked City was the underbelly that everyone knew about but seldom spoke of. "Homeless drug addicts still outnumbering the crack whores and gang bangers?"

"By a slim margin." Rex shrugged.

"Well if anyone could have found him there, it would've been you." She let her fingers trail through his hair, taming pieces here and there. "David doesn't know anything?"

Rex's eyes closed, and he shrugged lightly. "Nothing that he's saying, but my read on him is cloudy. They've got that twin thing going on."

"That twin thing?" Queenie repeated. "Explain."

"I'm not sure I can, but I've seen it before. It's like they came in to the world together and they know they'll always have each other so the rest of the world can fu—, er, go fly a kite." He shrugged. "They don't feel accountable to anyone but each other, and there's no expectation, no need to outdo each other."

"Like you, me and Cece when we were younger."

"Exactly. Except worse."

"Worse how?"

"Worse because of Diana." Rex ran through his observations of Bradford the night before for Queenie.

"Wow, so he gets her, but loves her anyway?" She realized how that sounded and attempted to make herself sound less judgmental, but Rex nodded before she had time to come up with an empathetic correction.

"Yes. And David understands Drake too well to try to correct his behavior."

Queenie frowned. "So, he might know something but he's just not telling anyone out of a misguided notion of loyalty to Drake?" Her hand slipped down to his neck and she started massaging the tension away.

Rex sighed, tipping his head forward to give her better access. "I hate to think he could be that stupid, but he's not exactly concerned either."

"And Diana?" Queenie worked away at a knot.

"I love my sister, but we both know she can be a real pain in the ass sometimes." Rex said, wincing slightly as she kneaded the tendon at the base of his skull.

*If you only realized the half of it,* Queenie thought. "No ransom note?"

"No. And that's all she needed to confirm that Drake's abandonment of her was deliberate. He's sending her a message and she's listening."

"You're kidding." Queenie stopped what she was doing and Rex tilted his face towards her.

"Wish I was."

"That's asinine," Queenie stood and paced the floor. "He could be anywhere, even —" She cut herself off, the thought was too awful to consider, focusing instead on Diana's selfishness. "Pain in the ass is an understatement," she said with more venom than she intended.

"When are you going to tell me what happened between the two of you?"

His observation caught her off guard. She manufactured a half-truth but before she could open her mouth Rex held up a hand.

"Save it, Queenie. I can tell by looking at you that you're about to bluff me, and I'd rather you didn't. If there's one thing I was always able to count on with you in the past, it was your honesty. Painful at times, for sure. But I'll take the pain of your truth over the pain of your mistruth. I've always been your friend, and now I'm finally more. Wherever our relationship goes, don't sabotage it by hiding things from me, okay? Especially not about my family. If I'd have known about Jasper's condition earlier, you bet your ass I would have come to see him before he died. Diana kept that information from me and I'm not sure I'll ever be able to forgive her for it. You don't need to lie to me about Diana, Queenie. I think I know her faults better than you."

She closed her mouth, uncertain of how much truth, if any, she was ready to part with. She finally settled for something that wasn't a lie. "Later. I'll tell you later."

He took her chin in his hand and tilted her face until she was looking directly at him. "Promise?"

"Promise." She leaned up on her tiptoes and kissed him. At that moment Queenie's cell phone broke in to a rousing chorus of '*I like big butts and I cannot lie*,' and blanched. "Cece chose her own ringtone."

He laughed and raised a hand. "I'm not here to judge."

She stuck out her tongue at him and answered. "Hey, Cece."

"Hey, yourself." Cece replied. "I need you to come downtown."

"To your office? No way, especially not at this time of night. Those awful clowns of yours will give me nightmares for days."

"Not to my office, to Juvie." Cece explained. "It seems like our girl got herself into a scrape with the boys in blue an—

"—What do you mean 'a scrape'? Is she okay?" Queenie's mouth ran dry and her heart sank. She barely registered Rex easing her on to the couch.

"Stop yourself, Queenie. She's here. I'm here. Now, we're just waitin' on you to round out the party." Cece's easy-going tone finally registered and Queenie forced herself to breathe normally. "You still with me, Queenie?"

"I'm here," she answered.

"You done with your fit of vapors, or should I send mama and Henry to get you?" If it were anything serious Cece probably would've sent Angel Baby and Henry along in the first place. *Jail. It was bound to happen, you are her mother, after all. Look at the bright side,* she told herself, *at least Cece wasn't calling from the hospital.*

"Will Henry bring the Bentley?" She said finally.

Cece laughed. "Considering the circumstances, I do believe he would."

"Another time, maybe. I'll be down in ten." She rang off, and turned to find Rex frowning at her. "What's wrong? Is Winnie all right?"

"She's fine, she's just in jail."

## ᴏ—Chapter Thirteen—ᴏ
꩜

By the time Queenie and Rex walked through the doors of the juvenile detention center, Cece was already there. Queenie spotted her friend's lean frame, still professionally attired in a pale gray suit, leaning against the counter chatting with the burly officer in charge. Two kids sat along the wall, mindlessly tapping away at their phones.

Cece laughed at something the duty officer said. When he looked past her, in Rex and Queenie's direction, Cece turned her head, eyes resting on Rex before meeting Queenie's look.

"The two of you together again in juvenile hall," she smiled. "It's just like old times. You should take a selfie."

Queenie rolled her eyes, not in the mood. "Where is she?"

"These the parents?" Officer Stucki reached for a clipboard.

"No," Cece straightened up.

"Mom?" Queenie's head swung around to see Winnie, whole and in one piece, standing in the hallway outside the door of the ladies restroom. Queenie was so relieved to see the kiddo, she barely registered Rex's hand on her shoulder. "She's okay, Queenie."

Queenie nodded, embracing her daughter. "You came," Winnie said.

"Of course I did," Queenie stepped back, but slid her arm through Winnie's.

"Of course she did." Cece and Rex replied in unison. Rex put a hand on Winnie's head and ruffled her hair. "You trying to give your mom gray hair? We thought you were in jail."

"That was my fault," Cece came to the rescue. "Turns out I didn't have all the deets when I called you. My bad." Cece grinned. "This is better anyway."

"Much," Rex acknowledged. "How'd you end up here, kiddo?"

Winnie ignored Rex's question, turning guilty blue eyes to Queenie. "Mom, I'm so sorry about the car. I'll pay for the damages myself."

"What happened to the car?" She asked, then decided it didn't matter. " Never mind, I don't care about the car. We can get another car. Was anyone hurt? Are you okay?" She checked Winnie up and down looking for signs of injury.

"You didn't tell them?" Winnie looked at Cece.

"That's your job, sugar," Cece chuckled, giving Winnie's cheek a pat. "Besides, they just got here. I didn't have time." She waved an airy hand at her friend. "There's nothing done here that can't be undone with a little money and a lot of paperwork."

At that moment another couple entered the sterile detention room, heading straight for Officer Stucki. "Where is my son!?" A shrill familiar voice demanded. "I insist upon seeing him."

"*That,* on the other hand," Cece muttered under her breath. Officer Stucki looked Cece's way, and she nodded, signaling with her hand that she'd be right there.

"You found him?" Rex asked Cece, Queenie registering that he was talking about Drake. "Not me. That was Wonder Winnie. That's why she's here. Just more proof that no good deed will go unpunished."

"You'll take care of him?" Winnie asked.

"If his parents will let me," Cece shrugged. "They haven't shown a lick of sense up until now, so don't get your hopes up, sweetie."

"Counselor?" Officer Stucki called out, a thread of desperation in his voice.

Cece put on her most professional smile and turned. Queenie watched as Rex's sister caught site of their quartet for the first time.

"Reggie? What are you doin—" Queenie met Diana's stare without flinching.

"You. I should have known you were involved in this." For all her rage, Diana paled when she laid eyes on Winnie, and Queenie recognized the fear in the woman's eyes.

*Gotcha.*

"Not at all, Mrs. Masterson," Cece interjected smoothly, easing across the short distance that separated the parties. "In fact, it was Ms. Hart's daughter that discovered the whereabouts of your son."

Diana scoffed. "She probably drugged him and trapped him in her house, like her mother did with my brother."

"Diana," Queenie heard the warning in Rex's tone, but Cece cut him off.

"Technically, it was *my* house that your brother was trapped in," Cece didn't miss a beat, "and he was less trapped, than unintentionally confined by a missing doorknob. And as for drugged, I don't think a contact high really counts, do you?" She looked at the parties involved, but only Officer Stucki had the presence of mind to agree with her. Queenie saw the wink Cece gave the officer and would've laughed if she weren't already vibrating with rage.

Diana took a step towards Queenie, a finger raised in fury. "If you think I'm going to let my son be dragged down by another generation of Hart women, then you are most certainly mistaken, Victoria." Diana's husband laid a restraining hand on his wife's arm.

*A cobweb restraining a rabid terrier*, thought Queenie. When Diana turned to Winnie, Queenie instinctively stepped between the two of them. "When Principal Yee hears about this you are through—"

"—That's enough," Rex cut through his sister's tirade, striding towards her and guiding her forcefully to Officer Stucki who looked ready to intervene. Unwilling to subject herself or her offspring to anymore of Diana's bitterness, Queenie took Winnie by the hand and led her outside, leaving Cece and Rex to deal with the mess.

Once outside the asylum, Queenie took a deep breath, letting the cool air wash over her.

"Mom, I'm so sorry."

Queenie threaded an arm through Winnie's and pulled her close, relishing the comfort the contact offered. "Save it, kiddo. I'm not sure yet that you have anything to be sorry about."

The automatic doors slid open behind them and Rex followed. He looked around until he spotted them and jogged over to where they were.

"I'm sorry about that," he shook his head. "You'd think she would've been more focused on finding Drake." He dropped a light kiss on Winnie's head. "Good job, Girl-lock Homes."

In typical teenage fashion, Winnie simply shrugged, but Queenie read the pleasure in her daughter's small smile. *And Rex charms another generation of Hart women.* Queenie turned to Rex, seeing his ambivalence.

"Hatfield or McCoy, Tex-Rex?" She asked bluntly, her attempt at humor rewarded with twin-crooked smiles.

"I've no idea which is which, but definitely, McCoy," he met her humor in kind. "If there's any truth to Star Trek then one of my descendant's will be doctoring in space. What could be cooler than that?"

Winnie giggled, and life started to feel normal again. "He's got you there, Mom."

*He's just got me, girl,* she realized as Winnie and Rex traded laughing glances.

"Star Trek defense noted," Queenie shook her head at the pair. "It's probably for the best. Cece will need an ally. I suppose you'll have to do."

Rex scoffed. "Cece's a shark. Diana has finally met her match. Catch up with you later?"

"You know where I live."

***

It was almost eleven before they finally drove the blue Beetle from the impound lot. Winnie sat in the back because the passenger side window had been broken and chunks of glass littered the seat and floor. Queenie drove, more because she felt the need to be in control of something, than any other reason.

"I positively long for a retelling of the day's events, sweetling. How long are you planning to keep me in suspense?"

Winnie launched into a description of her day, beginning with the lunch period where she'd encountered David, who showed what Winnie felt was a peculiar lack of concern for his brother's absence. Sensing David knew something, Winnie set about to describing in detail how hard Rex was working to find Drake. "That's when he told me his uncle should give up the search. Drake would be found when he wanted to be found."

"Ah, so he was a runaway, after all." *Inconsiderate little shit.* "Just out of curiosity what teenage interrogation technique did you employ to get David to reveal Drake's whereabouts?"

"Let's see... how about the fact that I'm uncommonly likeable and he couldn't resist my charm?"

"Undeniably true," Queenie agreed, suspecting there was more to the story.

"Also, I may have implied that Rachel showed some interest in David, and I would be happy to nurture that interest if I weren't so busy helping you at the store because Rex was running around looking for Drake."

"You lied." Queenie frowned at her daughter's reflection in the rear-view mirror.

Winnie just shrugged. "It seemed like the thing to do at the time."

"I wish I could argue with that." She acknowledged, still hating the fact that her daughter felt obligated to behave that way on Drake's behalf. "So, where was he?"

Winnie hesitated. "Um, a house on Lincoln and Sixteenth."

Queenie sucked in her breath. "You went into the Naked City by yourself?"

"It was daytime, Mom," Winnie made an attempt to explain, but Queenie wasn't having it. "Winnie, the Naked City doesn't keep daytime hours. It's the same dangerous hell hole sun-up or sun down." *Easy Queenie*, she chided herself. *No harm done. This time.* "Don't. Ever. Do. That. Again." She gripped the steering wheel and pretended it was Drake's neck. The role-playing was oddly satisfying.

"I won't," Winnie promised. "Today's experience was sufficiently thrilling to last for some time," she assured her mother. "He answered the door."

"Was he stoned?" Queenie asked, readjusting her imaginary stranglehold.

"You really want me to answer that?" Winnie asked, digging through her purse.

"Probably not," Queenie admitted, loosening her grip when her hand started to cramp. "So, how did the car end up in impound with a broken window?"

"I locked my keys in the car, and before I could tell him I had AAA, Drake broke the window. When the car alarm went off, the receptionist at Dr. Ziegler's office called the police."

"Dr. Ziegler?" Queenie asked, lost now. "How did we get to the veterinarian's office?"

"I had to take Bob Marley there because he ate all the brownies in Drake's bag. The chocolate was bad enough, but then Drake mentioned that the brownies were special."

"He had pot brownies in the car and Bob Marley ate them?" Queenie repeated out loud hoping it would make sense once the words left her mouth. "Nope. Still confused." She let her brain dive through the looking glass and make some creative leaps on it's own. "I'm assuming Bob Marley is a dog."

"A Chihuahua, sayeth Dr. Ziegler," Winnie answered. "He was living in the house where I found Drake, but he was in pretty bad shape, so I just took him."

Queenie sounded out her daughter's school note in her head: *Please excuse Winnie from school. She was up late after dog-napping a Chihuahua from a drug house in the Naked City while making a misguided attempt to save her idiot cousin.*

"Mom?" Queenie realized she was clenching her teeth, and relaxed, turning into their driveway. "I'm here." They parked and went inside. "So, the vet called the cops and they showed up?" Queenie acknowledged Cobra Bubbles with a head scratch and fished a treat out of the cookie jar for her. "Theoretically, Bob Marley had consumed any illegal substances by then, so how did you and Drake end up in the pokey?"

Winnie dropped her bag near the door, and closed it behind her. "They asked me for the registration."

"Which you didn't have because we don't have the papers yet." Queenie filled in. "The dots are finally connecting."

"Right. I think they would have let us off, but then the cops took a whiff of Drake and decided to search him."

"Don't tell me."

"Idiot had four joints stuffed in his pocket."

*Oh, Drake*, Queenie sighed inwardly. *Your parents must be so proud.*

"So, they gave us a ride to the big house, and I called Cece," Winnie gave a little shrug to signal the tale had reached it's end and headed to the refrigerator.

Queenie had to admit, except for the really poor choice at the beginning of her adventure, Winnie had a good head on her shoulders.

"Mom?" Winnie looked at her from the open refrigerator.

"Hush child, I'm trying to decide if I'm supposed to be mad at you." Sensing an opportunity in the offing, Cobra Bubbles wormed her way between Winnie and the open refrigerator.

"Mom?" Winnie repeated, and this time Queenie detected a thread of anxiety.

"Yes, kiddo?"

"What Drake's mom said about telling Principal Yee? Can she do that?"

*Knowing Diana, she's probably on the phone to the school board right now.* Just thinking about Diana was enough to make Queenie want to go honey badger on something blonde. She sidelined the thought and grabbed the dog's water bowl from the floor, busying herself with re-filling it. "She can tell him whatever she wants," Queenie said. "But I doubt he'll care very much."

"How can you be so sure?" Winnie's face was a mask of concern.

"Well, think about all of the times Drake has been in trouble," she pointed out. "He's still there."

"But his parents paid to keep him there," Winnie frowned. "I don't want you to have to do that."

"You could say we already pre-paid," Queenie topped off Cobra Bubbles bowl and set it down.

"*We* did?" Winnie asked.

Queenie nodded. "You know how in your freshman year you mentioned that the tech lab needed an upgrade because it wouldn't run your fancy illustration programs?"

"Yes." Winnie said. "But they took care of that and upgraded all of the hardware a month later."

"That is exactly the reason Principal Yee won't care about anything Diana Masterson has to say." Queenie nodded.

"Because of a new tech lab?"

"Because we paid for the new tech lab."

"*We* did?" Winnie's eyes widened.

"It felt like a necessary expenditure at the time, and it was tax deductible." Queenie explained. "A win-win all around. And it looks like it may afford us the added benefit of sweeping today under the rug."

"I remember Principle Yee saying it was over a million dollars! We can afford that?" Winnie's mouth dropped open.

"Well, you will remember that we had to survive off of macaroni and cheese that day," she reminded her daughter. After writing *that* check, Queenie had *felt* broke. "Cuts had to be made."

"Mom," Winnie crossed the kitchen and tucked herself into her mother's arms. "You're the ridiculously best."

"Don't let it go to your head," Queenie warned, returning the embrace.

"Never." Winnie promised.

"Great, now can you please get the dog out of the fridge? If she reaches Angel Baby's chocolate cake we'll have to make another trip to the vet's."

# ᗜ—Chapter Fourteen—ᗜ
### ♔

"Montgomery," Rex mumbled into the phone.

"It's eleven thirty, Major," the phone replied. "Keeping Vegas hours these days?"

*Leo.* Not about to spill his family issues on Leonardo Jackman's dime, Rex yawned. "Just catching up on lost time, Leo." He cleared his head and sat up, swinging his legs over the side of the bed. Eleven thirty? *That never happens.* "You have news?"

"Yvonne scored on Matson," Leo began. "Did a nickel as a jarhead, but got out when something more lucrative came along."

"He's a merc." Rex guessed.

"Not just a merc, an XE op."

*Why did I ever think living stateside would be simple,* Rex wondered. "Hell, XE, eh? Talk about going big." Mercs in general were a compassionless lot, Rex knew, but XE mercs would do anything for money, provided the pay was confirmed before the kill.

"Can't get much bigger," Leo agreed. "Yvonne couldn't nail down anything beyond Matson being muscle. And my digging didn't produce any special skills that would elevate him to sniper status, certainly nothing you couldn't handle, Major, but I'd think twice before going into business with him. Although, by the looks of it, he's been using the business as a kind of cover."

"Well, he does *consulting* on the side," Rex provided.

"Ah," Leo said on the other end. "Found a way to market his particular skill-set, I'm guessing."

"In more ways than one." Rex agreed.

"Some things never change, Major," Leo said. "Guys like that are always looking for an angle."

*He's going to be looking for it on his ass, if I have anything to say about it,* Rex thought. "Anything else I should know?"

"From the looks of his financials, I'd guess he's preparing to make some kind of move. Also, he landed in your neck of the woods at approximately oh-eight hundred."

"You have access to his financials?" Rex was taken aback.

"I have it all, Major. Yvonne was very thorough." Leo's tone implied a level of precision that had nothing to do with information, and Rex let it pass. "His record shows a few drunk and disorderly charges, which wouldn't mean much, but his discharging CO noted that Sergeant Matson had an unfortunate propensity for alcohol."

*No news there.* "I owe you one, Leo."

"You owe me two, Major. Don't forget the dog."

"About that," Rex recalled the way Cobra Bubbles had frozen over the pigeon corpse in the street two days earlier, and Winnie's vivid description of the dog's hobby. "Did she get any kind of *special* training?"

"Affirmative, Major. Army transport frowns on thinking of itself as a puppy taxi service. I had a friend in the canine unit do some work with her to expedite delivery."

"What kind of work, Leo?" Rex asked, already suspecting he knew.

"Cadaver classification, Major." Leo answered, the grin on his face translating through the phone line.

"That would explain why she's dug up every deceased childhood pet within a ten mile radius."

"Sorry, Major," Leo chuckled on the other end, not sorry at all.

"I bet," Rex said. "My thanks to Yvonne, and your dog trainer."

"Anytime. Good luck with the jarhead."

Rex pulled into the parking space in front of the Survivor Hutt, and headed inside. J.J. acknowledged him with a wave. "Aaron in back?" He asked and J.J. tossed him a nod. Rex bee-lined for the office, where he discovered Aaron pitching files into a duffle bag. The filing cabinets drawers were off their rails and the safe doors stood open, showcasing a vast emptiness.

"Taking care of loose ends, Merc?"

Aaron turned and stood with an answering grin than made Rex itch to loosen some of his teeth. "I always thought grunts were slow, but I have to say you've changed my mind."

Rex leaned against the doorframe and surveyed the level of panic in the mess Aaron had generated. *Somebody's on the run,* he realized. "Bring home a tail, did you?"

Aaron's grin dimmed. "How did yo—," he stopped himself.

There were always drawbacks with selling yourself as someone else's muscle. Among them was the reputation that went along with the job. XE, and the few companies like it, had a high turnover because its employees painted targets on their backs every time they took a job. And companies like XE hated competition. Take enough jobs and you became familiar, familiar faces were easy to find in a crowd if you knew what to look for. From his expression, Aaron had come face-to-face with his sell-by date. *Get out or get dead.*

"I'm done."

Rex shrugged. "Done here, anyway."

Aaron's laugh was harsh. "You know what? Fuck you, Rex." He slammed a filing cabinet shut. "You roll in here like the Prodigal fucking son who owns the place and everyone in it. Two days in and you're making sliding time with Queenie and parking your boots outside her door like you never left her behind to raise your kid. Well, to hell with that." Aaron shortened the distance between them. "If Jasper were here he'd probably shake my hand for this."

And that's when Aaron's fist connected with Rex's jaw.

***

207

Queenie sat in her office chair listening with half an ear to Nicholas DeMarco work through his investment pitch about the doughnut shop he wanted to open with her money. Her attention was diverted for many reasons, the least of which was that Nicholas's dark good looks would cause any woman to indulge in selective listening. He was no Rex, but Antonia and Dante's middle son could give Rex a run for his money in a fair contest.

The other reason was that he'd grown up in the restaurant industry and she'd guess his dear mama and papa had gone over every detail with Nicky before sending him in to face her.

And third, it was doughnuts. *Only a fool says no to doughnuts.* While she would admit to being a fool in many areas: love, occasionally poker, and definitely children. Food was sacrosanct.

A button on her desk phone lit up, accompanied by a beep, causing Nicky to pause and Queenie to frown. She didn't have an assistant, because she only used the office on the rare occasions like today when she needed a place to pretend to be a grown up. The only extension that would be calling her from inside the building was the security desk.

"Hang on a sec, would you, Nicky?"

"Sure, Queenie," Nicky sat back in the chair opposite her.

"Hart," she answered.

"Ms. Hart, it's Daniel from security reception."

*Daniel?* It took her a second to put the face with the name. She'd hired Daniel herself. He'd been a gang banger back in the day, and had done a dime in prison. His sister, Elena, had referred him to Queenie. Elena ran a Mexican bakery in the neighborhood that made empanadas that melted in your mouth. Queenie couldn't have, in good conscience, refused Elena anything after taking in to account all the happy memories her mouth had enjoyed in Empanada Land. So, Daniel had become the security/doorman for a building she rarely used.

"I'm kind of in the middle of a meeting, Daniel. Is there something I can do for you?"

"Of course, Ms. Hart, I'm sorry. It's just that a gentleman is on his way up to see you. And Mr. DeMarco is the only person on your list today." Queenie heard Daniel hesitate briefly before continuing. "And this guy looked rough."

*Rough?* Who did she know who fit that description? Aaron was her first thought, but he was still out of town as far as she knew, and he never came to the building anyway.

"And beat up, and angry." Daniel went on. "Definitely angry."

*Angry? That could definitely be Aaron,* she thought. *Probably worked up about Rex again.* "It's not ringing any bells, Daniel," Queenie lied reasonably, trying to put him at ease. "But if I have a problem I'll let you—"

The door to her office opened abruptly, revealing the roughest looking version of Rex that Queenie had ever seen. Nicky must have thought so too, because he rose reflexively and took a brave and foolish step between Queenie and Rex.

"Excuse me—," Nicky began.

"—I don't have business with you," Rex warned, looking past Nicky to Queenie. "Only with *her.* Now." If Queenie were a lesser woman, she probably would've been tempted to duck under the desk. But she'd grown up in a hard neighborhood, and reminded herself that she'd mastered her fight or flight instincts a long time ago. Rex was angry. With her. And he had cause.

Nicky interrupted her contemplation. "Queenie, who is this?"

"Ms. Hart? Everything okay?" A forgotten Daniel spoke in her ear through the receiver.

"Yes, Daniel, I'm okay," she assured him. "It's fine." *Maybe.* She hung up hoping Daniel wouldn't call the police, and waved Nicky aside. *Right, first things first, Queenie. Clear the room of innocent bystanders.* "Stop that. He'll hurt you and your mother will stop feeding me." She pinned Rex with a stare. "You. Have a seat," she gestured to the available couch.

"You," her gaze swiveled back to Nicky. "Walk with me." The younger DeMarco cast a doubtful look at Rex, then back at her. She smiled benignly as if large, raging, muscly men burst into her meetings on a daily basis. Nicky fell for it, picked up his satchel and followed her to the outer office where Queenie's secretary would have sat if she'd needed one, closing the door behind them.

"Queenie—" Nicky took her arm, concern etched into handsome features.

"Skip it, Nicky," she cut through what she was certain would be a well-meaning warning. "You have other things to think about right now."

"I do?" He froze.

"Yes," she nodded, getting him on track and away from ground zero. "Like a better name for your enterprise. Doughnut House is straight and to the point, but I think you should capitalize on your family's name. Maybe DeMarco's Doughnuts?"

He blinked. "You're funding me?"

"I'd be an idiot not to." *You're an idiot anyway*, she reminded herself.

Nicky's grin was infectious, and Queenie was smiling despite angry Ranger Rex in the next room. "Queenie, thank you!" He pulled her into a crushing hug. She returned the hug and extricated herself so she could breathe again. "We'll meet again in a week to firm up the numbers with Walton, my accountant, soon to be yours as well. I'll have him call you to schedule a time."

"Queenie, I'm speechless." His joy would've been infectious if not for Rex.

"Go! Celebrate!" She patted him on the shoulder. He gave her office door another doubtful look, and she reassured him. "He's harmless. Shoo."

He finally went, leaving her to face the dragon alone.

She turned the door handle to her office and went inside. Thankfully he was sitting, so she did the same. Queenie surveyed him for a minute, taking in the rapidly bruising eye, and swelling cheekbone. "This is a surprise."

"It's a day for them, apparently." Hazel eyes pinned her, daring her to look away. She could almost feel his rage in her bones. There was only one thing she could think of that would make him seek her out in this state. Cece had been right all along. As impossible as it would seem, Rex hadn't known. *But he does now.*

She took in the sad torn state of his clothing, alarmed at the bloodstains. "Are you bleeding, Rex?"

"Your concern is touching, Victoria. But it's not my blood," he replied darkly. "Were you ever going to tell me?"

*Right. Let's get to straight to it, then,* she thought. "Tomorrow night." Queenie answered. "Cece is taking Winnie out. I was going to tell you then."

He leaned in, head tilted, eyes narrowed. "What were you going to do? Shove a cigar in my mouth and congratulate me?"

"Rex—" Queenie began.

"—Does she know?" He demanded. "Does Winnie know that I'm her father?"

"Of course she does. I would never lie to he—" As soon as she said, Queenie wanted to take it back.

"—only to me." His accusation bit, and Queenie bit back.

"You haven't exactly been around for me to lie to."

"I've been here almost a week, Victoria."

"Yeah. A week in the last seventeen years," she pointed out. "Pardon me for not wanting to disrupt my daughter's—"

"*Our* daughter, Victoria," Rex corrected her. "Yours *and* mine."

*This is not his fault*, Queenie reminded herself, trying to keep the conversation from getting out of control. "Yes," she finally agreed. "*Our* daughter."

"You kept her from me this whole time," he grated out. "Her whole life she thought I abandoned her."

"Didn't you?" She threw her hands up.

"No." He ground out. "You are not going to lay this on me."

"Oh, c'mon, Rex," Queenie said. "You're a big boy. You know where babies come from. You must've known there was a chance that night—"

"—I am a big boy, and you're a big girl, Victoria. I would've expected you to reach out to me and let me know—"

"—After you'd already sent me that letter saying '*my choices had led us down different paths*'?" She reminded him. "You left and never looked back. What was I supposed to do? Chase you down? Take my moon-sized belly to the Army and have them run you to ground?" She heard the bitterness in her own voice, and tried to dial it back.

"I came back," he said.

"Seventeen years too late," she informed him plainly.

"No." He shook his head faintly. "Back then."

"Back then when?" She asked. "I've been living in that house since you left. I think I would've remembered you knocking on my door."

"For your father's funeral," he explained, forcefully raking a hand through his hair. "I never should've sent that goddamn letter in the first place. When Jasper told me that your dad finally

211

managed to drink himself to death I hightailed it back here. Jasper vouched for me so I could get bereavement leave," he explained. " Victoria, *I came back*."

Queenie felt the world she knew slipping away, bits and pieces of it being replaced with emptiness. "But you didn't see me?"

"Oh, I saw you," he laughed, the sound humorless. Restless, he shoved himself from his seat and went to the window. "I didn't make the funeral. My plane was delayed with weather. By the time I got in, Colin had already been buried. I went home to see you, and you were passed out on the sofa, hugging a fifth of Johnny Walker and a bottle of Valium." He turned to her, not bothering to disguise his pain and anger. *"That's* when I walked away from you. I looked back, Victoria. I just didn't like what I saw."

Queenie remembered that night. Two months had passed since her night with Rex, and two weeks since the letter. She'd discovered she was pregnant earlier that week, but had to shelve the issue because her father was finally succumbing to Cirrhosis of the liver. His passage and Rex's unborn child were all the impetus she'd needed to change her ways. The night she'd buried Colin Hart was the night Queenie had done her Scarlet O'Hara vow and sworn to never drink again.

"Rex," she started, but stopped, realizing she didn't know what to say.

He stood in front of her telling her that he'd seen her at her very lowest and couldn't find it in himself to prop her up one more time. She wanted to laugh, but suddenly all of the energy in her body had drained away.

"What?" His eyes narrowed. "How can you possibly say that you never lied to me? You've been lying to me this whole time."

"Rex—," she tried again.

"So, what was the other night? I'm good enough for a lay, but not father material—"

"—It wasn't like that," she said.

"Then tell me exactly what it was like, Victoria." Rex bit out. "I think I understand now why you were in such a hurry to remind me that I wasn't welcome anymore. You wanted me out of your hair so you could go back to your happy little life."

Guilt washed over her, but Rex wasn't finished.

"Christ! When did you even become the cold-hearted bitch you are today? The old Victoria understood things like loyalty and family and she wouldn't even think of keeping me in the dark about my only child." His long legs ate up the distance between them. "But you? You're not her anymore, are you? You manage people's lives up here. Hell, you've practically built your own boardwalk empire." He waived a hand toward the window. "You could've found me. Let me know. But you didn't. You just played me for a fool this whole time and I want an explanation for that, Victoria." He leaned over her desk, clenched fists supporting his weight. "You owe me that much."

*You knew you were an idiot for thinking this would turn out any other way.* Queenie let the hollow spread through her, filling her until she almost felt absent.

"I don't owe you anything, Reginald Montgomery," she bit out, quietly. "You tried your hardest to walk away from all of us without a backward glance. Whose fault is it that it turned out so well?" She didn't back down from his stare. "That night you're talking about was the first night in who knows how many years that I went to sleep with out company from Jack Daniels, or one of his other friends. Turns out it was a day for cutting ties, I guess." She shrugged shortly, hating the distance their past had put between them. "I still have that bottle of Johnny Walker, as a matter of fact. I take it out when I'm feeling down, and remember that things have been worse."

*In fact, I may be seeing it later.* Queenie felt all of the fight drain out of her and decided she was done. Done trying to make excuses for Rex and his family, done trying to outrun her past. Just done. She let the last card fall. "You want explanations? The line starts at your sister's house. Hopefully, what you find there will satisfy your curiosity." She dismissed him with a gesture and forced her attention to her laptop so she wouldn't have to watch him walk away. *Again.* "Close the door on your way out."

\*\*\*

Queenie surveyed the scene of the Survivor Hutt's office. J.J. had closed the store after Aaron and Rex had their blow out. A sign on the glass front read: NO Z.E.R.T. TONIGHT.

It was late, and Queenie should've gone home, but Rex was likely to be in her near proximity and she wasn't in the mood to deal with him again. Or ever. *You're going to have to deal with him sometime, girl. He's your junior partner now that Aaron has signed over his share.*

J.J. had broken the news over the phone. Aaron had sold her back his share of the business for a dollar before quitting the premises.

"You could have at least cleaned up, you bastard," she said to the mess.

"That was always your job, Queenie."

Queenie spun around to find Aaron's muscled form filling the doorway. His face was bruised, a particularly nasty split in his lower lip, and if his posture was any indication he was favoring his left side.

"You look like crap on a cracker."

He laughed, the sound turning into a grunt, a hand going to his side. "You should see the other guy."

"I have. He kicked your ass. Which saves me from having to do it." Just looking at him was painful. "Sit down before you fall down. I'll get some ice." Queenie pushed Aaron towards the chair and went out to the fridge in the backroom. By the time she got back Aaron was leaning back in the chair, eyes closed, presumably in pain.

*Good.* She unceremoniously dropped a towel filled with ice chips on his head. "You want to explain yourself?" She perched on the edge of the desk.

He adjusted the makeshift cold pack, one dark eye open in her direction. "I could ask you the same thing."

"*You* want to judge me?" Queenie laughed, but the sound was as hollow as she felt. "You lost the right to ask me anything when you shoved your nose into matters that didn't concern you and blew up my life like a paper target."

"Why didn't you tell him, Queenie?" Aaron sat up, still holding the towel to his face. "As soon as I realized that Winnie was his, I thought for sure he must've known and just bailed on you. I mean, you're a straight shooter, always have been. So, I just figured…"

The anger drained out of her and she sighed, leaning a hip against the desk. "So, you were avenging my honor, is that it, big guy?"

"You bet, babe," he started to grin, but stopped when his lip opened up again.

She grabbed hold of a lock of black hair and tilted his face in her direction, so he would know she was serious. "I don't need you to fight my battles."

"I know you don't, but I want to anyway," he adjusted the ice pack so he could keep the pressure on while he looked at her.

"Aaron, you just want to fight. That's not the same thing," she let go of him. "And this time I think you bit off a little more than you could chew."

He rubbed his jaw with his free hand. "Won't be doing that for a while."

"You and Rex deserve each other, you know that?" Queenie sighed, feeling like she owed Aaron an explanation. "I did tell Rex about Winnie."

"That lying son of a—" Aaron made to rise, but Queenie cut him off.

"—He just never got the message."

Aaron looked at her. "Come again?"

"It's complicated, and ancient history. There's no need to go over it. What's done is done." She looked around the room. "And overdone."

Aaron grunted again.

"I thought you'd be long gone by now," she made a half-hearted attempt to clear a spot on the floor with the tip of her shoe, then gave up.

"I almost was, but I left something important behind."

She stepped back and made a sweeping gesture around the office. "Well, good luck finding it in this mess."

He stood and shortened the distance between them. "Come with me, Queenie."

She held up her hand. "How many fingers am I holdin—"

"—Stop it, Queenie. I'm serious." Aaron plucked her hand out of the air and held it. "Come away with me."

"I'm serious, too. I think you may have a head injury. You're not making any sense."

"Queenie, I love you. But I can't stay here anymore. I've only been here this long because of you and Winnie as it is." He squeezed her hand. "I'm not good with roots, but I'll drop some for you. Just not here. Maybe in Florida. We liked it there. We could settle down, get a boat. You could play poker on the coast. There's big money out there. You'd have your pick of the whales."

Queenie was stunned. "And where is Winnie in all of this? While I'm running away with you?"

"Hell, she has Rex now. Why not give them some time to get to know each other?"

She could hardly believe what she was hearing: *Just leave your kid, you know, like your mom did.* Out of gruesome curiosity Queenie pressed him for more information.

"And Cece, and her mom? Henry? All of the other businesses in the Heights? What about them?"

"They're all going to have to learn to grow up one day." He shrugged and she wanted to punch him.

"Like you did?" Queenie jerked her hand out of his. "Aaron, you'll never change. You want me to run away from my responsibilities so I can make *you* my priority, is that what I'm hearing?"

"Queeni—" he made an effort to explain, but she wasn't having it.

"—Desert my friends and family? Abandon the only place that's ever been home to me? For what? To watch you drink away your days on the beach and worry that someday your past might catch up with you?" He paled slightly and if Queenie thought she could've managed it she would have throttled him. "Jesus, Aaron. *Really?*" She pulled away from him, but he grabbed her wrist and held it. "What? This was your big push? Go on the lam with me with me, babe. It'll be fun?"

"It's not like that," he winced. "Well, not exactly like that anyway. I'm not a fugitive."

*Yet.* She heard the unspoken word float between them.

"I don't want to know." She yanked her wrist again, but he held on. He was close enough now for her to smell the alcohol on him.

"Queenie, it's always been you for me. No one else will do. I love you. Enough to change, enough to become a better man. Give me another chance to show you."

She felt like she was caught in some kind of weird time-warp and wondered how many times her own mother had listened to her father say the same thing and believed him.

"I know there's this thing with Rex," he continued. "But forget him. He doesn't know you like I do. And he never will."

"Aaron, there is no thing with Rex." *Thanks in large part to your big mouth.*

"You're blind, you know that?" Aaron snorted. "Not just about him, but about everything. I'm offering to take you away from all of this. And you're going to stay for what? A misguided sense of loyalty to people who would sell you out if the money was good enough? You think these people are your friends? Your family?"

Queenie thought about Antonia and Dante, Nicholas and Morris White. "Yes, Aaron, they are my family. And maybe they'll go another way someday, but that's what family does. Don't you get it?" Queenie heard herself, and realized she'd probably have more satisfaction if she continued this conversation with a wall. Come to think of it Aaron and a wall were oddly similar; they were both supportive in their own blind ways. He didn't get it and probably never would.

She sighed, "I think you should just go."

He stared at her, his hand tightening on her wrist, and for the first time since she'd known him, Queenie felt real fear. *Great. Now I'm going to end up stuffed in a suitcase because I couldn't keep my mouth shut.* But Queenie had had it with the men in her life.

"Aaron, stop it. You're hurting me." Cobra Bubbles growled from the doorway. Queenie made a fist with her other hand and prepared to use it.

Aaron came to his senses and let go, shaking his head like he was trying to get the fog out. "God, Queenie, I'm sorry."

"I know," she rubbed her wrist. "I'm sorry too."

## ∽Chapter Fifteen∽
꙰

"At least *someone* punched him," Cece sipped her cucumber cooler and eased into her chaise. "J.J. says they must have been going at it for a while before he realized what was happening and busted them up. Once your side of this gets around, J.J. might regret breaking them up and make up for it by punching Rex a few times himself."

"It doesn't need to go any further than this, Cece." Queenie lay back in her own chaise, trying unsuccessfully not to think about the day before. "I don't want Winnie to hear about it."

Cece gave a derisive snort. "How's that supposed to work? You planning on keeping everything that happened yesterday from her?"

"Yes— No," she sighed. "I don't know." When the day from hell finally died and Aaron had finally blown out of her life on the same volatile wind that had blown him in, the vet's office called to tell her that the dog Winnie rescued from the pot-house the day before was going to pull through.

So, after school Winnie and Queenie picked up the scrawniest, ragged looking Chihuahua Queenie had ever laid eyes on. Apparently, before Dr. Ziegler's groomer had gotten hold of it, Bob Marley had sported an awful set of doggy dreadlocks that were shaven off at the vet's recommendation. What remained was a nearly hairless four-legged fawn colored bag of bones that was painful to look at.

The upside was that Cobra Bubbles had taken an immediate liking to Bob Marley, and Queenie suspected it was because the stray more than halfway resembled the things she'd been spending her free time searching out and digging up.

When Winnie retired with her canine companions for the night, and Queenie had a free moment to let the stress of the day finally impact her, she'd reached for the phone and out to her best friend.

Cece's answer to most things stress related was spending money and pampering. In short order she'd managed appointments for herself, Queenie and Winnie at her favorite spa, which was where the pair of them sat after their massages. Winnie was occupied in a facial, and still oblivious to the conversation Queenie shared with Rex.

"I still can't believe Aaron wrecked the store, tried to beat up your baby daddy and then sent you flowers asking you to run away with him."

Aaron's regret-me-nots had arrived that morning. Two dozen yellow roses with a card restating his continuing affections and the number to what her accountant confirmed was an off-shore bank account. Queenie shook her head. "You're telling me. I don't think he sent me roses once the whole time I knew him."

"How do you think he found out about Winnie?" Cece asked.

"Rex's name is on her birth certificate, remember?" Queenie shrugged. "It's public record."

"I warned you about that." Cece reminded her.

"I know," Queenie acknowledged. "You were right. You're always right. I should have listened to you, but I was feeling very sentimental at the time. I'd just had a baby. It happens."

"More like just mental." Cece said. "I'm never having kids. I've seen what the hormones have done to you."

"It's not the hormones, it's Rex," Queenie admitted, trying hard not to think about him.

"Speaking of G.I. Jackass, you think he's going to pursue a relationship with our girl?" Cece asked, her mild tone failing to disguise the ticking cogs of her litigious mind.

"She's almost seventeen. She knows he's her dad. I'm not going to stand in the way of them if that's what Winnie wants," Queenie adjusted the cushions on her chair, trying to get comfortable.

"I'm shocked you think I would suggest you should," Cece lifted a delicate brow in Queenie's direction. "I was just pondering the financial aspects of the relationship."

Queenie trailed Cece's line of thought. "You want to sue him for child-support?"

"Only if it would make you feel better, sugar," Queenie opened her mouth to object, and Cece continued. "Think about it, Queenie. How much better would you feel if you could burn twenty-thousand, or so, dollars of Rex's money on say, a trip around the world? Or a new car? God knows Whitey's old Crown Vic has seen better days," she shuddered. "I can't believe you still drive that thing around."

"I like that car," Queenie said, knowing Cece was just trying to lift her

spirits.

Cece nodded agreeably. "And I liked the Mohawk I had in middle school, but sister, there's a time and a place for everything." Queenie remembered the Mohawk and laugh out loud. "God, that was terrible."

"Wasn't it, though?" Cece grinned at her. "I don't know what my mama was thinking."

"She was thinking she needed to pick her battles." Queenie answered from experience.

"Probably," Cece agreed again. "And I'm picking mine with you. That car has got to go. I understand your affection for the god-awful thing, but it's a deathtrap. A deathtrap that has a whole new level of memories now that Rex has fully matured into the dickhead we suspected he might be all along."

"Cece—," Queenie began.

"Don't 'Cece' me, Queenie." Cece sassed a finger wave at her. "Right is right, and wrong is wrong. And right now his hot white ass is just flat out wrong. If he had the balls to go to his sister, then he's stewing in his own wrongness as we speak. Assuming she didn't try to lie her way out of this mess."

"That's a big assumption."

"Nevertheless, a secret like the one she's keeping can only be kept for so long before it starts to break down the bearer. Like Frodo and the ring all over again. I've seen it, believe me. And that woman is hanging onto her fantasy life by a thread. I think this week will be her new touchstone with reality. If Rex doesn't come around by Monday, then I'm suing his ass."

"I don't need, or want, his money." Queenie argued.

"I know you don't, Queenie. But I don't think he's going to give you what you really want. And at this point if he doesn't give you what you want, then I'm going to do what I know how to do, and take what we can get. I'm going to sue him, and you, me and Wonder Winnie are going to spend his money in Paris."

"Who's going to Paris?" Winnie asked, looking clean and fresh in her plush white spa robe. "Are *we* going to Paris?" She looked from Cece to Queenie. "When? When are we going to Paris? Can we go in the spring, during fashion week?" She looked hopefully at her mother. "Can we bring Jon? Can we go to EuroDisney?"

"See what you've done?" Queenie said to Cece.

"I don't care." Cece looked at Winnie. "Yes to everything, doll. We'll get started on it tomorrow."

"Really?!?" Winnie's squee reverberated through the spa, causing a few women to turn their heads. She gave a hop of joy, then hugged both of them, and sat on the edge of Queenie's chaise. "I can't believe this week. My dad, Bob Marley, Lady Gaga tonight and now this!" She clapped in a decidedly un-Winnie like fashion.

"Um, hello?" Cece sat up, her gaze fixed on the floor. "What is that, and why was I not consulted?" Winnie tucked her foot under her, but it was too late. "You let our girl get a tattoo without consulting me?"

"Absolutely not," Queenie sat up, looking at her daughter for an explanation. "Winnie?"

Winnie's eyes slid closed and she shook her head. "It was the only way I could get Drake to leave that ratchet drug den."

"Getting a tattoo?" Cece asked in disbelief. "He coerced you into getting inked?"

"It wasn't like that?" Winnie opened her eyes, blue gray eyes imploring them for understanding. "Drake wants to be a tattoo artist, but his mother won't hear of it?"

"I can imagine not," Cece said. "And sully the good Masterson name?"

"Exactly," Winnie sighed. "Turns out, the reason he's always wearing a stupid hoodie is because he's been practicing on himself. His arms are almost completely covered, Mom."

Cece whistled. "His momma must have flipped when she found out."

"She's never been all that stable as nearly as I can tell," Queenie said.

"Truth."

"Anyway, he's pretty good. Both he and David are crazy amazing artists. Apparently it's a well-known secret at school that if you want a tat Drake's your guy. He even tattoos their friends. When I found him he wasn't going to come with me, we argued about it, and he dared me. He said if I let him tattoo me he would go home. I told him okay, but whatever he tattooed on me he had to tattoo on himself."

"This just gets better and better," Queenie said to no one in particular.

"Please tell me you got a tattoo of Justin Bieber," Cece reached for Winnie's robe. "It would serve that entitled little shit right to have to walk around with that on his body."

Winnie laughed ruefully and slid her foot out for them to see. "I would have if I'd thought of it, Aunt Cece."

"What does it say?" Cece squinted, trying to make sense of the small black scroll letters.

"Ohana," Queenie read aloud, swallowing the same lump of emotion that threatened to choke her every time she watched Lilo and Stitch. *Family.* "It says ohana."

"Jesus, you're a softie just like your mother, aren't you?" Cece shook her head at them.

As much as Queenie wanted to deny it, she felt her throat close and her eyes well with tears. She jammed her eyes shut to stem the water-works, but it was no use. Her daughter's sentimentality mirrored Queenie's own feelings and her emotions chose that particular moment to take the stage. Queenie swept her legs over the side of her chair and sat up enough to bury her head in her arms before the sob she'd been choking back managed to escape.

"Mom!?" Winnie cried out. "What is it?"

As much as she wanted to comfort her daughter and reassure her, in that moment Queenie couldn't find the strength. *Goddamn Rex and Drake both.* She'd been such an idiot.

"Mom, I'm sorry." Queenie felt the chaise give as Cece perched behind her.

"It's not you, love. Don't you worry about that little bit of ink."

"Cece, what's wrong with her?" Winnie asked.

"Nothing that time won't fix." Cece said, stroking Queenie's back softly.

"I don't think I've ever seen her cry before."

"Well then, it's about time for it. A lot has happened lately, what with Whitey passing and your dad coming back. Then Drake going missing and you almost being in jail. I think she's finally reached her limit."

"Have you ever seen her cry before?"

"A few times," Cece said. "But it's been a while."

About seventeen years, Queenie realized. The last time she'd broken down had been over Rex. The moment was etched in her memory. About a week had passed since she'd read Rex's only letter to her and she'd had her first contraction. Whitey had taken her to the hospital where Cece and her family already waited, but the only person Queenie had wanted to see was Rex. It was at that moment she realized he'd meant what he said. He really wasn't coming back. And right there in the hospital lobby she broke down and sobbed like a little girl. Everyone but Cece chalked it up to drama of childbirth. Cece always knew better.

*Didn't you promise yourself then and there that you were never going to shed another tear over him? Man up, woman, you're freaking your kid out.* Queenie took a deep shuddering breath and her tears finally dried up. *That's better.* She wiped her runny nose with the sleeve of her spa robe.

"Ew, Queenie," Cece said. "I'm sure if the fine attendants in the spa knew you were planning on turning that robe into a biohazard, they never would have given it to you."

Queenie laughed weakly. "I'll have it cleaned."

"Have it burned," Cece suggested.

"Mom, I'm so sorry I didn't tell you about the tattoo."

"It's not you, sweetie," Queenie gave her daughter a quick squeeze.

"Are you sure you don't mind too much, Mom?"

"Of course, I mind, Wee." She eyed Winnie's foot. *You're too good for all of us.* "As soon as we're done here we're stopping at the urgent care on the way home and getting you a tetanus shot to go with your new ink."

***

Rex sat on his uncle's sofa, trying to man up enough to cross the street and talk to Queenie.

He'd stormed over to Diana's after leaving Victoria's, determined to get to the bottom of things. Diana took one look at his face and said: "Come inside."

She'd obviously been expecting him because she'd laid out a small box of photos and letters on the table. *All from Jasper.* All obviously containing photographs, the corner of Winnie's face peeking brightly up at him. Rex took one look at the contents and abandoned any pretense or courtesy. "Diana, why in the world would you keep something like this a secret?"

"Why?!? Is your memory so selective that you don't recall what she was like? The drinking, the drugs! Always strung out on one thing or another! Whatever prompted you to think a girl like Victoria would make a suitable bedmate, Reggie? What was she? A boyhood itch you needed to scratch?" Diana demanded, hands on hips. "You were finally going to be free of that awful place and then she somehow managed to manipulate you into a *baby*! What kind of future would you have had then?" She scoffed. "I know exactly what would've happened. You would've thrown away the next eighteen years of your life on a chemically dependent dropout because of a momentary lapse in reason."

"So, you were cutting my losses for me? Is that it? Is that what Victoria and Winnie were to you?" He demanded.

"I was doing you a favor, and you know it. Why couldn't you leave it alone?" Her look accused him. "And how do you think it's been for me? Having to hide your indiscretion from my sons and knowing that any moment somehow someone might find out the connection? Just look at what happened the other night with Drake. The officer reported he had marijuana on him. He's going to be on *probation*, Reggie! All because he was trying to cover up for that Hart gi—"

Rex reached his limit. "Don't you dare drag her into this," he warned, his entire body tightening into a live wire. "Your memory is as selective as mine, apparently: if the weed was Winnie's she would have failed the drug test right along with Drake. She didn't. Drake's problems don't have a thing to do with *my daughter*." Rex had listened to Diana's tirade and found himself completely lacking the patience to deal with her. "Please tell me you have registered by now that Drake ran away and David covered for him. That Winnie got David to tell her where he was so we could all stop worrying? That she risked her own safety to bring him out?" Just the idea of her wandering through the derelict Naked City made Rex want to strangle Drake. Anything could've happened to her there and Rex would've lost his chance to know her.

All of the anger Aaron had beaten into him earlier spilled out looking for its rightful owner. "Christ, Diana! You had no right!" His jaw clamped and he forced himself to unclench his fists. *Not that she doesn't deserve a good beating.* "You stood in your kitchen not a week ago berating our dead father for abandoning us. What did you do but make me abandon my own daughter? You had no right to keep my daughter from me, or Jasper's condition!" He thundered, and Diana took a step back. "You will never begin to understand what Victoria and I meant to each other, and thanks to you I've missed out on my daughter's entire life, and the end of Jasper's. There is nothing you could possibly say or do that will ever make this right between us." He went to the table and collected the things she'd laid out.

"Reg—," Even his sister's pet name for him was too much for Rex in that moment. "—It's Rex, Diana. It's been Rex since Jasper took one look at me and decided it suited me. It's going to say Rex on my tombstone, so get used to it."

He'd left her house carrying more anger than he ever thought he'd be capable of feeling towards another human being.

Now, back at Jasper's the rage had faded but that didn't change his situation. He slid the box she'd given him aside, the contents displayed on Jasper's coffee table, a montage of a life stolen from him. *His daughter's life.*

Photos of Winnie from birth to right before Jasper's death. Photos of her at the zoo, in the Christmas pageant, at her first dance. Sixteen birthday photos, every year accounted for without fail. Documentation in stages, courtesy of Jasper, Rex guessed. All meant for him, but kept by Diana out of a misguided notion of family.

He rustled through the photos, finding the one that hit the hardest. The first one, the one that started it all. He stared at the picture of a smiling Victoria, Cece at her side, the pair of them laughing at the photographer and holding up a sign that read 'Guess what?' with an arrow pointing at Victoria's burgeoning belly.

He took the version he had out of his wallet and compared it to the original. The pair of photographs were identical except that Diana had made a copy and edited out anything that indicated Victoria's condition. He was left with a pair of smiles from his two favorite people in the world. Somehow his sister's least favorite.

And he'd replied with that goddamn letter, which in retrospect was the height of youthful indiscretion for him. He'd just seen her at her worst, and he was at the beginning of his new life. With boot camp behind him and the future wide-open Rex had no idea that what he felt for her would stay with him. That he'd never shed the desire to be near her. He'd never want to be strong enough to let go of their shared past.

*Face up to it, Boy.* Jasper's voice echoed in Rex's head from memory. *No battle was ever won from walking away.*

*Is that what I'm doing,* he wondered. Battling? Come to think of it, he'd sat in the same chair nearly a week ago and felt the wall Victoria had thrown up between them. He'd wondered when she left, where the distance between them had come from. Now he knew. She'd thought he'd known about Winnie, because she'd done her best to inform him of her impending arrival. Even Cece had been testing waters when she'd asked him about custody or palimony issues. The night of the impromptu pizza party Winnie had jumped on the bandwagon and quizzed him about his fatherhood status.

They must have figured out that he was in the dark in pretty short order.

And when he extended the hand of friendship, Victoria had taken it. With reservations, sure, but she'd taken it knowing she'd have to tell him about Winnie at some point. But Aaron had stepped in and done it for her.

Rex rubbed the bruise along his jaw wondering if Queenie had less bite in her punch. Her punch maybe, but not her words.

*"Close the door on your way out." Denied, Rex. She put you out, Old Son. And in your place where you belonged.* He'd come at her on her own turf, what did he expect? His Colonel would be ashamed if he'd known Rex made such a rookie mistake.

*Wrong mentality, boy-o,* he reminded himself. You're not fighting an enemy. Victoria as an enemy would be a gargantuan mistake. When he'd walked away from her the night Colin Hart died, it had been with more hopelessness and regret than he could stomach. Knowing now what he'd left behind tripled the regret, but the hopelessness was gone. Tempered by hardship and time, Victoria Hart had grown into one hundred pounds of Irish force to be reckoned with.

And Rex wanted to reckon with her. Very badly. And for the rest of their lives.

But she'd made it pretty clear to him that the chances of that happening were slim, now. *Slim.* He'd faced slim odds before.

*But back then you were only in danger of losing your life. Are you man enough to risk losing Victoria and Winnie,* a thread of doubt niggled into his brain.

*There's only one way to find out, Boy,* Jasper's words encouraged him. And for the briefest instant Rex would have sworn he caught a whiff of his uncle's Old Spice.

***

"If you require any services during your stay, just dial zero, or text me at this number, Ms. Hart," Janelle, Queenie's personal butler at the Mirage lay a card on the marble side table in the foyer. "I'm available for your needs twenty-four hours a day."

"Then this should be the easiest shift of your week," Queenie dug through her wallet until she found a bill that would compensate for the dog hair and slobber decorating the perky butler's pressed gray slacks, pressing it into Janelle's hand.

Janelle slipped the tip into her pocket with the subtlety of a stage magician, producing a pair of doggy treats in its wake. "May I?" She asked, Cobra Bubbles sitting immediately at Janelle's feet, tail wagging emphatically, while Bob Marley, uncertain of what was happening, circled his canine companion, hopping over her tail as need demanded.

"You bet," Queenie said, wondering if Janelle always had pet treats on hand, or if she was just that good. Cobra Bubbles took the proffered biscuit with a gentleness that belied her size, while Bob Marley, presumably concerned about seeming invisible beside his gargantuan companion, began dancing on his hind legs to get Janelle's attention. "I see you, little man." Janelle knelt and waited until the Chihuahua took the treat before straightening. "If you'd like to schedule walks for them while you're here just call me. We have a private park for villa guests."

She left, closing the massive double doors behind her. Cobra Bubbles went to the doors, sniffing them before taking her tour of their new accommodation, Bob Marley following like a tiny skeletal fawn shadow. The duo padded across the travertine floor and out to the private patio to run a security check on the pool perimeter before returning and settling on the cushy leather couch.

"Don't get used to this," she warned the dogs. "It's just for tonight." Queenie rifled through her overnight bag until she found the dog bowls she'd brought, and went into the kitchenette to fill one with water, pausing when she saw that Janelle had already left a trio of bowls behind, one brimming with water. "Okay, maybe two nights." Queenie headed into the bedroom suite, tossing her bag on the king sized bed. Her phone vibrated in her pocket and she answered it.

"Mom!" Winnie squealed in her ear. "This room is bigger than our house! It has an upstairs! And a Jacuzzi!"

"And an amazing view," Cece said in the background.

After the spa, Cece and Winnie started planning their concert adventure. Queenie decided it would be easier for all parties involved if the pair of them just stayed on the strip where the concert was being held. She'd called the MGM Grand to see if a room was available. During the booking process the reservation specialist asked her for her name, and when Queenie had given it she'd been politely placed on hold and connected with the VIP host who proceeded to thank her for choosing their property and told her they had a suite available. When Queenie asked for a cost breakdown, the host informed her that because she was such a frequent guest at the MGM family of gaming tables they would be happy to comp her. It turned out that she had more reward points than she could use in a lifetime, so in addition to a free room, the food was taken care of as well.

After completing the reservation, her host asked if she needed any other reservations. Queenie realized that she had no desire to stay home all-alone with a brooding Rex just across the street. "Do you have anything that will accommodate a small horse and a large rat?"

The host didn't miss a beat, suggesting the Mirage villas. Queenie liked to play in their high limit room so she took it, not quite realizing that when the host said villa, he meant literally a villa. Turned out the Mirage kept a small neighborhood of completely private, individual villas for its high rollers and celebs.

"How's your room?" Winnie asked.

"It's okay," Queenie answered, standing in the door frame of the master bath and looking at the bottle of champagne resting in the wine chiller next to a tub that was only slightly smaller that the pool. *Maybe Cobra Bubbles and Bob Marley will decide to take a bath later.* She pictured them sitting back in the bubbles, a glass of champagne in each paw. *You're losing it, girl.* "You ready to go out on the town?"

"Yeah, I just wanted to call you since I won't see you again until tomorrow."

Queenie's heart swelled. "Aren't you the sweetest daughter a mother ever had?"

"Just until I get off the phone. Then it's hell on wheels."

"Of course." Queenie laughed. "A girl's gotta roll, after all. Have fun tonight."

"You too. I love you."

"Love you back, kiddo."

"I'm gonna go, but Cece wants to talk to you." There was a pause and some giggling.

"Girl," Queenie could hear Cece's smile through the phone. "It's over the top."

"Same here," Queenie grinned. "If only I'd known about this comp thing sooner."

"Use those bad boys up, but use your judgment. You get me?"

"I'm picking up what you're laying down." Not even Rex was enough to drive her to drink.

"How are you doing?"

Queenie wished she knew. Just don't think about it and you'll be fine, she kept telling herself. *Ah, denial, hold me tight and never let me go.* "Let's just say I've put a pin in Rex for the time being."

"My mama always said voodoo could do wonders for a girl's state of mind." Cece said half-seriously. "Just don't damage any parts you think you might want to use later."

"That ship has sailed," Queenie replied. "And what do ya know? It turned out to be the Titanic."

"Poor baby," Cece said with genuine regret. "Maybe you should get another massage tomorrow. They comp the spa too?"

"Everything, according to Janelle."

"Who's that?"

"My personal butler."

Cece whistled. "You're living high, now. You sure you still want to associate with the likes of me?"

"We're Shake and Bake, remember? We're stuck with each other."

"Nu-uh, sugar. In this outfit I'm El Diablo. That leaves you with the Magic Man. So, go make the tables rain, Queenie."

"You got it, Boss."

## ❧ Chapter Sixteen ❧
♕

Rex dropped his truck in the Mirage valet, wishing for the hundredth time that Cece had seen fit to help him narrow down his search for Queenie. He'd manned up and crossed the street three hours earlier, only to find Queenie and Cobra Bubbles gone. A query text to Cece garnered a simple response: Try the tables.

He suspected Cece most likely knew exactly where Queenie was, and also what had passed between them the day before. All things considered he was lucky she was willing to help him at all. Cece and Queenie should've been born joined at the hip. He had no illusions about his standing with either of them right now.

It was the noise that bothered him, he realized as he reconnoitered, searching out the high limit room. Too much time spent cultivating silence and avoiding crowded areas during his Army tours made him unfit for the masses of people herding through the Strip's Megaresorts. This was his eleventh stop so far in his search for Queenie. According to Google he only had twenty-one high limit rooms left to go. So far he'd batted zero, but as he forded a stream of people exiting a nearby showroom, Rex caught sight of a familiar black-haired figure beyond the golden velvet ropes separating the whales from the average tourist.

With an internal sigh of relief, Rex made his way to the entrance where a male suited attendant stood behind a podium and greeted him politely.

"Does sir wish to play?" The attendant inquired.

Rex paused, realizing for the first time that he'd been so focused on finding Queenie that he didn't actually come up with a plan once he found her.

"I suppose I do."

"Very good. And does sir already have a line established?"

At Rex's blank look the attendant nodded briefly as though agreeing with the nothing Rex expressed. "I take it sir has never played with us before?"

"No."

"Very good," the attendant smiled. "Here in high limit the minimum hand tonight is five hundred dollars, with maximum bet of fifteen thousand. To ensure the players will be compensated for their efforts, you may play from a house marker with an established credit line, or sir has the option of fronting with one hundred thousand in cash or chips. Does sir have a preference?"

*One hundred thousand in cash to play?* Talk about sticker shock.

"Would sir be interested in establishing a line of credit?"

*You can't win if you don't play, boy-o.*

"Why not?" He shrugged, hoping for once fortune would favor his boldness.

A discrete phone call from the attendant prompted the arrival of a sleek blonde. "Mr. Montgomery, my name is Sheila. I'll be your line executor this evening." Her smile was spare but sincere. "If you'll follow me, we'll expedite your line and get you to a table." Forty-five minutes later he'd been put through a financial background check worthy of the FBI, and, he suspected, barely approved.

"Very good, Mr. Montgomery." Sheila removed the small stack of paperwork he'd just signed. "Will you be taking out a marker for this amount?" The way she said it almost made him forget that it was his uncle's house he was getting ready to gamble away. *Without your girls, what good is the house, Rex?*

"I suppose I will, Sheila."

"Excellent," she rose, gliding around the desk and led him from the room back out to the podium and a familiar attendant. She smiled at the attendant, but unhooked the velvet barrier herself and directed Rex to pass into the inner sanctum of table games. "The High Limits room is at your disposal, Mr. Montgomery. I'll have your chips brought to you."

"Thank you, Sheila."

"My pleasure, Sir. And good luck to you."

Rex took a leveling breath and set his sights on Queenie's table. His heart rate increased, but he couldn't tell if it was because of her, or the fact that he was about to potentially make an ass out of himself and lose a mint in the process.

"No guts, no glory, Old Son," he muttered under his breath and took a purposeful step.

*\*\*\**

Queenie actually heard her stomach growl and wondered if it was time to take a break from the table. Lady Luck had been a serial dater all night, flirting with one player, then another, sometimes leaving the table all together, with the whole table folding and only the players in the blinds making any progress. Bandit had given up, leaving Queenie to play with Gypsy, Cowboy and Amazing Rando.

"I don't know about y'all, but I feel like I'm working for every penny tonight," Cowboy pitched his cards towards the dealer.

"After the pounding you took the other night, I can hardly believe you can stand to sit through this." Gypsy's cards followed Cowboy's.

"He doesn't have an ounce of quit in him," Queenie followed suit.

"Coming from you, Queenie, that's quite a compliment." Cowboy tipped his hat and Queenie rolled her eyes.

"Flattery won't get you your Gaga tickets back."

"Thought you'd be using them tonight. I'm a little insulted."

"Don't be. I gave them to my help."

Gypsy's lyrical contralto drifted across the table. "Ooh, girl, the size of your man-sacs defies my imagination." Her gaze wandered around the table. "And believe me when I say I've seen my share."

"Christ, it's not bad enough that the table is molasses tonight, I have to put up with this shit?" Cowboy looked disgusted.

Gypsy ignored him. "Maybe we need to cleanse it with something."

"Like sage?" Queenie asked, stretching in her chair.

"How about a cigar?" Cowboy slid one of his over-priced cancer sticks out of its tube and began the ritual of lighting it.

"Fresh blood." Amazing Rando spoke.

Those two words were enough to gain the attention of everyone at the table.

"That's a little extreme, isn't it, sugar?" Gypsy raised a perfectly penciled brow.

"No." He clarified vaguely, his chin lifting slightly, directing the table's attention. "Incoming."

"Jesus, Rando," Cowboy blew out a cloud of acrid tobacco. "Don't be so goddamn chatty. It ruins my concentration."

Through the cloud of cigar smoke, Queenie recognized a familiar face. Her heart jumped into her throat and she forced it back into place. *This cannot be happening.* Her first instinct was to make her excuses and flee, but she crushed the urge knowing if he'd pursued her here, Rex would most likely follow her anywhere.

"New blood indeed." Gypsy's smile melted into the sultry red crescent of a predator. "Hello, handsome."

Queenie watched as Rex took the open chair, the high limit attendant pausing behind him to lay out stacks of chips. Finished, he paused briefly before turning away.

"Charlie," Queenie called out. The attendant turned and Queenie grabbed an orange chip from her stack and tossed it to him. Charlie caught it. "Thanks, Queenie."

"Ooh, you're a green one, aren't you, handsome?" Gypsy leaned towards Rex, fully enabling her cleavage. "It's customary to tip the help."

Rex drew two orange chips from his own stack and slid them towards Queenie. "My thanks, and interest paid, Queenie."

Gypsy helped the chips along and Queenie retrieved them hoping no one noticed the trembling of her hand. *Get it together,* she scolded herself. *He's no different than any of the other fat-*

*wallet-whales you've hunted. If he wants to swim in your waters, let him.*

"You ever play big-boy poker before, handsome?" Gypsy asked.

"Don't answer that," Cowboy warned. "And you might as well tell us your name, or *he'll* keep calling you 'handsome' all night."

"Never mind him, he's just jealous," Gypsy sent Cowboy an artful pout. "No one's called him handsome since Reagan was president."

Cowboy blew a stream of blue smoke in her direction, "Gypsy, if you—"

"—Rex," Rex announced, cutting through the dissention.

"Rando," the Amazing Rando murmured, rhythmically tapping the table with one finger in a pre-hand ritual everyone except Rex was already familiar with.

"Cowboy." Cowboy nodded.

"I'm Gypsy," Gypsy dropped a strategically placed hand on her bosom. "And you know our little Queenie, thanks to Charlie." She made a sweeping gesture to the diminutive Asian gentleman behind the table. "And this is Mr. Lin, our dealer. If he's good to you, then it's expected you'll return the favor."

"If the cards don't turn soon, his kids will be going hungry tonight." Cowboy grumbled.

"His son is a dentist, idiot," Gypsy shook her head.

"Don't call me an idiot, bitch." Cowboy scowled.

"Don't let the sexual tension fool you, Rex," she spoke to Rex in a stage whisper. "Cowboy *hates* our alone time."

Amazing Rando cleared his throat and looked pointedly at Rex.

"You're holding up the table, sugar. Mr. Lin needs you to ante before he can get the ball rolling." Gypsy settled back in her chair, picking up a purple five-hundred dollar chip, fingering the curve suggestively. Rex followed Gypsy's lead and tossed a purple into the pot.

*You are so out of your league, Tex-Rex. And it serves you right.*

Queenie sat back and waited for the bloodletting to begin.

***

The cards stayed fickle and after being relieved of nearly half of his pot Rex couldn't tell if he was finally hitting his stride or if the novelty of taking his money had worn off for the other players.

"Two pair," the dealer announced, pushing a stack of chips in his direction.

"There you go, sugar," Gypsy said encouragingly as she tossed her cards in.

"Thanks," Rex sorted his chips, sparing a look in Queenie's direction. She ignored him and he swallowed his frustration. She'd yet to really acknowledge him, beyond the occasional pitying head-shake when he lost a hand. *You need a way in, boy-o. And fast.*

"What brings you to town, Rex?" Cowboy asked, relighting the tip of his cigar.

"My uncle died. I came to tie up some loose ends."

"Sorry to hear that, love," Gypsy gave him a sympathetic look before anteing. Queenie followed suit, and Lin dealt. "You expecting it?"

"Came out of the blue really. Whitey was a tough old soul. Marine. He raised my sister and me after are parents died, and I guess I thought he'd live forever."

"Semper Fi, brother." Amazing Rando said, offering Rex a quick salute.

"Heart attack?" Gypsy asked.

"Cancer." Rex looked at his cards.

"Tough break. He have family here to take care of him?"

A pang of regret stabbed at him. "My daughter and her mother. Some family friends."

"Your sister?" Gypsy asked, taking a peak at her cards. Queenie made a delicate snort and Rex watched Gypsy slide a curious glance her way.

"No. She's not that kind of sister."

"Sounds like an ex-wife I once had," Gypsy peeked at her cards and threw a chip in the pot. "Bitch to the bone. Probably the reason I'm like I am today."

"How the hell do you figure that happened?" Cowboy asked, adding to the pot.

"I have a competitive nature, Cowboy, and maybe this is my way of letting Debbie know that I'm more man *and* more woman than she could ever be."

"Makes sense," Cowboy said to everyone's surprise. Gypsy tipped her head prettily in his direction, then turned her attention back to Rex. "So, you got a baby momma. You still with her?"

*Thank you, Gypsy.* "I aim to be, ma'am."

"Ooh, I love a man with purpose," she said huskily, pursing her lips Jessica Rabbit style. A general chuckle floated around as Mr. Lin dealt a card to the table and flipped it: Ace of hearts.

"What if she doesn't want you back, Tex-Rex?" Queenie finally spoke, signaling her intention to stay in the game by tossing a thousand dollar chip in the pot.

*It wasn't what you wanted to hear, but did you really expect another reply after yesterday?* Rex opened his mouth to reply, but was interrupted.

"What woman in her right mind could resist this, Queenie?" Gypsy reached over and pinched Rex's cheek playfully, tsking over the bruise Aaron left him with. "Even with the shiner, he's still a stone cold fox. You might think of giving him a run if he doesn't get his lady-love back in the saddle." Queenie's reaction was an indelicate snort that earned a bark of laughter from Cowboy.

The call around the table was matched by all and Mr. Lin dealt another card: two of spades.

"The jury's still out on women having a right mind to begin with," Cowboy jibed. "You sure you want *her* back, boy? There had to be a reason you left her to begin with."

"No reason to be proud of." *It's now or never.* "Because I was a coward, Cowboy." Rex said baldly, earning looks from everyone at the table except Queenie, whose gaze remained steadfastly on her cards. "She had problems. Problems I couldn't fix, so I fixed the problem by rejecting her."

"Ouch," Gypsy tsked disapprovingly. "Props for the honesty, hon, but that's the problem with a man's idea of love. It's so often conditional. And I'm speaking from experience here."

"Give him a break, Gypsy. You know women aren't always sweetness and light." Cowboy scoffed. "Most of the damn time they're wells of bitter darkness. Expensive, dark, damn wells." He checked his cards, and pushed them away. "Like this hand. I'm out."

Amazing Rando withheld comment, but followed suit in folding, leaving it to Rex. Rex called, more out of the desire to keep Queenie in the game than anything else.

"She could be that too," Rex added, recalling his chilly welcome back from Queenie, and her resolute dismissal of him the previous day.

"Then why would you want her?" Queenie asked, speaking to her cards.

*Why indeed, Rex?* It was the same question Cece had asked him in her office, the same question he'd been asking himself for what seemed like years.

"Because I can't stop wanting her, Queenie." She made the mistake of looking at him and their gazes tangled. "I've wanted her since I knew what wanting was and I've never been able to stop."

An uncomfortable silence descended on the table and Queenie broke first, but not before igniting a spark of hope in Rex. *Still cold, but not the Ice Queen. I can work with that.* Gypsy looked from Queenie back to Rex, an unspoken question in her eyes.

"Despite all of the wanting you left her behind with your *petite enfant*. You must have talked since then. My ex and I have two kids and she's always wanting to talk to me about football games and doctor's appointments."

"I didn't know about the baby until I got back a week ago." *Goddamn your selfish hide, Diana.*

Amazing Rando let out a low whistle. "Your life sounds like one of those Mexican soap operas my girlfriend's always watching, man."

"That's a tough one." Cowboy agreed. "If she didn't tell you back then, then why would you think she still cares about you? She probably has another guy by now. Hell, a couple of them."

"Yeah, Rex?" Queenie picked up a stack of chips and raised the pot by two thousand. "Why would you think she still cares about you?"

The dealer lay out another card: ten of hearts.

Rex didn't even look at it, just matched Queenie's bet. "She tried to tell me, Cowboy, but my sister interfered. And I know she still cares about me because she didn't ride me out of town on a rail at the first chance. Which she could have easily done."

Gypsy bowed out. Leaving the bet to Queenie, who raised the stakes by pushing a tower of chips into the pot, then allowed her gaze to linger on his stake before pointedly raising her eyes to his as if to say: 'Better talk fast, Tex-Rex."

*Want to see what I'm made of, Queenie?* It was just another hopeful sign as far as Rex was concerned.

"Maybe you're reading too much into it and she was just being nice." Queenie suggested, arching a fine black brow in his direction.

The four of hearts appeared on the table and Rex matched Queenie's stack, inwardly blanching at his rapidly diminishing pile, still unwilling to back down. "Not really her style. She went out of her way to make me feel at home. Letting me to sleep on her couch when I showed up completely hammered. Introducing me to her daughter, even though I didn't know who she was at the time. Inviting me for dinner and letting me babysit her dog."

"Don't trust no one with my Herman," Amazing Rando said.

"I'm with Rando on this one Queenie," Cowboy agreed, sitting back in his chair seemingly oblivious to the drama playing out in front of him. "It sounds like she's got it bad for him, even if she's not coming clean about it."

"Even if she does, boys, how do we know our Rex can commit?" Gypsy tossed out. "He said himself he ran the first time. He talks about wanting her, but wanting something isn't the same as loving it. Maybe his Juliet is holding back because she's afraid he doesn't know the difference and can't go the distance." Gypsy, not bothered by having to pay attention to her cards, settled into her seat, lying folded hands on crossed legs and looked at Queenie. "Could that be it?"

Queenie shuttered her expression against him, shrugged softly and raised again. "Maybe."

Mr. Lin laid out the last card. Jack of hearts.

"What do you say to that, Rex?" Gypsy asked softly.

*Maybe.* It was the 'maybe' that did it. Rex could work miracles in the vast space that a 'maybe' left him. A 'no' would have been definitive, but a 'maybe' was halfway to a yes.

He faced Queenie even as she ignored him, wanting to give her a clear view.

"I'd say she knows me better," he began. "I'd say I made the biggest mistake of my life by running away the first time, but I'm a quick learner and losing her once was enough of a life lesson." The thought of having to walk away from her again left a lump of emotion in his throat, but Rex forced it aside and continued. "I'd say she needs to take a chance because what we have is real and everything up to this point was just a test. A test we passed. I'd tell her that when it came to her, 'wanting' and 'loving' have always been the same thing, and I'm ready to go the distance. And I'd tell her she needs to believe me, because I'm all in whether she wants me along for the ride or not." Rex pushed his remaining chips towards the pot. "What do you say, Queenie?"

No one spoke, all eyes drifting to Queenie.

Queenie looked at her cards, then at the river of cards on the table. "What about Diana?"

"She can go fly a kite in an electrical storm." Rex said without pausing.

"You really think this is a thing?" Queenie finally looked him in the eye and Rex knew he was close.

"I think it's the only thing, baby."

"Let's let the cards decide, then."

Gypsy took a quick breath. "Queenie…"

"Fine." Rex agreed, his pulse speeding up as he watched her commit towers of chips to the pot. "You sure you can afford to lose?"

Queenie bestowed a mysterious smile on him. "I like my odds, Tex-Rex."

"Bet is called, show your cards."

Queenie turned over her cards: the queen of hearts and ten of spades.

"Pair of tens," Cowboy shook his head. "All-in on a shit hand like that? Must be love."

Rex showed his hand.

"Heart straight." Mr. Lin announced, sweeping the winnings towards Rex whose grin had nothing to do with the money.

"Together they have one hell of a Royal Flush," Gypsy pointed out as she studied the cards.

"Queenie?"

"Together we're unbeatable, Rex. Who am I to argue with Lady Luck?"

## ᄋ—Chapter Seventeen—ᄋ
🐚

"These are some swanky digs, Queenie," Rex closed the double doors of the villa behind them, barely sparing a glance at his surrounding before reaching for her.

"Like them?" She asked, allowing herself to be caught.

"Not as much as I like you," Rex grabbed her by the hips and drew her towards him, pinning her to the door. He dipped his head to her, capturing her lips with his own. Queenie melted into the kiss, her hands slipping beneath his shirt, urging it upwards. Rex broke the contact to oblige her, pausing long enough to pull the shirt off and give her the access she wanted. Her hand glided up his abs and around pulling him back. Just the heat of her palm against his flesh was enough to stoke his arousal and Rex groaned. Wanting to share the pleasure, this time it was his turn to make short work of her clothing.

He freed her of her top, savoring the naked expanse of skin available to him, modest lace lingerie showcasing the twin treasures he'd been dreaming of since their last encounter. He dipped back in, teasing the sensitive skin of her neck, trusting his fingers to free what his tongue wanted to taste. When her bra finally came loose, Rex kissed a hot trail to his goal. As he latched on to one sensitive tip, Queenie moaned over him, her hands tangling themselves in his hair, pulling him closer.

"Oh, my g—" her sentence ended in a gasp as Rex took one nipple between his teeth, teasing and sucking it to rigid tightness. Deciding he didn't want it's mate to be jealous, Rex moved on, languishing similar attentions on it's partner. As his mouth worked, his fingers set out on another mission to free Queenie of her clothing. When they'd breached the defenses of her jeans, Rex slipped them down and off, along with her panties.

In one motion, a sensitive nub still in his mouth, Rex rose, his hands gripping the firm curve of her rear lifting her to meet him and bracing them both against the door. He broke contact with her nipple and straightened. She gripped his shoulders, one hand pulling his face to hers to resume their kiss where it had left off.

Unable to wait any longer, Rex's liberated himself from his own clothing with a free hand. He broke the kiss and searched out his lover's eyes.

"Queen—."

"Yes, Rex," she cut him off. "Right now, if you don't min—"

He slid home into the warm wetness of her before she could finish, pleasure infusing him from the inside out. Queenie gasped, her breath short and ragged. "Oh..."

With her tightness surrounding him, Rex let the natural rhythm of their passion take over, urging them both to the next level. Every thrust brought a fresh wave of pleasure, forcing him onward until he knew he couldn't hold back any longer. He felt Queenie strengthen her grip on him, her breath coming short and fast.

"Right now, Rex," she cried out, her nails digging in to his shoulders. That final demand left him undone and he lost himself in her.

They stood as a single unit pressed against the oak doors of the villa trying to catch their breath. In the silence they heard the murmuring of voices on the other side of the door along with some light laughter and finally applause.

"Oh, hell." Queenie buried her head in Rex's should in mortification, but Rex only chuckled. "At least they were applauding," he hoisted her over his shoulder and turned, giving the room a quick search before successfully locating the bedroom suite. "Look on the bright side, thank god the door held."

"It was all the bright side, Tex-Rex," she said. "Is this your equivalent of dragging me off by my hair?"

"I've taken enough beatings this week, thanks." He kicked the door closed behind him and dropped her unceremoniously on the bed, luxuriating in the sight of her naked form against the rich fabric of the duvet. "Does it make me a voyeur if I can't stop looking at you?"

She smiled, a wicked glint in her eye. "I think you'd have to be looking at me through the window to be a proper peeper. At the very least, the bedroom closet. Or maybe the internet."

"Are you on it?" The idea surprised him.

"Of course," she clarified when his eyes widened. "Not like this. I'm wearing clothes."

"That's a shame. Then I'll have to pass," he sprawled on to the bed beside her. "I like this view much better." He slid an arm beneath her and pulled her on top of him where she made herself comfortable. "You're really on the internet?"

"You never checked?"

"I never thought of it, to be honest. I know it sounds silly, but WiFi isn't as available in remote parts of the world." Rex explained. "Did you? Look for me, I mean?"

She shook her head. "No. There didn't seem to be any point to it. You'd made your point when you left."

"Too well, I think." Rex let his hands wander across her back, fingertips caressing the curve of her rear. "Let's promise each other to talk about this every day so I can recall what an idiot I've been. I'd hate to forget."

"Deal. I take it you had a chance to speak with your sister."

"Less speaking than yelling, but yes."

Queenie lifted her head to look at him. "She yelled at you?"

"The other way around." Her eyes widened and he shrugged. "It's about time someone did after the way she's treated everyone."

"Well, look at you, Tex-Rex. Only here a week and already straightening up this lawless town. Whitey would be proud."

"He would have chewed my ass for this whole mess, and you know it." Rex sighed. "Did you know he tried to send a picture of Winnie to me every year?"

"Really? I had no idea?"

"Diana gave me a box that he'd forwarded to her thinking she'd send them along."

"He must not have known her very well."

"It's easy to underestimate crazy, sugar."

"You're preaching to the choir, soldier."

"I think Uncle Jasper just wanted to believe that she would eventually do the right thing."

"And she did."

"Don't do that."

"Do what?"

"Say it like that. Like what happened didn't have meaning, or affect us."

"It affected us, but we survived. I can't carry your sister's choices around with me Rex. Been there, done that, have the sobriety chip to prove it. There's only room enough for a select few inside my head and she doesn't make the cut."

"When did you know?"

"That she didn't tell you?" His nod prompted her. "Cece and I put it together earlier this week, after she figured out that you had no idea you had a kid." Queenie explained. "It really couldn't have been anyone else. Not Whitey, he wanted you to know. The only other person who could have kept that kind of thing from you besides Uncle Sam was your sister."

"Whitey knew the whole time?"

Queenie nodded. "Of course he did. It was never my intention to keep it a secret."

*No. She wouldn't have.* "He must have thought I was the biggest ass for never coming home."

She stroked his arm. "Don't do this. Don't try to back yourself into a life you didn't have with choices you couldn't make. You knew him better than that, and in the end he got his way. You're here now. It's not too little, or too late."

Rex realized how close it had been. He almost hadn't come back. Diana had been so reassuring when she emailed to say she'd handle the business end of their uncle's passing. He'd almost missed the train again. Would have if Diana had her way.

"Ten-hut, soldier." Queenie brought him back. "You're awfully far away for a man with a naked chick on top of him." She sat up, repositioning herself meaningfully. "What's a girl have to do to get your attention?"

"I don't know, why don't you try something and we'll see if it works?" He took in the full spectacular view she offered. "I think you'll find you have my full attention now."

She smiled, letting her fingers gauge the truth of his words, enjoying his sharp intake of breath as her hands stroked the sensitive flesh of his member. "That is much better."

He groaned. "I'm not complaining."

"Now that I have your attention, let's see how long I can keep it." Queenie dipped her head, letting her mouth take over where her hands left off.

"Queeni—," he choked out. She ignored him, savoring the salty taste of their lovemaking on his skin, admiring the lines of his body in the moonlight, letting her hands tour the length of him. Her fingers hugged the rigid softness of him, stroking the core of him until he groaned. "Queenie…"

She was gratified by the power of his plea and gripped him firmly. "Not yet, Rex." Queenie followed her lover's example, one hand straying up his chest to tease a sensitive nipple, while the other held him steady as she took him in her mouth.

Her tongue caressed the rigid velvet of his manhood, pausing now and again to circle the engorged tip. Rex moaned, lust rooting him to the bed. His hands slid into her hair, guiding her mouth along him from base to tip. Her hand gripped him harder, the rhythm of her mouth increased. When she knew he was close, Queenie pulled away, tearing a groan from him and took control of his pleasure, establishing a rhythm and then slowing, eliciting a moan from her lover. She repeated the act several times, before drawing off of him with measured patience. Rex's gaze tangled with hers, the heat in them matching hers.

In one motion, Queenie straddled him, allowing the full length of him to fill her. A deep groan slipped from him and he reached a seeking hand towards her, caressing the fullness of one breast, teasing the tautness he found.

"Not this time, Tex-Rex," Queenie took his hand by the wrist and brought it over his head. She dragged its partner up and pinned him with her weight. The full length of her lie stretched across him, her face inches from his, her aroused peaks grazing the hard muscled of his chest. With a patience she never suspected she possessed Queenie began a languorous rhythm with her hips, reveling in her sudden power. Rex made a half-hearted effort to free himself before giving himself over to her control.

Queenie rewarded them both by increasing her tempo. Rapture seared through her, urging her onward. Unwilling to hold off any longer, she increased the rhythm of their passion. His breath came in short gasps now, and Queenie, knowing he was close, increased the pace of her desire, trying not to let the sensations rippling through her outstrip his.

"Queenie!" He cried out beneath her, his hips rising to meet her demands. Rex finally gave himself away; releasing his passion to the same ocean of pleasure Queenie was drowning in. The pressure in her body built, strained by the ache of desire in every nerve ending in her body. Just as the sensations threated to drown her, pleasure exploded in her and the world dropped away.

When the wanting ache had passed, leaving only contentment behind, Queenie rolled off of Rex, tucking herself in beside him.

"Queenie?" He said finally.

"Hmm?" She drew lazy circles on his chest with her fingertips.

"Do you love me?"

The words left his mouth and she realized she'd never said them aloud. "I suppose that depends."

"I'm listening." His hand rested on the small of her naked back, warming the flesh beneath his palm.

"People say they love each other all the time. I'm not sure what they mean. What I feel for you is like—," she paused, trying to find the right words, "—the breath before the brakes, or the last heartbeat before a first kiss, if that makes sense." *I sound like a crazy person*. She shrugged it off. "It's a feeling I've only had for you, Tex-Rex."

"It will have to do." He tipped her face in his direction, hazel eyes meeting hers. "I'm going to marry you."

"That's a nice idea, but I'm not really marriage material." she said, dizzy with a mixture of physical pleasure and happiness. *If I wake up right now and find that this is all a dream, I am going to burn this hotel to the ground*, she thought.

"You should try everything at least once," Rex said. "Who knows? You might enjoy it."

"Tempting, but it would ruin my reputation as woman of ill-repute. I'm pretty high ranking in the group right now."

Rex chuckled, "Maybe it's time to pass the crown to someone else?"

"Hmm," she pretended to think about it. "What do you have to offer besides these abs and a dysfunctional family?" She traced a finger across his six-pack.

"A pony?"

"Ponies are my kryptonite," she laughed. *Dream, or not, I'm going with it,* she decided. "Now, I have to say yes."

"Then let's do this before you come to your senses and change your mind."

"Right now?" She asked. "Um, we're naked, and it's two in the morning."

"It's Vegas," Rex said, kissing the top of her head. "Isn't this the marriage capital of the world?"

"You don't seriously want to go right *now* do you?"

Rex thought for a minute. "We should probably wait until Winnie and the rest of the gang are available."

"Good idea. And we need to find a place."

"And an Elvis," Rex agreed.

Queenie ignored him. "And a dress."

"Do you really need a dress? Can't we find someone to marry us like this? It has to have happened."

"You're an exhibitionist all of a sudden?"

"It's the first time I've ever had something worthwhile to exhibit," he said stroked the curve of her breast.

"Hmm, nice try, but the nudist nuptials are out. We'll have to regroup and make some plans." Queenie let her hands drift over Rex's abs again.

"Plans," he closed his eyes, opening them again when a scratching sound came from the direction of the door. "What's that?"

"The dogs, most likely," Queenie started to rise, but Rex beat her to the punch, striding naked to the door and opening it to reveal six pounds of Chihuahua and Cobra Bubbles.

"Who dis?" He looked at Cobra Bubbles, waiting for a reply. She wagged her tail and licked Rex's hand before bypassing him to hop on the bed. Bob Marley followed, waiting expectantly for someone to lift him up. Rex obliged, depositing the canine next to Queenie.

"That's Bob Marley," she explained.

"I didn't see you for one whole day and you replaced me with that?"

"It was a long day," Queenie filled him in on the recent happenings, including all of the details of Drake's adventures that Queenie guessed the teen most likely omitted.

"So, pot brownies, tattoo, and Bob Marley. Those the high points?"

"About rounds it out, yep." Queenie stroked the dogs.

"She making up for lost time?"

"Let's hope not."

"You know I'm going to have to kill Drake now, right?"

"Let's make that plan B," she said to Bob Marley. He wagged his tail in agreement.

"He's not coming to the wedding," Rex told the bed-at-large.

"Probably for the best." Because that would mean Diana would be there and Queenie never wanted to see Diana again. *Maybe waiting isn't such a good idea after all.*

"You're thinking about eloping aren't you?" Rex nodded, a knowing twinkle in his eyes.

"Maybe."

Rex pulled on his jeans, pausing to pick up something from the floor. "Whose Janelle?"

"The butler. Do you need butlering?"

"Doesn't everyone? I'm no different than any other common schmuck dwelling in a Mirage Villa." She watched him pick up the phone.

"See if they can send us a pizza. I'm starving."

"My good loving no dou—," he shifted gears realizing someone had picked up the phone on the other end. "Nope, not you Janelle, sorry about that." Queenie laughed out loud at his gaffe and he gave her a mock scowl. "I bet it does happen all the time, thank you for being so gracious. And yes, you can help me. I need to get married."

"Rex."

He waved her off. "I will indeed be marrying Ms. Hart. Tomorrow if you can manage it. Maybe ten people in attendance." He listened to something Janelle said, then looked at Queenie. "What time is dinner at Angel Baby's?"

"Five."

"Two-ish," he said into the phone, then paused.

"Yes."

Pause.

He nodded into the phone. "We'll get the license before hand. Okay."

Pause.

"You choose," he smiled broadly. "Why yes. I would *love* Elvis to perform the ceremony."

Queenie rolled her eyes at him, but couldn't stop smiling.

"No, I don't have one yet. I'll let you use your discretion, you sound like a woman with impeccable taste." He dug a piece of paper out from his pocket that Queenie realized must be his chip receipt. "Heart-shaped and under a hundred thousand if you don't mind."

Rex grinned at her and Queenie swallowed the lump in her throat. He was buying her a ring. His grin strayed from her to the dogs.

"And two dogs need to be in the ceremony."

Pause.

"No. No wedding clothes for the dogs. Just maybe something to dress their collars up? I think that's it." He snapped, remembering. "And a cheese pizza to our villa as soon as you can manage." He rang off and squeezed back into bed. "You thought I was going to forget the pizza, didn't you?"

"Not you."

"I'm never going to forget your pizza again, Queenie."

"I'll hold you to it, Tex-Rex." She pulled his head down so she could kiss him. "Rex?"

"Your majesty?"

"I could live without your pants right now."

"And done."

# About the Author

Julia Bidwell is a Las Vegas native, and an unapologetic romance addict with a fondness for clever dialogue, hunky heroes, and happy endings. When she's not writing contemporary smut she's reading it, or thinking about it... or she may even be sitting in front of her telly marathoning 1990's BBC murder mysteries. She gets daily inspiration from her very own Prince Charming, a darling teenage daughter, and a collection of furry friends with more personality than most people she knows. You can contact her at jules.bidwell@gmail.com, or via the usual methods (FaceBook, Twitter, etc.).